KILLER TRACKS

KILLER TRACKS

A MISTY PINES MYSTERY

MARY KELIIKOA

First published by Level Best Books 2025

Copyright © 2025 by Mary Keliikoa

This novel is entirely a work of fiction. The names, characters and incidents portrayed in it are the work of the author's imagination. Any resemblance to actual persons, living or dead, events or localities is entirely coincidental.

Mary Keliikoa asserts the moral right to be identified as the author of this work.

First edition

ISBN: 979-8-89820-033-6

Cover art by Christian Storm

This book was professionally typeset on Reedsy.
Find out more at reedsy.com

To Robb, Always

Praise for Killer Tracks

"Keliikoa is the Queen of immersive small town mystery. *Killer Tracks* is cleverly plotted with deftly drawn relatable characters who face off with a deadly threat from the past."—James L'Etoile, award-winning author of *River of Lies* and the Detective Nathan Parker series

"Mary Keliikoa's *Killer Tracks* is a wonderful addition to the Misty Pines mystery series. Great pacing, strong plotting, and compelling characters. Highly recommended!"—Bruce Robert Coffin, international bestselling coauthor of The Turner and Mosley Files

Prologue

Click. Slide. Clang.

If he never heard that sound again, it'd be far too soon. That, and the sleepless nights under a threadbare wool blanket that chafed his exposed skin, the looming threat of death…in the yard, the shower, the halls to and from the cafeteria or his cell.

Death and desperation seeped from the pores of this godforsaken place. So thick he could almost taste it. No amount of soap, no amount of ritual, would rid him of the stench that clung to him—though he'd be willing to try.

It was over now. Dying among these second-class men would not be his fate. A man of his intellect, a man far superior to the minions around him, deserved better than what he'd endured these past years.

He'd eagerly reeducate those who believed otherwise. They'd all see it by the time he was through with them, just like those that came before.

Click. Slide. Clang.

A voice echoed off the concrete walls.

"Inmate 22-A-4242. Gather your crap. Time to go."

He stood, hands to his sides.

"Ready to face the world?"

He remained silent. None would get the satisfaction of his acknowledgement.

The voice continued. "They gave you a goddamn Hail Mary. Bleeding heart liberals anyway. Don't screw it up."

He bowed his head to obscure his smirk.

"Right. I know your type. You're innocent." The guard continued rambling. "That's what all you convicts say. 'I didn't do it.' 'I was framed.'

'It's unconstitutional.'" The guard's voice dropped to a growl, prickling his skin. "Tell that to the victims and their families. I'd reckon less than one percent of you bastards got a legit claim."

The guard had forgotten betrayed, of which he surely had been. But he shrugged, not to agree, but to stave off the urge to wrap his hands around the guard's throat. So close to freedom…

Whether he was innocent or not had no bearing; it had not been among the criteria for the help he'd received. Being wrongfully convicted qualified. According to the junior team that had embraced his cause when he'd written the letter, they agreed that's what had happened in his case. Even if it took them ten years, he loved a system that allowed more loopholes than the cable-knit sweater Mother had dressed him in for school.

"Sell it to someone else, you psycho," the guard snapped. "Bet you money. We'll see you again real soon."

A jagged smile crossed his face. The guard had part of it correct—but he'd never be back here. Next time, he'd be less gullible.

And he intended to snuff out anything that could hurt him, like the light of every other woman who hadn't seen his worth.

Chapter One

Some days, it didn't pay to get out of bed.

Sheriff Jax Turner had experienced more than his fair share of those mornings in the past six years. First, when his daughter Lulu died from leukemia. Then, when his marriage dissolved—more like shattered into a million pieces. Followed by a couple of cases that had tested his limits of trust. They'd destroyed some, too.

Today was different.

Abby Kanekoa, his ex-wife with whom he'd shared the gutting grief of those past years, had offered hope for reconciliation—the chance to glue a few of those pieces back together. It would never be the same without their little girl…but perhaps they could create something new.

Leaving for the mountains just after Labor Day was less than ideal. Though with the tourist season coming to an end in Misty Pines, and Abby was due for a vacation at the Bureau, it was the best time. Deputy Rachel Killian, his new hire and right hand, was turning out to be as capable as he'd hoped. Applicants for filling the gaps at their station had been sparse. Few, it seemed, wanted to work these days—or work at the often cool and foggy Oregon coast. He'd at least been able to get most of his young crew on full-time payroll, so Rachel had help.

Bottom line, getting away was Abby's idea. He would not tell her no.

Now to get through the pep talk with the team. The two major events of the past year had allowed them to punch a few notches into their experience belt, but wisdom and reliance on gut instinct were born with time. Leaving them to run Misty Pines without his guidance had his muscles taut.

He entered the sheriff's office with his duffle flung over his shoulder.

"Oh, hon, don't tell me that's all you're taking for the week?" Trudy said. Jax's long-time secretary, and overall, Team Mother to him and his ragtag group of deputies, lifted the headset off her ears.

He suppressed a smile. "Glad to see your accident hasn't made you any less opinionated."

Eight months had passed since the event that had nearly stolen her from him and the team. A warm and fuzzy Trudy would be hard to get used to—he was grateful he didn't have to learn.

Trudy rested the headset around her neck. "Looks like Abby hasn't given you any clue about where you're going."

"Other than the mountains, not much. I've tossed a few essentials in my truck."

"Like?"

"A good book and a board game." He smiled. "A couple of bottles of wine." She arched her brow.

"What? I'm assuming she's arranged for us to be at some luxury resort."

"You think so?"

"Abby likes her massages, saunas, breakfast in bed." Not to mention time basking on the deck with a steaming cup of coffee. For being a tough, no-nonsense woman, and a hell of an FBI agent, she liked the finer things—and she'd earned every damn one of them.

"And what do you like?" Trudy asked.

He chuckled. Not much of what he'd just mentioned. "Roughing it."

"Hmmm…and she arranged this for the two of you to reconnect?"

His smile faded; he dropped the bag at his feet. "Are we camping?"

Trudy laughed and shook her head. "When it comes to women, you do take a minute to catch up. Might I suggest a few more items?"

"Like a tent?" He'd have to dig it out of his garage, which wouldn't take long.

"No. But a communication device might come in handy."

"Abby said something about our phones being off for the week." He shifted on his feet. "Are you saying we're headed somewhere with no service?"

She returned to her desk in response.

Of course they were. Several interruptions to his and Abby's conversations had come from the station over the past months. Too often, when they'd just settled into talk or were on the edge of a sensitive topic. Tourist season was like that every year, with the random fender bender, a too-loud party on the beach, a drunken brawl at the pub. Some infraction demanding his attention.

Added to that, Brody had slid his motorcycle on wet pavement and nearly dislocated his shoulder in the spring. Garrett had a few interviews in Portland, one in Seattle. Matt was called in to stock shelves by his boss at the IGA grocery store when they were short-staffed, which had become more consistent.

Time with Abby had been the price, although the last time they'd carved out a night together still brought a smile to his face. Maybe this trip signaled her intention of wanting more quality *togetherness*. That thought alone made having limited phone access worth it, regardless of where they went, even as the uneasiness of being out of contact with his crew niggled at him.

He flung the bag back over his shoulder and headed to his office.

The click of claws on the linoleum sounded behind him.

"Boss." Rachel and Koa, her black lab, came out of the kitchen. "You all set?"

"Almost. Picking Abby up soon for what appears might be a wilderness retreat."

Rachel laughed. "Don't look so concerned."

"I'm not."

"Uh-huh. That's why you have a crease between your eyebrows."

He rubbed the spot. "Guess I'm not fond of surprises."

"Never have been myself, but I have a feeling you'll have fun."

"According to Trudy, I will. Hope Abby does." It was sweet she'd chosen a place that appealed to him—more imperative if she enjoyed herself. She'd never been one to sleep on the ground.

"Believe me, she did good."

"Take it you know where we're headed?"

"Not precisely."

"How about a hint of what you do know, so I'm better prepared?" Having spent far too much time in the dark, he preferred to be ahead of things these days.

She did a zipping motion in front of her mouth. "I get that it'll be difficult for you, but try not to worry. The men and I have everything covered."

He nodded. Letting go of the wheel would never be easy, and in law enforcement things could change quickly. But Rachel was solid, and he trusted her… despite his former partner Jameson not agreeing with him hiring his only daughter. Jax had made the right call; he stood by it. There should be no hesitation about him and Abby taking a week for themselves.

"You'll get a hold of me if there's a problem?" he said.

"You won't have any way…"

"I'm taking the satellite phone."

Rachel folded her arms over her chest. "Suppose that's smart after the last trek in the wilderness…"

"Exactly my thought."

Rachel pursed her lips, likely recalling that day when radio silence had left her and the team wrought with worry as they waited for word on whether Jax and Abby were alive. But Abby should understand his decision, if it came up. Probably better it didn't.

"Let's do a briefing before I head out," he said.

Rachel winked. "The men are waiting for you in the strategy room."

He chuckled. That's why there'd been no sign of them when he'd arrived.

In his office, he set his duffle bag on a chair, and retrieved the satellite phone, burying it near the bottom in a T-shirt. Once he checked his email for the tenth time and cleared his desk, he started toward the meeting room, until he heard voices in the reception area.

Trudy was holding open the station's door. The men were grabbing their gear about to file out, Rachel and Koa behind them.

"What'd I miss?" Jax said.

Koa turned at the sound of his voice, trotting to his side. Jax squatted next to her, draping his arm gently over her back.

"Nothing to worry about, boss," Rachel said.

"Just a routine traffic revision, chief," Brody said. "We've got it." He'd gelled down his wispy brown hair today, making him look young. Too young.

"I've got forty minutes before…"

"Oh no you don't, Jax Turner," Trudy said. "It's a half-hour drive to Abby, and you will not be late."

"I—"

"We've got it, Sheriff," Rachel said, calling Koa to her. Koa didn't budge.

"Koa's siding with me on this," he said.

Rachel lifted a brow at her black lab, who promptly returned to her side. *Fine.* Jax stood. He'd wanted a team he could rely on, and he had one. So why did he feel left out? "Who's in need of traffic revision anyway?"

"Fire department," Trudy said.

"There's an apartment complex on fire at the edge of town," Rachel said.

Battalion Chief Mike O'Brien rarely requested assistance. With the remaining tourists eking out the last of their holiday weekend, there could be a traffic log, he supposed.

"I'll go with you," Jax said.

Rachel held up her hands in a stop gesture. "Please. Get out of here and have a good time."

Before he could protest, Rachel was out the door, and Trudy shut it behind them. Through the glass, Jax watched his team slide into two of the patrol cars.

"You heard your deputy, hon. Get your stuff and head to Abby's. And don't come back until you and that saint of a woman have worked everything out."

Trudy was right. He needed to check his ego. Misty Pines could handle a week without him.

A call came through Trudy's headset, which she tapped to answer. She settled behind her desk as he grabbed his bag, her voice fading as he walked outside.

"Yes, Mrs. Harper. Just a small fire. Nothing to worry about."

Chapter Two

Rachel had arrived at work with her hair down and feeling the effects of too much red wine from the night before. She and Janelle, her girlfriend for the past year who'd encouraged her to apply for the deputy position, had argued over Rachel working too much. Preceded by a fight she'd had with her father about moving to Misty Pines in the first place. She'd expected he'd get over that and give it a rest; putting a hundred miles between them had made zero difference.

He wanted her back in Portland, and she'd be damn sure he didn't get his way.

Succeeding here mattered—and she had, to some extent. The team treated her like one of the boys; even Garrett, the deputy who'd felt more deserving of her position in the beginning, had come around. Trudy was like a surrogate grandma who Koa adored. Didn't hurt she kept a drawer full of dog treats at the ready. And Rachel loved Sheriff Jax like an uncle—even if everyone compared them, like she was a "chip off the old block."

She only smiled when it came up, knowing she was her own person. Still, she'd considered Jax family from the time he was her father's partner, and he'd kept her under his wing since taking a chance and hiring her. He appreciated her, something Portland's higher ranks never had, but he stayed in charge.

Until today.

With Jax gone for a week, she'd have a chance to demonstrate what she could do, who she could be to him. She should be excited— *was* excited—if for no other reason than to prove to the people of Misty Pines that she lived in no one's shadow. But in the last month, she'd begun to realize Jax had been right to ask the question he had during their initial interview nearly nine months ago…would the small-town vibe be too slow-paced for her?

If she were being honest…

"Where you want us?" Brody said, appearing at her patrol car window and breaking through her thoughts.

"Give me a sec."

She climbed out, leaving Koa inside.

The black lab let out a pitiful whine before she could close the door, pacing the backseat. Rachel ducked in and ruffled her neck; she'd given her a potty break at the station.

"What's up, girl?"

Koa cocked her head, then barked.

She never acted needy, yet she'd glued herself to Jax, and now this. Perhaps the men in bunker gear with masks hung around their necks had unnerved her.

Although Koa knew how to read the room, too. *You feeding off my cranky vibes this morning, girl?* "I'm okay, Koa. I'll be close by." With no smoke drifting toward the road, Rachel rolled down the back window further so Koa could catch the breeze coming off the ocean. "We'll go for a run tonight near the beach so you can chase those seagulls later. Promise." The exercise and outlet would be good for them both.

Rachel returned her thoughts to Brody's question and where to station the men as Matt joined them.

"Thought we were being called to a complex fire," Matt said, yawning.

"Too many late nights?" Rachel said.

"Too many jobs."

She nodded and looked toward the eight-plex at the end of the street, not sure how Matt did it, working both as a deputy and a night grocery stocker. She could hear Janelle now if she took on a second gig.

But Matt had been right to ask the question. Two of Misty Pine's three fire rigs blocked the road in front of the complex. Eight of the ten-man volunteer crew were on scene, but she only saw Chief O'Brien at the base of the sidewalk. No visible flames or smoke came from the building. There didn't appear to be much traffic buildup, either. "Above our pay grade to question the request."

"Probably came from Marks so he could watch us run around like rats in a car engine again," Brody said.

None of them were fans of Commissioner Troy Marks, including Jax most of the time. But they were no one's rats. "Fire and Rescue direct made the call." The Battalion Chief was doling out orders to his men. As the leader of this crew until Jax returned, she should act more like him. "And regardless, we're here to assist. Matt, drink more coffee and take Glendale Road. Brody, ease traffic onto Sherman from there."

"Yes, ma'am."

She winced. "It's Rachel."

"Rachel." Brody flashed a smile. From the start, he'd welcomed her as an addition, but lately he'd seemed more in tune with hot rods and motorbikes. His off-duty gig at Len's Auto suited him.

But Rachel wondered when they'd get more help. Seemed a bit overkill to have them all doing traffic control. Garrett was lucky he had the day off.

With a glance to confirm Koa was good—she had her nose sticking out the window—Rachel strode to join the man in charge and told him where she'd posted the deputies. "Anywhere else you'd like us, Chief?"

"That'll do." He was appraising the building; she followed his gaze.

"Fire already under control?"

"Hasn't started. Caller was mistaken or wanted to get our attention…like we had other places to be." He huffed. "Though one tenant felt nauseous with a pounding headache. Another thought they'd smelled gas. Could be nothing, or something. Either way, they were smart enough to clear out of their apartments. I'm keeping everyone at a suitable distance until we know what we have."

Rachel had encountered traffic rubberneckers and curious bystanders on the regular in Portland—human nature prevailed, small town or not. But with plenty of first responders on scene, this task hardly required her entire team.

Guess it would make for a good tall tale over a pint of beer later. It seemed all the residents of Misty Pines were desperate for some action.

"Where are the tenants?" she asked.

"Across the street." He nodded to a small, huddled group.

"Is everyone accounted for? I see four people from an eight-apartment complex."

"An upstairs occupant is believed to be at work." He clipped his words—clearly not liking the questions. "The couple who lives across the way are on vacation, and one of the downstairs units is vacant, according to Winona." The Chief pointed to a long, dark-haired woman wrapped in a blanket in the group.

Rachel recognized her as an employee at the gas station on the other side of town. "Where are you on confirming if there's a leak?"

"How about you go and manage the traffic?"

"How about you answer the question?" She matched his tone. When working in Portland, she'd met more than a few like O'Brien.

He cleared his throat. "We're still searching. That said, this place is decades old, has faulty pipes, and doesn't exactly meet today's code." He frowned and spoke into his radio to the crew inside, turning his attention away and dismissing her.

About to respond, a flash of black darted past her. It moved so fast she had little time to register as it entered the stairwell that divided the two sides of units.

The Chief growled. "What the...?"

Rachel whipped around toward her patrol car long enough to see the back door wide open. Dread crushed her chest as she lunged forward.

The Chief clutched her upper arm, stopping her momentum. "No one else in that building without my say so."

She shook herself loose. "Koa!"

The sound of feet pounding on the pavement exploded from behind. "I'm so sorry," Matt said, his face red and contorted.

"What did you do?"

"She was clawing to get out. I was afraid she'd rip up the interior." He swallowed hard. "I thought she had to do her business."

Koa wouldn't have reacted that way unless she'd sensed something. Or someone. There'd be no other reason for her to go inside.

And Rachel had missed it. Thinking too much about the pace of the town, not being enough. Of stepping out of Jax's shadow. Wrapped up in her own clouded thoughts of her girlfriend's accusations and her father's demands. "Are you sure the building's empty?" she said to the Chief.

"Fairly. We're still in the process of confirming what the neighbors told us." The Chief grabbed his walkie. "Team report. Where are we—?"

The rumble beneath them caught Rachel's attention first.

"Clear the area," the Chief ordered.

As he and Matt stumbled backwards, Rachel went forward. No one told her where to go when it came to Koa.

Before she'd gone a step, a blast of glass and heat erupted from the front window of the bottom apartment, slamming her to her knees.

She watched in horror as flames licked the building and black smoke snaked to the apartments above.

Chapter Three

A view of the ocean filled the side window as Jax drove to Abby's townhouse in Cannon Beach. Traffic crawled most of the way. The rare hot summer had drawn in the tourists, but at least they were heading out of town, giving Rachel and the team less to handle. Unfortunately, those tourists were on his same route.

At least as far as the "Y," where he veered south towards Abby, and the visitors drifted toward Portland.

He arrived at Abby's ten minutes late and knocked with a fair amount of trepidation.

"You're here," she said. Her rigid body language had him preparing to defend himself.

"I—Yes. Sorry…traffic was heavier than expected."

She waved him off, a citrusy smell wafting off her. Perfume? That was new.

"You're telling me," she said. "I went for bagels this morning, and the cars were bumper-to-bumper on the main strip. Didn't realize it extended into Misty Pines."

"Me either, or I would've set out sooner." He let out a breath. "Now do I get to know where we're headed? Trudy offered only slightly more detail than you have." He sniffed, taking another whiff of this fresh scent Abby must be trying out. He could get used to it.

She lifted her finely sculpted eyebrow. "You're like a kid at Christmas. I told you it's a surprise, and why are you sniffing?"

"You smell good."

"You and Olek."

Jax almost eye-rolled, then thought better of it. Abby's partner, Olek, had come through for him and Abby when they'd needed him earlier that year. "How is Stretch these days? Still pining for you?" Okay, maybe he was curious about the status of their partnership.

"Busy moving our offices."

"Your offices are moving?" Another recent development, apparently.

"We're merging with West Shore. Our SEO's retiring, and rather than replacing him, they're shutting down the satellite. It's not like West Shore is far, and it will put me closer to Mom."

"Dora will love that."

"Hope so. She still has a few good days. Since I never know when those will occur, however...." Abby's voice drifted off.

Jax brushed Abby's arm and gripped her hand. His own mother had abandoned him and his father long ago, and his father had died of a massive heart attack. To witness the gradual disintegration of someone to the point they no longer recognized who their loved ones had once been to them, would be heartbreaking.

She cleared her throat. "Anyway, remind me to pick up a thank you gift for Trudy for being the emergency contact for the home this week while we're gone."

"Ah, so there will be places to shop?"

She smiled, giving away nothing. "As for the move, budget cuts these days are inevitable. Even in the FBI."

"That they are." Or budget constraints. Misty Pines had voted down the budget increase that would have provided the extra staff Commissioner Marks had promised, along with new equipment. Hopefully, they'd loosen their purse strings the next go around. "Back to our trip. What kind of surprise?"

"One where we'll be spending the next few days alone to reconnect and see where we are."

He'd wanted to hear those words for so long. "Not even a clue of the location?"

She sighed, a sign she was done with questions. "Nope. Other than it's remote and we'll have no distractions."

Jax nodded. He'd never known Abby to enjoy being so disconnected from work or life, though people changed. Wish he could say he had. Whether it came back to bite him, he had no regrets about bringing the satellite phone along.

"Don't look so scared. We'll be fine."

"It's not that. It's just the first time I'm leaving Rachel and the crew in charge without access to me."

"We've seen Rachel in action. She's quite capable. Besides, Trudy's there."

"True." He chuckled, thinking of Trudy mothering Rachel like she did him. "Okay, so phones won't be working. At least I'll have my firearm."

The skin pinched between her eyebrows, stepping him back.

"What?" he said.

"Being armed is unnecessary."

"You never know."

She dropped her arms to her side. "Jax, we're just going into nature." She released a heavy breath. "Wouldn't it be nice for two seconds to pretend we're normal people?"

Maybe FBI protocol differed from a beat cop's practice, which was to always carry. They were both seasoned enough to know danger lurked everywhere.

"Normal people take guns to the wilderness regularly. What if we encounter wildlife?"

"Then a handgun would kill the animal or injure it, which would be worse. How about we avoid killing or hurting anything this trip."

There it was. "Always the goal." He reached for her hand again. Her stress from the events of earlier in the year radiated through her skin.

She closed her eyes and held his hand. "You're right. I'm being silly. We should have something."

"How about a compromise? Where's your dad's shotgun?"

"In the garage's cabinet, but it hasn't been used in years."

"Better than nothing, though, and loud enough to scare anything off if necessary."

"Probably true. Buckshot's on the shelf next to it."

That settled, they gathered the rest of the food and supplies necessary for their getaway. Jax had won that round, but Abby's comments about being normal felt off. Or perhaps it was him on the edge because of leaving his deputies, and the fire. He could check in with Trudy on that, but that would be seen as not placing much faith in the team.

And despite their differences, Commissioner Marks would never allow the town to go up in flames.

Abby found a country music station for the forty-minute drive. Not his preferred classic rock, but that gave her a headache, and the jazz she leaned into put him to sleep. This weekend appeared to be about finding common ground, though the mountain range took care of the music choice within ten minutes. They rode the next half-hour in silence, Abby fiddling with the window controls.

"Okay, what gives?" he finally said.

"Nothing," she said as they passed a gas station and grocery supply store. The first signs of life he'd seen in the last thirty miles.

"It doesn't feel like nothing." He tapped the steering wheel. "If you've changed your mind and being this far out makes you uneasy, we can find a boutique B&B closer to town. That is, if you promise not to drag me in for some mani/pedi." He chuckled to lighten the mood.

She didn't smile; his mind drifted to Lulu. Only she'd painted his nails, the memory of her choosing the pinkest sparkly color for him that last Saturday morning before the diagnosis.

He swallowed.

Abby folded her hands in her lap. "No. A different setting is what we need. It'll be great." She looked out ahead. "Take the next left."

Canyon Bluff Road. Known for being rocky and dusty, Jax lowered the speed to a crawl, glad to focus on the path and the steady climb. Soon, sparse trees became thick forest crowding in from both sides. "Where the heck are you taking us, Ms. Kanekoa?"

"You'll see."

Now Abby gazed out the window, smiling. He relaxed some. He'd never been out this far, but was aware of the area's remoteness and the landslide on the main roadway that had made it inaccessible this past year. "I'd heard this mountain was closed to the public."

"It is, until next weekend."

"Are you looking to get us arrested?" he said, finding himself excited about the prospect of where the road led.

"Nope. We have the entire mountain to ourselves."

An entire mountain—that had some appeal. And they didn't bring a tent. He had an inkling of where they might be headed. He pushed the speed, ready to be there, only to hit the brakes time and time again as he maneuvered around ruts and rocks. Despite the repairs required to make the road passable from the slide, much still needed fixing.

Finally, they'd gone as far as they could—the top of the world.

"The fire lookout's still here?" He parked at the base of a boulder wall. "I thought they'd decommissioned this place." He'd read about the updated tower built last year, located more central to the forest. Newer or not, if fire ever came their way, he'd much rather have rock surrounding them like this.

"They used this for the ranger station, which also got moved to be close to the tower." Without another word, Abby jumped out of Jax's truck and trotted up the rock stairs laid out inside the wall.

He followed to the ample cabin perched far too close for his liking to a sheer rock cliff. Keeping a respectable distance from the edge, he skimmed the expansive view. A slice of the Columbia River lay below, with vistas of shrub steppe between.

"What do you think? It's ours for the week."

"It's beautiful."

"It really is. Now get over here, and we can take a picture."

"How about we take it from here?"

She laughed. "You're still afraid of heights after all this time?"

"Heights are fine. It's the falling part that concerns me." He turned around and flashed a smile. "Let's get that picture after we're settled."

"That works."

Jax headed for the truck, assessing the forest. Bears should shy away from coming out this far as long as they kept food sources out of sight. Then again, the miles-deep evergreens could be home to countless other critters who might not be so shy. *Quit thinking the worst.* Trudy's words flitted through his mind. He was prone to that, and he'd have to channel his inner Trudy for the week.

"Looks like we'll have plenty of hiking options," he said, but Abby had disappeared inside the cabin.

Jax grabbed the bags. When he entered, Abby was staring at the kitchen. He followed her line of sight. "What's wrong?"

She placed her hands on her hips, rotating left, then right. "There's a bowl in the sink, and a pillow on the floor."

"And?"

"The road here has been closed since last year, and we're supposed to be the first guests in this place, which just got renovated."

"Maybe a worker spent the night to work out the kinks."

She strode into the kitchen. Peered under the sink. The garbage can liner hadn't been replaced. "Maybe." Yanking a bag from the roll, she lined the can.

When she stood, Jax wrapped his arms around her, resting his chin on her shoulder, not minding her fine black hair tickling his face. "I can see those wheels spinning. Wouldn't it be nice if, for two seconds, we pretended not to be law enforcement? To be like a normal couple?"

"Using my own words against me now?" She faced him, leaned in, and closed her eyes. "You're probably right about it being a worker."

"Sounds reasonable to me." He hugged her again, then let her go, suddenly chilled. "How about I start a fire and get this cabin feeling like home away from home?"

"I'll get something on the stove. I'm starved."

Outside, Jax returned to the cliff side of the cabin. He drew in the fresh crisp air as he surveyed the scenery. Abby had chosen a peaceful place for their time away. Isolated with gorgeous views. Abby being the most gorgeous of them. But so little in his life remained peaceful for long.

It could be Abby's unease that had him on edge. Or his own. He could hear Trudy now. *Pull it together, hon. We can survive a week without you.* Rachel had echoed the same thing.

But no matter how many mantras he repeated, he couldn't shake the feeling that even with the best of his intentions, something unwelcome had already begun again.

Chapter Four

Rachel braced in terror for the next blast to rock the apartment complex. When none came, she scrambled to her feet, dizzy, her ears reverberating.

Emergency personnel cranked to life as the Chief, less than a foot away, screamed into his radio. Sound fought through a mountain of cotton to reach her, but his face, reddened and pinched, suggested no one had answered. Two more firemen raced for the building that she'd yet to see anyone come out of, including Koa.

Her heart ricocheted. About to move toward the building, pressure on her arm startled her. Matt was attempting to pull her back. She stood firm, laser-focused on the stairway, watching for Koa to emerge.

Only seconds had passed since the explosion, but far too long. She twisted out of Matt's grip and ran toward the stairs, falling in line behind the two firefighters. As they reached the top, they turned into the apartment on the right.

With no sign of Koa, she raced down the hall, screaming. "Koa. Come."

But her ears rang; she'd never hear if Koa responded. And could Koa hear her screams? Having experienced the blast while inside the building, she could be equally deaf.

Rachel checked one apartment where the door was askew, but found nothing. Koa *had* come this way—one more apartment to check. Since no flames had reached the top level, she sped toward it. The door was open.

Inside, Koa—standing guard over a man, her posture rigid and alert. *Thank God.*

She rushed to her, fighting back tears of relief that her companion appeared unharmed. Not to be said about the man on the floor whose eyes were wide open, his mouth agape, his skin pale. Blood, black and drying, had oozed into a puddle at the back of his head.

He might have fallen… although she would've expected to find his body crumpled, less flat. Almost like it was laid out that way. Staged?

Something else on his body caught her attention, but she had no time to examine further until they declared the building safe.

"Koa, come," she said, motioning her hand, showing the same command.

Koa trotted around to Rachel, who dropped to her knees and embraced her friend, who was trembling. Rachel quickly inspected her head, her body. Satisfied there were no visible injuries, she stood and gathered Koa in her arms.

"Sorry, girl." But there was no way she'd risk Koa not hearing her and getting into more danger.

Water hoses were dousing the flames in the downstairs apartment as she came down the stairs and into the opening. Matt and Brody met her, helping her ease Koa to the ground a safe enough distance from the building. Both wore deep worry lines; she'd seen that look on them before, not so long ago, when they thought Jax had died.

Chief O'Brien had been sputtering obscenities at her since she'd cleared the stairs. Hearing clearly was not required to decipher the words coming from his mouth.

Now he marched her way. "What the hell were you thinking?"

She took Koa by the collar, in no mood to argue, and got her back to the patrol car, securing her in the back seat. Matt had followed, still apologizing.

"Don't touch this car again. Got it?" she said.

"Yes, ma'am."

"It's Rachel."

"Right. Sorry."

How did Jax do this? She drew in a breath, fighting the urge to unleash on the deputy. Koa was safe. "We have a body upstairs. Call the medical examiner and get him en route."

"On it," Matt said.

By the time she'd gone back towards the building, the Chief had already forgotten about her and was directing his team to attack the fire from the rear of the structure.

"There's a body in the back, top left apartment," she shouted. "No one's to go in or out of that unit."

The Chief straightened; his face paled. "Christ, I left the big city because of crap like this." He stretched his neck. "You think you got a crime scene on your hands?"

"ME will be here shortly to make the official call." Though she'd seen the blood. The body. She'd also been a first responder at a few homicides in Portland. More often then, she'd be diminished to guarding the premises or a witness the moment the detective arrived. But she knew.

She was also aware of how Jax liked to keep outsiders out of their business, which meant they'd be investigating this themselves.

Being around the action had her adrenaline at full tilt and relishing that Jax would be gone for the week—whether he'd see it that way or not. When she proved herself beyond capable of handling this matter, he'd have to relinquish some of that control and give her more to do.

As they waited for the firemen to make the building safe enough to re-enter and the ME to arrive, Matt and Brody kept the traffic moving around barricades, and she called Trudy.

"Need to know the owners of every unit at Pine Crest Condos, in particular 206," she said.

Rachel's brief visual of its sparse furnishings gave her the sense that Bruce Hatfield was a bachelor. Not that her apartment in Portland boasted much more than a futon and bean bag chair.

Rachel missed that old apartment. Living the minimalist lifestyle had worked for her. She could pick up and leave when necessary, or feel like she could. And Janelle had plenty enough for them both. Too much. Perhaps that's why she'd been looking around at places of her own—a fact she'd yet to share with her girlfriend.

She shook her thoughts when a red vehicle with an official Misty Pines logo on the door pulled next to hers. Fire Marshal Gregg Stout was a stump of a man. He lumbered out of his seat, dressed in gray coveralls, and headed toward the Chief.

He and the Chief were talking with a good 'ole boy motions of a slap on the back and a hearty laugh as she approached. They'd no doubt shared more than a few beers at the Tip Top Tavern. Most of the old-timers in town gravitated there.

Either way, after Chief O'Brien's earlier dismissal, it was time to make sure they knew she was acting sheriff.

"ME's on the way," she said, approaching, her hearing cleared. "I'll be the lead investigator once he's made his determination on the body."

"Body?" Marshal Stout said. "Well, hell, Mike, you might've led with that when you called."

"Just found out myself," the Chief said. "But Sheriff Turner should get his ass down here and act like the sheriff he was appointed to be. After your stunt of running into the building, missy, I don't trust you anywhere near this scene."

Missy? *Huh.* A snippy retort formed in her head. She bit into her tongue. Her first week on the job, Jax had warned her about her quick temper.

But this was a crime scene now.

"He's out of town. I'm in charge. That upstairs apartment's mine until further notice."

She turned on her black-soled work boots and waited at her car with Koa, directing Brody to get the tenants, shaken by the blast, over to Osprey Café until she could get their statements.

Chapter Five

Jax appraised the sparse wood supply stacked at the side of the cabin. It would be out long before morning. September at sea level might be comfortable, but not so much at this elevation, and Abby hated the cold.

As he gathered the pre-cut wood, his face quirked into a half-smile. Abby snuggling closer in bed would be a plus, but things could easily go the other way. He'd already seen signs of her being stressed with her plans not unfolding the way she'd expected, much like they had another time.

On their honeymoon, they'd opted for a coastal town further south. The ocean hummed in the background and soothed them from the start. The sea's brackish smell, combined with the firs and pines surrounding him, had the same effect.

The hotel was the problem. The one she'd chosen was like something he and Jameson had been called to countless times to break up fights and drug deals in northeast Portland. Sparse shrubs and chipping paint from the constant assault of saltwater and mist had greeted them—nothing like the sweet cottage feel that the website had boasted. If only it had stopped there. The lumpy bed and damp towels had proven to be his unflappable Abby's undoing.

It wasn't just the accommodations: it was that she'd seen none of it coming. Until that moment, he'd never seen a chink in Abby's impenetrable armor.

Her breakdown had been brief. She moved into action, getting on the phone and having them packed and into a nicer motel within the hour. Pivoting and getting through any situation with grace had long been among

Abby's strengths. But whether he'd like her to cuddle close, Jax had no intention of witnessing that again this weekend over something as easily fixed as having enough firewood.

When he returned inside with his arms full of split logs, Abby was appraising the living room.

"Still settling in?" Jax let the wood roll onto the brick pad in front of the woodstove.

"I can't stop thinking that someone's been here. It's bugging the hell out of me."

"Thought we decided a worker raided the place and did a lousy cleanup job."

"Turns out there's more."

"Such as?" He scanned the room, searching for what she'd discovered.

"There's a half gallon of milk in the refrigerator."

He knelt on one knee and arranged the wood into a pyramid. "Doesn't that prove my theory?"

She folded her arms over her chest. "Maybe…."

"We found the door locked when we arrived. No broken windows. No signs of forced entry."

She glared at him.

Okay, he sounded like a cop right then. "All I'm saying is, it's no big deal. Just throw out the milk."

She went into the kitchen and grabbed a pan from under the stove top. "It's just weird."

"And highly unprofessional," he said. "But this is the Forest Service, not a five-star hotel." That didn't come out right. "I mean, the road's been closed. They're not officially operating. And I'm good with it." He smiled. "In fact, I'm great with it."

She put her finger in the air, halting him. "Here's another theory. I got the dates wrong." Her brow creased with clear frustration at that idea. She shook her head. "Things have been crazy at work, and I got confused. Maybe the travel agent double-booked and here we are breaking into someone else's week. They could show any time and demand we leave."

"Did you find clothes in the closet or drawers?"

"No."

"Then there's nothing to worry about." He could feel her stress rising by the lift in her shoulders. "If someone does show, we'll deal with it then. Worst-case scenario, a hiker found a way in, spent the night, and moved on."

"And they had a half-gallon of milk in their backpack?"

"I'm only offering scenarios. Maybe the contractors left the milk. The options don't have to be linked."

She shrugged. "I suppose if we're up here, it's not impossible that a hiker would ignore the signs and come through."

"Likely more than one this past year."

She lifted her chin. "I just wanted everything..."

"To be perfect." He stood and strode to her, wrapping her in his arms again. "Which it is. I realize you did this for us to spend time together. But we could be adrift in a dinghy in the middle of the ocean, and as long as I'm with you."

"I know, but—"

He did know. It was more than not seeing this coming. It was losing Lulu and not spotting the signs of their daughter's sickness sooner. Neither of them would ever stop replaying the *what-ifs* of that for as long as they lived.

The attack on Abby earlier that year, after she'd let her guard down, only fueled that insecurity.

He kissed her cheek and returned to the fireplace. "If it makes you feel better, I'll take a look around," he said. "We could use more firewood."

"We're out?"

"Nah, there's plenty." A white lie in this situation seemed warranted. "With the temps dropping tonight, I figure we'll be keeping it stoked."

She nodded. "Better to be prepared. I'll go with you."

He tensed. "How about I get this fire raging and wrangle a few more logs while you start that pot of stew you'd planned instead?"

She bristled. "I'm fully capable of taking point."

Point? "It's just firewood, Babe."

She let out a breath. "And I'm the one who said to leave the badges behind."

She chuckled.

There she was.

"Fine. I did say I'd start lunch, and I am hungry."

He smiled. "Me too."

Jax hunched to open the fireplace wide. Warmth radiated from the ashes. *Huh.* A hiker or contractor's employee might have started a fire while they were here, but he'd expect it to be cold by now.

"How did you find out about this being available again?" he said.

"Express Travel, you know, next to the bookstore?"

"Martha. Sure, she's been planning vacations for years."

"She has and was so excited to pull a few strings to get us here before the public."

"Then I'm sure it's all fine. We're here now, so let's enjoy. I'll get the firewood, and you get to cooking."

"Like a good little woman…."

They'd never lived a traditional life together, and he rather liked it that way. "Not in a million years." He sniffed. "I'm happy to start the stew if you want to relax. I'll get the wood later."

Her face wrinkled. "Uh, yeah. No. This is not the Lean Cuisine meals you have in your freezer."

"It's Marie Callender, lady. Don't mess with what we have going. Although nothing compares to your luau stew." Braised beef and taro leaves. His mouth watered thinking about it.

That got another smile from Abby. "That's because it was my Tutu's recipe. Get me my fire and I'll feed you. This time."

Jax found an ax outside leaning against the cabin, happy to do as he was told.

Abby was right, though. Every sign suggested someone had stayed there recently. Like he'd attempted to convince Abby, that didn't mean they'd be back.

If only he could persuade his gut.

He clutched the ax and made his way toward the forest to find some wood.

Chapter Six

iles away from the prison, he stood at a distance, breathing in his newfound freedom. More than anything, in the gray icy walls of his cell, he'd missed the full view of the sky. The wind on his stubbled face. The scents as they sailed through his nostrils. Even dead fish and pine smelled better than the prevalent excrement, sweat, and desperation of incarceration.

Though he hated the vastness of the ocean, he also felt it was a kindred spirit. That it could look so beautiful, yet cunning. That it could sneak up on its admirers and drag them down with no warning. Death could happen at any time; the ocean snuffed life out of the unaware without the slightest emotion.

It just was. Like him. His ways not cruel, just what they were.

Although he'd never acted alone—provocation had spurred him. Like betrayal did now.

But then, he tried to explain his reasons to the women that were chosen. That their actions had created their situation. It was their biases. Their judgments. Their rejections. Their shunning of him on a basic level. Admittedly, sometimes it was simply their beauty.

To him, they were all the same. As such, they'd paid the same price.

Of course, they'd plead to avoid the inevitable. Their voices, high and shaky, and shredded with terror once they realized their fate. That's when he'd wrapped his hands around their delicate necks and tightened. Until they…

Shut.

Up.

What happened after was not his preference, but he reveled in it, nonetheless.

He wiped the spittle that had formed at the corners of his mouth.

Now he was free again. And in time, he'd be united with who would become his next victim.

Lost in reverie, he'd almost missed seeing the young officer carrying a black dog from the apartment building.

Give or take a few years, she was about the age of the others…maybe older. Long through college now. The orders she doled out were like the backhands his mother had given him—the men's faces reflected that.

She was in charge; the men quivered.

Something about her shot yearning through him—he wanted to control her.

His outward face remained serious and concerned as cars passed, and people stopped to see the chaos. Inwardly, he smiled. More firefighters raced to the building.

He dug his nails into the meat of his palm.

He had to behave for a while.

Chapter Seven

Rachel kept eyes on the fire marshal as he entered the downstairs apartment where the blast had originated while Matt continued to direct traffic. When the marshal reappeared, she hustled over so as not to miss his update. It appeared a faulty propane heater in the vacant back apartment could be the culprit, although determining the official cause would take weeks.

"Every damn one of these tenants is lucky that carbon monoxide didn't do them in first," the marshal said.

"Who'd be stupid enough to fire up propane inside a closed room?" the chief said.

"That'll be a question for the landlord. Appears work was being done to get the apartment ready for rental. Could have been drying the place out. Not sure of anything yet, other than common sense ain't so common these days."

"Wouldn't there need to be an ignition to create the explosion?" The men turned to Rachel as if they'd just seen her for the first time.

"Right. Gas leaked into the front apartment via vent and likely found its ignition source there. A candle's flame would do it. Luckily, that tenant wasn't home, or you'd have two bodies to contend with," Marshal Stout said.

One was more than she'd expected—and more than enough.

The smoke damage guaranteed the tenants wouldn't be returning to the units for the near future. She'd let the fire marshal or chief break that news to those affected. In the meantime, the few she'd seen huddled on the street corner had disappeared. If Brody had done as asked, they'd be comfortably waiting at the café until she released them.

The medical examiner arrived in a marked car, and a woman in her late forties climbed out and approached Rachel. "What you got?"

"A body on the top floor," she said, giving the woman a second look. "I was expecting someone else."

"Shocking. No worries. I didn't expect you, either."

"Excuse me?" Being new to Misty Pines shouldn't warrant sarcasm.

"Dr. Shocking. Grace is fine. Miller retired, and I'm it. I assisted the sheriff in your last homicide."

Rachel chuckled at how she'd immediately thought the worst. Maybe Jax was right that she should pull back on her reactions. "I was only interviewing then."

"See you passed the test." She smiled.

"That I did." Although this crime scene felt like one itself.

Once the firefighters deemed the carbon monoxide levels safe enough to enter the building, Rachel led the ME upstairs. They pulled on rubber gloves and foot coverings before getting to work.

"Lucky for you, murder scenes are taking precedent," Dr. Shocking said from her squatted position near the body.

"Why lucky?"

"You don't keep up with the news?"

"Try to avoid it when possible."

"Self-care. I like it. Nothing but depressing crap anyway. But our office is short-staffed and overworked. Translation—a complete mess. Miller got out while he could. The number of drug deaths has skyrocketed. I can barely keep up with the pile of bodies at the morgue. Murders, however, jump to the front of the line."

Smiling would be inappropriate, but her gut had read it right when she saw the body. She'd be lying if she said a murder investigation hadn't appeared at the right time. It was the kick in the rear to feel like she could make a difference in this town. "Lucky me then."

"That's what I said."

"Any ideas about what happened to our victim?" Rachel said.

"From the current state of the body, probably deceased anywhere from eight to thirty-six hours. I'll venture somewhere in the middle since there's some pooling and softening of limbs."

"Cause of death?"

The doctor focused on the man's head. "Blunt force trauma, perhaps. Scalp wounds bleed profusely, which can be misleading." She inspected closer from different angles. "There's brain matter, suggesting considerable force behind the hit."

Rachel winced at the detail. "Not something that would happen naturally, I take it?"

"If he rammed his head into a concrete pillar, sure. But..." She circled her finger. "I don't see any pillars, and the location of the wound suggests someone stronger got the best of him. Likely taller, too, though that can also be misleading."

Rachel appraised the room: no visible blood splatter or signs of struggle. The man also had no coffee table or sharp corners that he could have fallen onto.

Leaving the doctor to continue her work, Rachel began her own. She headed for the bedroom first, hoping to find an ID. The wallet on the nightstand belonged to Bruce Hatfield. The picture matched the man in the other room, although this one showed him full of life, and with a warm, but impish grin.

Though a license hardly told the whole story, Bruce Hatfield looked happy. Clearly, something had gone very wrong to change that.

Rachel tucked the ID back into the wallet and dropped it into an evidence bag. Trudy had yet to confirm the name on the lease, but at least she had her victim's identity. What she didn't find were indications of a struggle or altercation. Like the living room, this space was neat and clean, except for a hair tie on the floor next to the dresser.

Could belong to Bruce. Though matted, his hair was longer. Not sure it was long enough to warrant a tie, but she bagged the item and strode into the bathroom. She immediately stepped back at the sight, her stomach revolting, and joined Dr. Shocking.

"Found where he was likely killed," she said. "I'll get some crime scene tape run and get the forensics team from West Shore out here." She might be the lead investigator, but she had no intention of screwing up any further evidence the scene might hold for the DA when they nailed the killer.

Dr. Shocking was still inspecting the body, distracted. "Sounds good."

Rachel was about to leave, then spotted a shelf near the wall-mounted TV that contained framed photos of a once young baseball athlete. Bruce, probably in his mid-teens. The team trophies he was clearly proud of were intact.

"Any chance a baseball bat would cause the damage to our victim?"

The ME leaned closer to the head wound. "Won't know until I get him on the table, but it might turn out you're right on that. Our deceased have a name?"

"Bruce Hatfield. He was thirty-five."

Dr. Shocking gazed at the body. "Well, Mr. Hatfield, hopefully you can help us figure out who did this to you."

"What do you think about the cuts on his arm?" Rachel said. She'd noticed them and something on the man's chest earlier. Their last case had severed feet washing ashore. This one had knife marks, which could be self-inflicted even if the injury to his head hadn't been.

"Deep enough to be painful, nothing more." Her eyes became slits as she narrowed in on his chest. "Huh."

"What?" Rachel said.

Her face turned stoic. "I'd rather not say until I complete my post back at the facility." She stood and called her office, but her jaw was tight as she paced in front of the apartment door.

Downstairs, Grace Shocking vanished into her car and left without another word. Rachel instructed Matt to secure the apartment until they retrieved the body. He'd also stay nearby while the crime lab worked their magic.

Only one fire engine and its crew remained, and traffic control was no longer needed.

"Another murder?" Brody said after confirming the tenants were at the café. He'd stood at Rachel's patrol car, caressing Koa's fur between her eyes. Now he looked paler than normal, awaiting an answer.

"Yes. Bruce Hatfield by way of blunt force trauma, likely. We'll know more soon."

"Damn." He shook his head.

"You know him?"

"Of him. He used to play in the minors until a knee injury took him out."

"Didn't know you were a baseball fan."

"Not me. My brother."

"Didn't know you had one."

"Lots of things you don't know about us."

Ouch. Though fair. "At some point, we'll have to change that."

"Cool." He looked toward the apartment. "Sure is too bad the sheriff will have to cut his vacation short. He'd been looking forward to it."

She didn't answer.

"You're not calling him?"

It would be hard to show Jax she could handle a case if she called him right out of the gate. "Not yet."

"I don't know, ma'am—Rachel. That could turn out bad, like driving your car without oil."

"Do you want to be the one that interrupts his romantic getaway with Abby when they might finally reconcile?"

"Well—"

She raised her hands in surrender. "You're braver than me."

Brody shifted feet. "Suppose we could wait. A day or two."

"That's what I'm thinking. The man should be able to have a break without us running to him every time."

"Sheriff never rests."

"He certainly doesn't. Besides, there's not much to tell while we're waiting on forensics to do their part and for the ME to issue her findings."

"True…"

"How about we interview some witnesses to see what they might know about Mr. Hatfield in the meantime?"

He hesitated, then nodded. "Okay, but just so you know, if the sheriff blows a gasket…."

"Right. I'm on my own." Like that was something new. "Let's go."

Chapter Eight

Jax kept an eye out for any signs they weren't alone on his way to the surrounding woods, the warm ashes in the fireplace on his mind. The anonymous visitor hadn't been gone long before their arrival, which was unsettling, despite what he'd told Abby.

He stretched his neck to dispel the tension. What was most important was they were gone, with nothing to indicate they planned to return. He could spend the next hours and days trying to solve the puzzle, or let it go—not be a cop this week like he promised. Enjoy the moment with Abby.

What he did notice was the air had changed some since they'd arrived, turning to a slight yellowish haze. Fire season had been hell this year, and there could be a few active around this part of the state or next door, in Washington. The winds could carry smoke in from just about anywhere nearby, including Canada. If it were close enough to be worried about, he'd expect the smoke and haze to be much denser.

Like the time he'd built a bonfire for Lulu. Before he'd nearly smoked them out of the house, he and Abby had roasted marshmallows with their then three-year-old. He could still see his daughter's eyes as she watched the fire dance, grinning from ear to ear. It was short-lived after he threw a couple of wet pieces of wood into the pile. Smoke blanketed the backyard, forcing them inside, and Abby teased him to never give up his day job.

"It's okay, Daddy," Lulu had said, coming to hug him. "I think you're the best, no matter what."

Lulu was a caretaker from the start. The thought of the world never knowing such a tender heart would break him if he let the memories linger.

Which he couldn't. This weekend was about him and Abby and what he hoped would be their new beginning.

A bald eagle soared overhead. A bird that often mated for life. He took that as an omen as he reached the forest where he scanned the towering pines and firs, some of them fallen. The winds that blew through this region, regardless of the season, had done some of the work for him. He could've saved himself the trouble of bringing the ax.

Leaning the tool against a moss-laden fir, he went to work tossing the fallen limbs into a pull pile. What he really needed was a wheelbarrow, which he hadn't seen at the cabin. At least he'd work up an appetite for Abby's delicious stew.

He cradled the first load close to his body and started up the hill and into the clearing. As he neared the cabin's woodpile, the aroma of braised beef wafted out, causing his stomach to rumble. One more load and he'd get inside to enjoy it.

He dumped the wood and turned, noticing his truck sitting at an odd angle.

Not again. He rounded his truck to the passenger side to confirm what he already suspected, and sure enough—the back tire was flat.

He huffed and turned back to the clearing, looking for signs he'd missed someone on his return to the cabin. Signs of anyone wreaking havoc on his tire. A potential suspect in his last case had done just that to all four tires not so long ago. But here, the area offered few real places to hide, except inside the forest where he'd come from. He saw no one now or in there. Though it was a long stretch of trees, with several pathways.

Would he ever stop thinking the worst? More likely, a sharp rock had been the culprit. The long and winding dirt road up this mountain had been full of them.

With no plans to leave in the short term, he'd deal with changing the flat later.

He hustled back to the forest for another load of limbs and wood chunks when he caught sight of movement and something red about a hundred yards away from the pile.

A branch cracked behind him.

He wheeled about, nerves buzzing, and crouched low near a fallen log. A squirrel leapt from one fir to another, its bushy tail flicking in his direction.

Pull it together, Turner.

Seemed he had a bit of his own PTSD because the last time he'd been in a similar environment, he'd been waiting on edge for a shot to catch him unaware.

Now he stood, beginning to doubt it possible to leave one's law enforcement baggage in the rearview, as Abby'd suggested. At least for the traumas.

Glancing out ahead, he saw that same red again. Probably nothing, but better to know than to guess.

Ax in hand, he traipsed through the forest, stumbling on knots of ferns covering the mulch-covered ground. As he grew closer to where he'd seen the flash of red, his feet tangled in the underbrush of dead vines. Catching himself, he rounded the tree. A red ribbon, tied to a low-hung limb, flapped in the breeze. The kind forest rangers or loggers might place if they were working to thin out the material to stave off potential fire hazards.

Jax rubbed his eyes to get a grip. The ax hung to his side as he made his way back to the pile of wood. Either he was getting old and senile, or the drive had made him more tired than he realized. Honestly, he'd been go-go-go for so long, he couldn't remember the last time he'd stopped and relaxed.

Or to deal with the mental wounds from his last case, and the one before that, and all those that had come before, which clearly still lingered. He raked his grimy hand through his hair with the thought of what he'd be like in ten years when he was already having issues now.

It might be time to hang up his badge. Most law enforcement checked out at twenty years to let someone fresh handle the job. He'd passed that benchmark a while ago. He did have Rachel now. But if he struggled to leave the team for a week, how would he give up complete control?

Something to think about. Later. He'd dawdled enough, and Abby would wonder where he'd gone.

He grabbed another batch of logs, sure the pile had been more substantial twenty minutes ago. *Huh.* His focus landed again on that squirrel, who held a nut in its claws and gnawed away without care. Jax's thoughts had drifted in ten different directions. More likely, he might be losing it.

Heading back to the cabin, he thought of Abby, who was younger by a decade. Did she look at him as too old? He'd never thought about that before, but so much had changed between them.

He tossed the wood into the pile and returned to his truck, tired of worrying. He wasn't so old he couldn't fix a damn tire—he might as well do that first.

Chapter Nine

Rachel made another call to Trudy before she'd crossed the street with Brody toward the diner. The fire chief might have updated the tenants with the disappointing status of their building, but social services would need to assist, and Trudy had her own network of helpers in town. Between the two, the tenants would be taken care of before nightfall.

After confirming a plan, Brody and Rachel stepped into Milly's warm diner, buzzing with customers. The smell of chicken pot pie and fresh coffee hit her nose first, then her stomach. She'd barely eaten today and felt the wobble in her legs.

Milly must have read her mind. "Let me get you deputies something to go. The usual work?"

"Thank you, Milly," Brody said.

Rachel nodded, already picturing the turkey on fresh-baked sourdough, a wedge of pickle on the side. "Appreciate it."

The four tenants she'd seen on the corner were down to three and huddled in a booth. Missing was Winona from the gas station.

"What's the story, deputy. We getting back in tonight?" the oldest woman of the group asked.

Guess she'd beat the fire marshal and chief over to deliver the news. "I'm afraid that won't be possible, Ms…?"

"Dorothy Abernathy." The woman rested her hand on her chest, like she was holding something in place under her floral housecoat.

"Ms. Abernathy. I'm sure the fire chief will be by shortly to let you all know the details."

"Any word about what caused the explosion?"

"There's some theories, but nothing solid yet," Rachel said.

"Sounds about right." The man who spoke had black spiked hair. Snake tattoos ringed his sagging biceps and had faded with time. "You bureaucrats are all the same. No one likes to commit."

"Just don't want to lead you astray, mister...?"

"Chuck Pullman."

"Mr. Pullman."

"Just Chuck."

"Nothing's definite. What I need from you, all of you, are statements."

"Probably that man in 206 started it," he said.

"Mr. Hatfield?"

"Yeah." Chuck slid back into his plaid insulated jacket and blew on his coffee. "Something's not right about him."

"Can you expand on that?"

"It's just a feeling." He huffed. "Keeps all kinds of weird hours."

So did she, depending on her shift. She'd come back to Chuck. "Who lived downstairs where the explosion originated?" Rachel said, pulling out her notebook.

"That would be my place," a woman dressed in running tights and a windbreaker said. "I'm Melissa."

"And you were out?"

"Gone for a run. When I came back, my place was crawling with firemen. Can you imagine if I'd been home?" The color drained from her face.

Rachel had imagined it: Melissa was lucky. "How well did everyone know Mr. Hatfield?"

"Not well," Melissa said. "Wait, you said...did." She scanned the room, appearing to only now realize he was not among them. "Is he okay?"

"No, ma'am. Mr. Hatfield is deceased."

They glanced at each other before focusing on the coffee cups in front of them.

"That's terrible," Dorothy finally said. "I didn't think the fire got that far?"

"Had to be the gas we smelled," Chuck said. "That'll kill you."

"What gas?" Melissa said.

Chuck gave her the rundown of the weird odor.

"Winona hadn't felt well and told Chuck, who called it in and cleared the building," Dorothy said.

"It's terrible that something happened to that guy," Chuck said. "But like I said, he worked weird hours and wasn't that friendly in between."

"He kept to himself, Chuck," Melissa said. "That doesn't make a person unfriendly."

Chuck shrugged.

"Did he live alone?" Rachel asked.

"You want what's on the lease application or the truth?" Chuck said.

"Truth works," Rachel said.

"Well…" Dorothy's voice dropped to a whisper. "When he was at work, I was pretty sure I'd heard someone upstairs. I live right below him you see."

"Probably the rats. How many times have we asked that good-for-nothing landlord to fumigate the place," Melissa said, her nose wrinkling.

Dorothy seemed to think about that. "That could be true."

They broke into a conversation about shorting the landlord his rent, although he'd throw them out if they did.

"Who's the landlord?" Rachel said, interrupting them.

"The staff at Landmark Company is who we generally deal with, but the owner of Landmark is the Commissioner," Chuck said.

"Commissioner Troy Marks?"

They nodded.

Great. She'd hoped to avoid him in Jax's absence. It was enough to see him and Jax go at it. She had no desire to be on the man's radar. She jotted the information into her notebook. "Speaking of tenants, I'd seen Winona on the corner with you earlier. Does she live in the complex?"

"Winona's my great niece, and she had places to be," Dorothy said as a little furry head popped out from her housecoat. A yorkie, with its brown and black silky fur and eyes that protruded from its tiny head. "This here is Mighty."

"Cute," Rachel said, though she'd always gravitated to big dogs. "So, your niece lives with you?"

"Occasionally," Dorothy said, "when she's on the outs with her boyfriend."

Rachel's focus drifted to Brody, who'd struck up a conversation with what appeared to be a local at the counter, dressed in work boots, stained jeans, and an oversized sweatshirt. Brody lifted his chin.

Rachel returned to her group of witnesses. "As to Mr. Hatfield, did anyone hear anything odd the last couple of days?"

They shook their heads.

"You said you thought someone might be upstairs, Dorothy. Was that recently?" Rachel said.

"Yesterday, actually."

"Was it footsteps you heard, or an argument? Fighting, perhaps?"

"Wait. Didn't you say the fire or gases got to that young man?" Dorothy said.

"I didn't say that."

Melissa cowered back into the booth. "Was he attacked? Should we be concerned for our safety?"

"I can't say at this point, but—"

"Then why aren't we allowed back in?" Dorothy's lower lip protruded as she stroked the fur on Mighty's head.

"Smoke damage, isn't it?" Chuck snapped. "We'll likely be out for weeks if that's the case."

Keeping these tenants on track was like wrangling cats. "As to your safety, Mr. Hatfield appears to have been the target," she said. Whether evidence suggested that or not, it was better to allay their fears than fuel them. "Again, did you see anyone or hear anything suspicious?"

They shook their heads in unison this time.

"If you want answers, start with his workplace," Chuck said. "They're a rough bunch at the docks. He could've had a run-in down there and it came home with him."

"He worked at the marina?" Melissa said. "That explains why he smelled like fish."

They were back to chatting about the price of cod at the market now. She understood the concept of interviewing people separately, but it didn't appear any of them had much to offer.

Rachel handed them each her card. "I'll be in touch if I have more questions. If you think of anything in the meantime, please call."

They barely acknowledged her departure as Melissa began filling her neighbors in on her daughter living in West Shore, and that she had an extra room where she could stay. Chuck might have an old buddy he'd bunk with. Hopefully, Trudy could help Dorothy and Winona.

Rachel joined Brody, still talking with the man at the counter.

"This gentleman thinks our victim might've been a drug dealer," Brody said.

"What makes you say that?" she asked. Rachel thought of the slash marks on the man's arm and the partial one she'd seen on his chest. Self-inflicted had been her first thought, but if this guy was right, they could be a statement, too.

"He works at the docks at night, and there's no telling what's coming and going out of there," the man said. His focus was straight ahead, then at his coffee.

"The marina encompasses an entire stretch of the river," Rachel said. "Any idea where or for who?"

"Nope."

"So, you're basing your opinion on him working nights?"

"That, and town talk."

Until Chuck had mentioned the rough crowd down there, she hadn't heard anything negative before. "On the commercial side of the marina, or the charter side?" Rachel asked.

The man nodded.

Not helpful. "What's your name?"

"John."

Rachel glanced at Milly, who was placing her and Brody's sandwiches in a bag. She caught her eye, but Milly looked away. Could be some history between the two worth circling back on later.

"Well, appreciate the info."

Rachel grabbed the bag, handing it to Brody, before slipping Milly a twenty.

"What did you think of the guy at the counter?" Brody asked as he and Rachel stepped outside.

"This town is full of people who like to offer opinions. Why? Did you recognize him?" she asked.

"Thought I saw him a few days ago near the beach park when I was out on my motorbike. That's why I approached him at the counter. Don't recall seeing him before that, but we have a lot of outliers in the area. There's that homeless camp south of the state park, too."

Rachel nodded, sensing what Sheriff Turner must sometimes feel. A vast area to cover with only a few of them to cover it.

With the building tenants believing Bruce Hatfield was odd and kept weird hours, and the man at the counter suggesting something shady was happening at the boat docks, it was a place to start. She'd avoid Commissioner Marks as long as she could.

Chapter Ten

Jax pulled the spare tire from underneath the truck and tossed it on the ground at the same time a vehicle ambled up the road their direction. He recognized the US Forest Ranger logo on the side panel of a state-issued SUV. As the truck parked and a tall man stretched out, he smiled.

"Samuel Hanover. Thought you'd be retired by now. How the hell are you?" Jax said. Sam was somewhere in his mid to late sixties, given the gray outnumbering the dark on his head, unlike Jax, who'd maintained his mostly sandy mop.

"What the hell, is right. I'd heard someone had rented the place pre-opening of the area. Wouldn't have guessed in a million years it'd be you. Took you for the slumming sort." Sam let out a laugh that suited his ample frame—deep and boisterous. He approached Jax with an extended hand. "Good to see you, my friend."

Jax wiped the tire grease on his jeans and shook Sam's hand. They'd run into each other several times over the years in town, had dinner more than once. Most recently, in February, when a call for hiring recruits for seasonal work had gone out. "You got that right, but I'm here with Abby."

"Well, that makes more sense." He laughed again and bumped Jax's shoulder. "Real glad to see things might work out between you two. Evie will be glad to hear it."

"How is your better half?"

"Oh, she's great. Still putting up with me after forty years. Figure she'll be eligible for sainthood soon."

"Think you're right, and probably wishing you'd retire by now."

"I'd only be underfoot and messing with her committee meetings and bridge parties. Then I'd surely be in trouble. You retire, you die."

Jax straightened. He hadn't thought about what he'd do to fill the gap when he left law enforcement. He possessed no other marketable skills, except for changing tires, and only because he'd had far too much practice this past year. Abby's view of him might change since she'd still be working…. "So, what brings you out? Forestry department responsible for the overhaul of this station?"

"God no. That project got privatized, and you won't catch me complaining. My new digs are just fine."

"Where are you located now, anyway?"

"Just over five miles east by way of the lower road. The forest trail cuts off about a mile of that."

"Good to know."

"You need anything, you come find me."

"Don't expect to be leaving for anything but firewood to keep Abby warm. Speaking of which, she's making her Hawaiian stew, and there's always plenty to share."

"Mmmm. Hard to say no to that, but afraid I'll have to. Got rounds to finish. Besides, it's best you lovebirds keep reconciling. Didn't mean to disturb you. Just seen the smoke coming from this direction, and thought I'd check it out, what with the dry summer we've had."

"It's been a drought year for most of the state," Jax said.

"You know it."

He did and was glad Abby wasn't outside to overhear their conversation. Setting aside being a cop was easier when you weren't chatting with another officer, or, in this case, a ranger. "You patrol this part of the mountain often?"

"When the public's around, sure. Not so often since that road's been closed. I've spent a fair amount of time surveying from my eye in the sky."

"Is that what they're calling the tower?"

"I do. I care little about what anyone else calls it. It's the best place to see a problem before it's a problem."

Jax liked Sam's thinking. "Smart."

"Damn straight."

Jax shifted. "Before you go, any chance you've seen anyone around here earlier today, or yesterday, from that tower?"

"I only just clocked in this afternoon. Nothing caught my attention on the way here, though. Why? Has someone been messing with the place? We had a vandal incident a month ago when some kids ignored the closure…."

"No vandals, but I'm not sure about the other." He explained the few things they'd found that were disturbing. "Almost appears someone was using the place before we got here today."

"Hmmm. Happy to check the log at the station in case some hikers came through. See if my counterpart saw anything unusual or noted activity he failed to mention. I'll swing by tomorrow if I find anything."

"They got you working tomorrow, too?"

"I'm here for the next few days. Flu's taken out a few of the crew."

"Gotcha. Well, if you find something, I'd appreciate it."

"Sure thing. But I wouldn't be too worried if I were you. There've been plenty of contractors working on the place, renovating and cleaning graffiti. Probably hustled to finish and got lazy. If not that, you know how *no trespass* signs work."

"Damn magnets for those who think it's a suggestion rather than a rule."

"You know it."

Sam winked and was down the driveway and out of sight before Jax could gather his tools off the ground. He'd just tightened the lug wrench on the bolt to change the flat tire when his name came as a screech from inside the cabin.

He clamored to get upright and sprinted inside, where Abby stood in the entry to the bedroom, a butcher knife in her hands. "What's wrong?"

"That."

He joined her in the doorway and peered into the bedroom, where two beady eyes peered back. Blinking. The creature's pink nose twitched, likely deciding whether they were a threat. "It's an opossum."

"I know what it is," Abby said, rigid. A slight tremor in her hands.

"It's harmless as long as we don't corner it."

"I'm aware of that, too."

"Then why are you shaking?"

"I'm not shaking. The fire went out; it's freezing in here."

Not that cold. "Okay," he said, but before he could suggest he get a broom or give the creature some space, the animal disappeared under the bed.

Abby lowered her knife and dropped to all fours. "Wow. Okay. You'll want to see this."

Jax crouched to look under the bed. No opossum, but a trapdoor was slid to one side. They got up and together shifted the bed to reveal a person-sized hole which dropped straight onto the ground and out.

Chapter Eleven

Rachel and Brody arrived at the marina to find several cars in the lot. A few empty trailers attached to trucks awaited their owner's return, but most rented out slips for the season. The charter fishermen did anyway.

There'd been no cause on an official level to visit here in recent months, but Rachel had run this direction several times since arriving in Misty Pines. The briny smell and hustle of the area was appealing. Boats would be motoring in or out. The day's catch carted off the dock or sold right where they were cleaned. The true vibe of a coastal community, complete with squawking seagulls swirling overhead waiting for scraps to be tossed and barking seals sunbathing on the farthest end of the docks.

While the town itself moved at a slow pace, there was usually activity here. Though not so much today.

"What are we thinking?" Brody said.

"From what I've witnessed, the charter boats return across the bar between two and four o'clock." At nearly three, Rachel had hoped to hit the sweet spot of vessels still offloading their catches and cleaning, and those arriving. "Perhaps Mr. Hatfield worked on one of them."

"Based on the odd hours, he might have worked commercial," Brody said.

"Possibly, but with a good mix here in the marina, it's a place to start."

They headed toward the main ramp that led to the docks. A shack, maybe twice the size of a toll booth, stationed near the top. Rachel stopped and tried the door. Locked. She cupped her eyes on the glass. The lights were out, and the red light of a coffee pot illuminated one corner. Someone could be returning at some point.

Rachel continued to the ramp, and Brody followed.

The closest she'd ever been to a boat prior to moving to Misty Pines was the Portland Sternwheeler, when she and her parents had gone on a Christmas cruise one year. She might have been nine? No, ten. Her BFF, Blake, had come along as he was staying with them that week. His parents had decided the Bahamas, alone, fit their idea of the perfect holiday. Later, it came out they'd hoped to save their marriage by getting away. They divorced before summer.

Despite their shortcomings, her parents were at least still married. Happily, from what she could tell. Their biggest argument might be about her, or what her father deemed were *her choices*. She'd never thought it was funny that her best friends had often been boys. Mostly, there weren't a lot of girls in the neighborhood. But she also got boys on a different level. Maybe because she had no interest in them, knowing that early on, they didn't have all that messiness associated with her chasing them.

Now, as she looked at Brody, the flex of the ramp under them like walking in a bouncy house, she once again felt like one of the boys. Accepted. She intended to keep it that way and not screw up this investigation.

She scanned the docks as they'd descended the ramp. Over half the boats were still out, the other half void of people. Then she spotted someone on top of a good forty-foot fishing boat named the Titan.

"Hey," she yelled to the man as they approached. He was slightly younger than Rachel, wearing orange waders and clasping a hose in his hand. The splash that launched off the boat deck in their direction missed them by an inch.

"What's up, officers?" He lowered the hose, letting the water continue to flow over the edge.

"Wondered if you might know a Bruce Hatfield?" Brody said before Rachel could respond.

"Heard his name before, maybe. Doesn't work for me, if that's what you're asking." Another splash, and Rachel side-stepped it.

That one had been on purpose. "Care to turn off that water?"

The man's look slid down her body. "No problem, ma'am."

Brody side-eyed her.

"It's Deputy Killian. When you're done, please come down here so we can chat, Mr....?" She casually put her hand on her vest, resting above her gun.

He hung the hose through one of the bow's overflow slots and hopped off the boat before shutting down the water stream. "Friends call me Robby. And sorry about the near miss. Didn't mean any disrespect."

Right. "None taken," she said.

"You check with the Protocol?" He craned his neck toward a trawler tied off three docks over. White with blue trim, desperate for a paint job.

"Just getting started. What do you know of Mr. Hatfield?"

"Not much. Like I said, he doesn't work for me, but deckhands change boats like they do underwear."

She'd expect no less of an analogy from this guy. "He one of those deckhands?"

"Not that I know of."

"How's his name come up then?"

"Not sure it has. I only said it sounded familiar."

He was already stepping on her nerves. "Appreciate the direction of the Protocol." Maybe they'd find someone more cooperative there.

"Sure. Though you might not find them around yet. They head out at night."

"They hauling fish?" Brody said.

"Yup. Lingcod. Tuna. Rockfish. Probably depends on what jumps on the boat." He winked at Rachel.

Either the guy was oblivious to *bug off* signals, or he was telling her something else.

"They're commercial?"

"Charter."

Fishing restrictions were not in her wheelhouse or her jurisdiction, but she believed those could be legally caught. Regulations would limit the amount allowed, however. Night might make that harder to monitor.

"Thanks again," she said.

"Then there's the yellow monster over there," he said, pointing to a boat on the other side of the marina.

"They a fishing boat, too?" Brody asked.

"No. They guide the ships in."

"Guide them where?" Rachel said.

"See those freighters?" He lifted his chin to the open water.

She and Brody set their gaze beyond the basin entry.

"Sure," Brody said.

"How you think they got here?"

Rachel straightened. "They floated in on the water." She could do sarcasm, too.

He smiled. "They get led in. That's what Big Bird does. They specifically work at night with a special crew that brings ships from the Pacific into the Columbia River. Bar's treacherous, and it takes an experienced pilot to avoid running aground. There's actually a few of those pilot boats. And commercial boats. Charter boats...."

"I see," she said. "So, Mr. Hatfield might have been on one of those pilot boats. Or he worked on the Protocol. Or somewhere else." Robby's game was clear—Bruce Hatfield could have worked anywhere but here, and they could knock themselves out trying to find where.

He snorted. "Yeah. Except over there, I know the pilots. He's not one of them." He spat on the deck. Charming. "Doubtful he did anything but tie off and clean boats." That made some sense given Bruce's bare bones apartment. "If nothing else, check with Aggie in the shack. She might have a better idea."

"Shack was dark when we passed," Rachel said.

He shrugged. "Probably out for a smoke and making rounds. That's why she's the person to ask. Not much goes on here that she's not at least privy to."

"Good to know, Robby."

"You can call me Rob."

Guess they weren't friends. "We'll be back in touch if we have more questions." She didn't wait for a response.

"Got a feeling that Rob's not telling us everything?" Brody said as they started back.

"I sensed the same."

"You did?" Brody said, smiling. "I mean, yeah. I think so, too. I didn't like the way he looked at you, though. Then to throw out the possibilities. Why didn't he start with this Aggie if she's the person who knows everyone?"

"Good question." They arrived at the shack to find it still dark, and the door locked. This time, the coffee pot light had gone off. *Huh.* It could have been on a timer and automatically shut down. "Could be he knew she wouldn't be here to ask."

"We going to hang around and wait?"

"Let's check with the Protocol and the pilot ship and decide then."

They slipped into Rachel's patrol car to drive to the other side of the basin. She'd left her cell phone in between the seats and checked it before starting the engine. Having missed a call from the ME, she launched Voicemail.

"Deputy Killian, this is Grace. Shocking." She chuckled, and Rachel smirked—this woman liked to mess with people. "Just calling with an update after doing a preliminary autopsy. There was an odd marking on the body that reminded me of an old case. I need to pull that file before giving you a definitive, and I'd like to follow up on something in that regard once I have it. Just wanted to give you a heads up. If it's what I think it is, we could have a serial killer on our hands."

Chapter Twelve

Jax secured the trapdoor in the bedroom, and Abby had said little more about it. The theory that Sam floated—kids messing around—had some merit. A young group of people would be drawn to a warm cabin to hang, especially if they could easily get access.

Either way, no one would be getting in while they were there. Not with the logs Jax had placed over the opening. If they tried, they'd make enough noise to alert them.

Now, he and Abby were back enjoying their getaway. Few things calmed Jax, but a roaring fire and Abby reading a book while he sat with his thoughts, was one of them. That and a full stomach.

"That stew might've been one of your best."

"It needed more ginger."

"It was amazing."

She gave him a small smile. Something was on her mind that had nothing to do with the lack of spices in the stew, the hole in the bedroom floor, or their getting settled at the cabin. He could tell from the quiet ride to get there, the intensity with which she'd held that knife in the bedroom.

"Everything good at work? You'd mentioned the move?"

"It's all good."

"Hmmm. I only ask because you've seemed a little…" No one liked to be told what they were, but—. "Well, you've seemed off."

"How so?"

"Choosing to come out here, to start. After what happened earlier this year—"

"Back on the horse, as they say."

"Yeah, if you ride horses, which you don't, and you've never enjoyed the outdoors." She stared into the flames, not giving him anything. "While I'm not complaining...."

"Yes, you are. You don't like it."

"Of course I do. The woods, the solitude—this is my element. You, not so much." He shifted. "What's really on your mind, Abby? I get we've had a road back to each other, but I'm feeling good about where we've been heading. Aren't you?"

"Yes. Obviously." She swept her hand across the room, then resettled into the crux of Jax's arm.

As she took a few breaths, the expansion of her ribs pushed against Jax. God, he loved this woman.

"But there is something," she said.

"I'm listening."

A knock came from the front door. She raised herself off Jax and looked at him. They could be hearing things. Another knock. Nope. No mistaking that.

One part of the cabin had a good number of glass panes, but they'd pulled the blinds, and a curtain masked the window in the front door.

"Are you expecting someone?" he said.

"Yeah, I ordered Thai." She rolled her eyes.

He smirked, then grew serious. Could be Sam back already with something.

Abby remained on the couch as he approached the door, stepping to the side. "Who is it?"

"Hey! My name's Hannah. Saw the light on. I'm a neighbor, sort of." She chuckled, and Jax could hear the long-drawn-out release of her breath. "I'm sorry to bother you. My phone's not working."

He glanced at Abby, who was standing now, leaning on the sofa arm, and shaking her head in disbelief. He agreed. Besides the fact the woman shouldn't be here with the area closed to the public, she'd clearly done no research about the lack of cell service.

Short of an emergency, Jax had no plans to disclose the satellite phone in his truck. He and Abby were doing well; she was about to confide in him. His inability to be completely cut off from the world wouldn't be the reason for the night to turn otherwise.

Jax opened the door to a woman in her thirties, maybe younger, older. Hard to tell with the shadows cast from the porch light.

She had a sheepish grin. "Hope I'm not interrupting."

Shoot. He'd neglected to smooth his hair and button his shirt. "You're fine. What's this about a phone? Everything okay?"

"Oh yeah, completely. It's just my boyfriend's supposed to join me, and I came out ahead to set up camp. I'm supposed to give him the exact location, and now I can't do that."

A romantic interlude not going according to plan was far from an emergency. "You know the area isn't open to campers until next week?" Jax said.

"Gosh, no, I didn't."

"You didn't see the sign at the entry?"

Abby came up behind Jax and tugged on his shirt. Right—no being a cop this weekend.

"I guess I might have," Hannah said, "but there were no blockades on the roadway."

Jax nodded, looking to get back to the sofa with Abby. "Well, wish we could help. It's not just your cell, though. There's no service out here."

She glanced at Jax, then back toward the road. "Hadn't thought of that. Assumed since this was an abandoned ranger station…" She rubbed the space between her brows. "He may show on his own anyway." She shuddered.

"Why don't you come in and take the chill off?" Abby said.

Jax forced a smile, knowing better than to argue. "Sure, come on in. Fire's blazing."

"If you don't mind? When I said he might show, I don't mean tonight."

"No problem. You can warm yourself, if nothing else, before you head back to your camp. Tomorrow, you can drive down the mountain and call him from there. Or perhaps it's best you find another location."

She nodded. "Good idea."

"You hungry?" Abby said.

Hannah came inside, stepped past Jax. "No, just ate, but thanks. Coffee would be great, though?" Her eyes flicked to the right, toward the kitchen.

Jax had eyed a Keurig in the corner when they'd arrived.

Before he could mention it, Abby was in the kitchen. "Dark or light roast? We have options."

Jax tracked her movement. Very accommodating—and not her usual self. She almost seemed glad for the distraction and not to continue their conversation.

"Dark would be amazing." The woman peeled out of her jacket and strode to the fireplace, rubbing her shaking hands together over the radiant heat. "This is a cute place. You two honeymooners?"

Abby dropped a pod into the machine and hit the button, then winked at Jax as she joined him in the living room. "Kind of. So, tell us about your boyfriend. Sounds like you two haven't camped in this area before. Why here?"

"Oh, that's easy. Have you seen the views?" She laughed. "I mean, you must have, right?"

"The Columbia River below is one of a kind," Jax said.

"Yeah. We've only seen it in pictures. Or I mean I have," Hannah said.

"Where you from?" Abby asked.

"Oh, um, Portland area. So, obviously, the river runs through some of that area, but it doesn't look like this. And I lived in Seattle, too."

"What part of Portland?" Jax asked, thinking of the Columbia River Gorge. There were many places in the Portland area to get glimpses of the river's beauty that equaled what they had at the coast.

"You know, all over."

Well, not everyone traveled around either. Could be a city girl. Or she was leaving a few pieces out of her story. "We used to live there," he said, reining himself in.

"Nice. Anyway, my parents used to bring me to the area, and we always drove past the Camel Mountain signs." She looked away. "My boyfriend thought this would be the perfect place to hang out. Guess he didn't realize it was closed either." She clasped and unclasped her hands.

The coffee beeped, and Hannah jumped, almost startled. Abby turned to go to the kitchen, but Hannah moved that way first. "I'll get it," she said.

"I don't mind," Abby said.

"Please. I insist. You've been so kind to invite me in, I won't make you wait on me, too." Hannah slid the cup out of the coffee machine and opened the drawer just below it. Jax watched as she grabbed a spoon and then placed her hand on the refrigerator. She pulled it back and turned.

Jax and Abby stared at her.

"Need some milk?" Jax said. He had no idea what Abby was thinking, but he had an idea it might be the same thing.

Hannah sure seemed to know her way around their kitchen.

Chapter Thirteen

Serial killer? The medical examiner's words had clicked through Rachel's head as she and Brody approached the Protocol and the *Big Bird,* only to find no signs of anyone home on either. With no one else to speak with, they returned to the station.

After giving Koa a long break, Rachel came in to find Trudy on the phone. "We've gone through this before, hon. Likely a raven got those socks this time."

Trudy's eyes were closed, her head resting on the back of her chair, face lifted toward the ceiling. Rachel chuckled, and Koa trotted over to Trudy, resting her chin on her lap. Without looking, Trudy reached into her drawer of treats, then gave a couple to Koa, all the while staying tuned into the caller.

The small-town issues of Misty Pines were many, and generally innocuous. A dead body in a building with a gas leak and ensuing explosion were genuine activity around here. Rachel was ready for that, unless it turned into a serial killer.

Brody had said nothing when he overheard the ME's suspicions, but he didn't have to—he'd have called Jax right then. But until Dr. Shocking was sure about what they had, and shared that information, there was nothing to report. Rachel would keep moving. Trudy appeared to have a good handle on the rest.

"I understand, but…." Or maybe not. "Yes. Okay. Absolutely. I'll send a deputy. I'm sure it's nothing." She ripped off her headset. "Either I'm getting old, or these people are getting nuttier."

"What's the problem?" Rachel said, unstrapping her flashlight so she could sit more comfortably in the desk chair. Koa trotted to her and curled at her feet. Brody had disappeared into the back of the station.

"It's Allen Schmidt and his wife, Betty. Betty's always been a bit of a worrier. Enough that she's generally agoraphobic. Which means—"

"She's afraid to go outside."

"Correct. But Allen's a good egg and he's fenced their yard off and she'll go far enough to hang their clothes in the summer. Even has a glass of lemonade on the back porch occasionally."

Rachel appreciated the backstory but shifted in the chair. "Something different this time she went out?"

"Hmmm," Trudy said. "Appears her husband's pants and a sweatshirt are gone. Along with some socks. Now the last time the socks went missing, it was the crows, so I told her—"

"Except this time, we have a fire on the edge of town, along with a homicide."

She cocked an eyebrow. "True enough, hon."

"By the way, did your church group figure out where Dorothy and Winona will stay while the complex is off limits?"

"Sort of. Dorothy's staying with me. Winona has gotten back with her boyfriend again, and if that falls apart, I have another spare room."

"Frank good with that?"

"He's in Boston for the week, visiting his brother, who took a fall. I'll enjoy the company. A few of the other ladies are prepping meals, so I won't have to."

"Thank you for taking care of that." It was nice to see the community pull together. Portland had its helpers, but nothing beat a small-town network. "What's the Schmidt's address? Probably a good idea to send Brody to check it out, just in case."

Trudy cleared her throat and handed Rachel the information. "Sweetie, Betty's quite fragile. I'd hate for someone with less—"

Rachel nodded, getting the gist. "Thanks, Trudy. I'll handle it myself."

Trudy smiled. "And eat something before you waste away. Don't make me mother you like I do Jax."

Rachel stood and smiled before tucking the flashlight back into her belt. "Like I could stop you."

"There is some truth to that. You out for the night then?"

"After the Schmidt's, I have another couple of stops, and then yes. Garrett will run the night shift. I'm a phone call away if needed."

"Matt said he could be available for overflow tonight, too. He checked in after the forensics group took over. He got your evidence logged."

"Appreciate him stepping up, but that man needs to rest. I'll put myself on the overflow. And I'll be interested if they find anything on that hair tie."

"DNA will take about seventy-two hours. I'll try to expedite and make sure you get the report." She put her headset back on. "You're doing great, by the way," she said. "Keeping the team on task. Organized. Jax would be proud."

"Thanks," Rachel said, but didn't agree. Her interrogation skills at the diner hadn't given her much, and Rob at the docks had provided less. Now she was waiting to hear from the ME on what they had, because she had no theories of her own. Jax would have plenty by now.

With Koa in the backseat, she pulled into the Schmidt's single-car driveway, realizing they lived on the same street as the complex fire. The house was well-kept with a manicured lawn and colorful spinning wheelies in the front yard. "Back in a jiff," she said to Koa.

A man north of seventy answered the door.

"You're not Jax," he said.

"I am not."

"Where's Jax?"

"He's—"

"Betty. Darling. It's not Jax. You okay with that?"

"Who is it?"

Rachel tucked her hand into her vest. "Deputy Rachel Killian, ma'am. Trudy sent me. Jax is away, but he's left me in charge." She added a smile, hoping it projected in her words. She'd come across plenty of people who questioned her in the past, or were hesitant to let her in. Usually, she could work around that resistance since they'd called for help. But there was no way around the fact she wasn't Jax.

"I guess if Trudy says she's okay."

Or Trudy. "She does," Rachel said.

Allen stepped aside.

The interior reflected the care of the outside—it was as neat a pin as her grandmother would've said. Doilies on the cushions and an old TV on a solid end table. And something sweet and yummy wafted in the air. "I understand you have concerns about some missing clothes."

"Not concerns. Theft." Betty emerged from the kitchen. "You hungry? Just pulled some banana muffins from the oven."

"I'm good," she said, her stomach disagreeing. It was frowned upon to accept, or she might have. "But the clothes?"

"Yes. Trudy has good opinions more times than not, but no ravens got to these. Someone stole them. I don't go out much, you see. When I do, I observe and remember everything. Including where I put things."

"Where were the clothes, ma'am?"

"Hanging on the clothesline. Come see for yourself."

Allen trailed as Betty led Rachel to the backyard. She pointed to where several jeans hung now.

"I already know what you're thinking," Betty said. "How can she be sure?"

"She is," Allen said. "Woman has a mind like a steel trap."

"Yes, I do. He has four of the same pairs. He works at the hardware store, and they have a uniform."

Allen went on to describe his tan shirt with his name tag. "Been wearing the same thing for twenty years."

"Yes, he has," Betty said. "And as you can see, there are only three pairs of jeans out there. Along with his four shirts. There's also only one sweatshirt."

"I assume there were more before?"

"Yes, two."

"When did you notice them missing, Mrs. Schmidt?"

"It's Betty, and it was a couple of days ago, I suppose. I didn't report it then because I wanted to go through everything first. Just in case the old mind *was* faltering."

"Or if a bird got them," Allen offered.

"Right. It has happened before with smaller items, but these are far too heavy."

"Now you're convinced someone took them?"

"Correct," she said.

"About mid-day, we heard something," Allen said. "I'd come home for lunch, and Betty here makes the best tuna on rye there is."

"It's the celery," Betty said. "Along with the sweet pickles." She winked.

Rachel smiled. "What did you hear exactly?"

"Not quite sure. Just something. But we'd just settled onto the couch to catch an episode of The Price is Right before I had to get back to work."

"A woman was about to spin that big wheel," Betty said. "We don't spend money on all those extras where you can stop the picture and come back to it."

"I see," Rachel said. The couple reminded her of her grandparents, and she had to hold back a smile. "Was anything else missing?"

"No."

"Was there anything special about the jeans that would help me identify them if I came across them?" A complete long shot, and the report would likely get tucked away in short order.

"Oh, I can tell you that," Allen said. "I spilled some damn engine oil on them at the store the other day."

"Careless fool," Betty said. "I tried to get it out, but try as I might, a black streak ran down the side."

"I liked the design." He winked. "That's why I wouldn't let her throw them away. The pinstripe makes me look dapper. That aside, I'm not sure why the thief would snag that one."

"Probably didn't see it," Betty said.

That pinstripe sounded familiar. Had she seen those jeans at the fire scene? Or in the café? Not at the docks. "And the sweatshirt?"

"Got that in Vegas. Zips up the front."

"Yeah, had a convention and left me home," Betty said, pouting.

"Asked you to go."

She waved him off like this was an ongoing argument.

But it wasn't their interaction that had Rachel bothered. Hadn't she seen those jeans and the sweatshirt just described on the man at the café that had directed her to the docks with a theory of the drug activity happening there? The man Brody had seen at the beach park?

She was almost sure of it.

Finding out who he was just became a priority.

Chapter Fourteen

Jax walked Hannah outside. The darkness consumed the forest ahead, in contrast to the bright cabin. The cloudy night sky offered little illumination until his eyes adjusted.

"You need me to accompany you to your campsite?" he asked.

"I'm good. Thank you. Experienced camper here."

Not so experienced, or she would have known more about the area she was coming into. "Still, might be good if you tell me which direction you're headed and where your camp is."

She pointed out ahead, meaning just about anywhere, including the forest. Clearly, she wanted her privacy. Fine—if she afforded them the same. If Sam came by again, he'd make him aware of the interloper, and he could do with her what he wished.

Though he thought back to the sounds he'd heard earlier when chopping wood. The missing kindling he'd prepared—or what he thought was missing—the open trapdoor, and her familiarity with their kitchen. He could say something or not make a big deal out of it. Nothing was taken and no real harm done. Plus, he could hear Abby in his head. The way she'd tugged on his shirt for him to stop being a cop.

"Well, if anything comes up, you know where to find us," he said. "Always happy to help a neighbor."

She smiled. Almost sad. "Thanks. I'll give you a shout. But I'll be good, I'm sure." She shifted feet, tentative. "Can I ask what you do for a living?" She shifted again from one foot to another. "You two seem like real nice people."

It's not like they were ashamed of their profession. "Law."

"Both of you?"

"Different branches, but yes. What about you?"

"Nothing like that." She shifted again. "You guys have a great night. Thanks again for the coffee."

There was a hint of regret in her voice. "Everything okay, Hannah?"

She turned toward him, this time with a smile. "Absolutely."

Jax's eye twitched as he watched the young woman leave on the gravel path, her flashlight bobbing. At the forest line, she turned left right. Must be where the trail Sam had mentioned began. Soon, the night swallowed her light.

When Jax came in, Abby was curled on the couch. "Okay, that was weird. Something feels off about her." He dropped onto the sofa next to her.

"You probably made her nervous when you grilled her about where she lived."

"It was an innocent question. Besides, she was nervous on her own and eager to get away from that part of the conversation."

"She was, but again—"

"She also seemed to be a bit too knowledgeable of our kitchen. You saw that, right?"

"Of course." Abby sat up. "You didn't ask her about that on the way out, I hope?"

"No. Thought about it, though."

"Me too, but utensils are often near the coffee machine, aren't they? At least close to where the plates are."

"I suppose, and it's not a big kitchen. But she reached for the fridge like she knew there'd be a half gallon of milk waiting. Most people would never assume that or be so blatant about it."

Abby shrugged. "Nervous energy could've gotten the better of her. And people have different levels of social boundaries. Not everyone guards their frozen dinners like you do."

He didn't smile. "Different in that some don't have any, you mean?"

"That too. The fact she came right in, for example," Abby said.

Abby had invited her in, but arguing wasn't how he saw any part of this night going. "I see your point."

"Again, not saying she's not odd. And she absolutely was who used the cabin before us."

"One hundred percent." Thankfully, they agreed on that.

"But if she's out here on her own, expecting her boyfriend to show tomorrow…." She rocked her head. "I'm just saying I could see her concern and why she'd find a haven. No woman likes to feel vulnerable."

The conversation might have drifted away from Hannah. "Perhaps. But you'd also think if you were coming to this area, you'd know you won't have cell service and be prepared. Not to belabor the point, she did ignore the signs. Which is trespassing and—"

"She probably thought it was harmless, and maybe romantic to have the mountain to themselves. Like me." Jax flushed, liking the sound of that. "Lacking cell service doesn't always stop people from enjoying the outdoors. Let's face it, not everyone has access to satellite phones."

Jax tensed. "No. No, they don't."

She tilted her head to the side. Waiting?

He smiled.

She bumped into his arm. "Geez, Jax, I already know. Might as well fess up."

"What?" he said, determined to play dumb as long as possible.

"That you brought one. And since there're people here we didn't count on, it was smart."

He chuckled, relieved. "How'd you know?"

"Trudy called me soon after you left the station. Said not to be too hard on you because it was her idea."

Of course, she had. Jax settled on the sofa. "In fairness, I had no idea where we were headed."

"I'll give you that. So, where's this phone?"

"In the truck."

"Under the seat with the handgun?"

"No. I only brought your dad's shotgun. The phone is in my bag in the back of the cab. Which I should get inside now that you know about it."

"Or you could follow me to bed, and I can communicate with you another way." She rose off the sofa and walked to the bedroom without looking back.

Okay, then. Jax placed another log on the fire and turned off the lights. Before he joined her, he peeked through the shades. Everything was quiet, as it should be.

After the events of earlier in the year, everyone came under suspicion; he should have asked Hannah more questions. But those same events had drained him of energy, and he was desperate for a break. Abby had good senses, and if she felt things were fine, then they were.

So why hadn't the hair on the back of his neck stopped tingling since Hannah came to their door?

Chapter Fifteen

Rachel left the Schmidts, heading straight for the café. When she'd been there earlier and spoke with the man at the counter, Milly had slid her a weird look. She'd intended to circle back anyway. Now she hoped it would give her a clear direction of where to begin in locating the potential thief.

Before reaching the café, however, she had to pass by the apartment complex with plywood boarding the bottom window where the explosion had occurred. The restaurant would close soon, but the upstairs where Bruce Hatfield's body had been found was illuminated; a couple of rigs belonging to the forensics team remained in the parking lot. Not wanting to miss an opportunity for new information, she slipped on booties before entering the apartment to join them.

The man running the show greeted her dressed in a white Tyvek suit and mask, which he slipped down under his chin. "Deputy Killian. What brings you back?"

"Just checking to see if anything stood out while you were working the scene?"

"Not much to speak of. There appears to have been no forced entry. I'm sure the medical examiner will have her theories on what caused the death, but blunt force was at least a contributor. The blood spatter pattern in the bathroom is lower than expected, implying the man was sitting when struck."

"A surprise attack?" A horrible way to go, as if there were a less horrible way.

"Not likely." He motioned Rachel toward the bathroom. "Come, look at this."

The earlier glimpse of the crime scene had been plenty. She followed anyway.

He pointed to the bathtub. "What do you see?"

Blood splatters low, like he'd mentioned. Also, a sticky substance on and around the knobs. "Residue?"

"Yup. Duct tape would be my guess."

"Our victim was restrained inside the tub?"

"Appears that way."

And utterly helpless when his captor ended him. Bile rose in her throat. "Clothed, I imagine, since that's how he was found?"

"Yes. Blood consistent with a physical attack was present on his clothing. The odd part is the killer moving him from this room into the main living space."

She'd thought so, too. "Any fingerprints?"

"Those of the victim, of course. Another set that we'll put through the system. If there's no match, we might be able to determine whether they belong to a male or female."

That would be helpful; she suspected a man had caused this based on moving the body with no disturbance elsewhere. If Jax were here, however, he'd remind her not to make assumptions. She backed out of the room; the tech followed.

"We also found something else of interest." He held up a bag containing a rag. "This was likely used to keep him silent. It might also have contributed to his death, but—"

"Not your department."

"Bingo. We'll make sure you have a preliminary report by morning from our end, and a fuller one in a few days."

Stopping by here had been informative, and overwhelming. She'd told Brody and the boys that she wouldn't call Jax. But the facts and supposition coming her way had her so far beyond her depth, she might have to.

There was one other person who could guide her, but that was a last resort.

She checked her phone for messages on her way into the café. Dr. Shocking must still be looking for answers. She'd push off calling anyone until she knew more.

The small bell attached to the door dinged with her entry. The sandwich provided by Milly hours ago had long since dissipated. Now the smell of something buttery, with a hint of onion and potato, hit her nose. Clam chowder. Her mouth watered, but she couldn't give in. Janelle would be whipping up dinner and expecting Rachel to eat.

The café was empty except for a young man sitting in the corner with a laptop, and a mop bucket at the far end, a young waitress ready to clean.

"We're closed, Deputy Killian," the girl said.

Sadie, if Rachel remembered correctly, and a recent graduate from high school. "No worries. I'm here for Milly. She still around?"

"No." Sadie stopped mopping and pulled out a few chairs. "After the café cleared out and things quieted down, she left, not feeling well."

Feeling ill could have been the reason for her weird look earlier. Probably wishing no one else would come through the door so she could get out of there.

"Hope it's nothing serious," Rachel said.

"No. The treatments sometimes make her nauseous."

"Treatments?"

"Oh, you didn't know? Chemo. Milly has breast cancer."

Rachel's insides crumpled, thinking about her mother's health scare a couple of years ago. The toll it had taken on her. She needed to call her mom and check in. Sometimes she held her responsible for the poor relationship with her father, and that was unfair. "I didn't know. I'm sorry to hear that."

"She's going to be okay. She tells us that every day, and I believe her." Sadie smiled.

"I have no doubt. In the meantime, maybe you can help me. When did you come on shift?"

"Been here all day. In the back restocking some and helping the cook, but here."

"There was a man at the counter when the building tenants came in.

Another deputy and I were speaking with him."

"Don't know about that. Like I said, I was mainly in the back. But a guy did camp out in the corner that showed up right after Milly left."

"How was he dressed?"

"Sweatshirt. Jeans."

"Say Vegas on the sweatshirt?"

She nodded.

That sounded like the guy. "He give you any problems?"

"Nah, just the creeps. That's why I called my boyfriend, Cory. That's him sitting behind the computer."

The young man peered over his laptop and lifted his chin. He might have played football at one point, given his broad shoulders. "Always good to follow your gut. But was there a particular thing that bothered you about the guy?"

"Staying most of the day, for one. He seemed focused on what was happening at that complex. I didn't talk to him much. Just refilled his coffee cup ten times. Maybe he had nowhere else to be."

If he was a drifter, that might be true. "You said most of the day, when did he leave?"

"About ten minutes before you walked in."

Shoot. He could still be in the area. "Thank you." Rachel set her business card on the counter. "If you see him again, I'd appreciate you call the station. I'd like to talk to him."

"Sure thing."

"And make sure you lock the door the minute you're closed in the future. It's safer," Rachel said, feeling uneasy that she felt compelled to remind her with the recent happenings.

Sadie winced. "I will. Milly's told me that a few times, too, and I forget." She grabbed the keys that had been inside her apron pocket and followed Rachel as far as the door.

Outside, Rachel strode to the end of the parking lot, scanning the road that led away from the restaurant. Hands on her vest, she did a quarter turn, searching. Another quarter turn.

No signs of him or anyone else. If she'd have come straight to the café, she might have caught him. Next time, she wouldn't allow herself to be taken off course.

As Rachel approached her car, Koa was barking, her focus out the window. Rachel spun around, expecting Koa was alerting her to someone's presence. A couple of crows took flight from the top of the café.

She chuckled at her jumpiness, and at Koa, who'd been off since this morning. Regardless, Rachel's gut said she had to watch herself, a feeling she'd felt often when working in the city, not once since arriving in Misty Pines. Until now.

Chapter Sixteen

The man, dressed in his borrowed jeans and sweatshirt, had spent much of the afternoon sipping his coffee from the small corner booth, staring at the street, and at the busyness of the complex. As the sun lowered in the sky, the café had illuminated. He sank further into the cushioned seat.

He'd watched as the young deputy entered the house down the road from the fire. The one he'd *shopped* from. He hadn't counted on them calling the police. People were more aware here than in the bigger city.

A fact he wouldn't forget.

Inside the warmth of the restaurant, he'd found refuge, expecting to stay until later before making it safely through town.

But the deputy had returned to the complex.

"What are you looking for, Ms. Killian?" he muttered under his breath.

The young waitress approached him. "More coffee?" Her wisp of a boyfriend sat in the corner. He'd appeared after the owner left.

As if he had the ability to protect this girl.

"No, Sadie, I'm fine."

"Okay," she said, her eyes darting to her boyfriend. "We're about to close."

"I'll finish what I have and be going then."

A few minutes later, he slid out of the booth, laid a five on the table. Outside, he inhaled the chilled air, feeling the sting in his nostrils. He strode to his rental car a block down and slipped inside, where he kept eyes on the complex.

Soon, the deputy emerged from the stairwell. Looking back at her car, where her dog waited. Then back at the restaurant.

"Where to now, deputy?" he whispered.

Her gait was long and assured. So many of those he chose started that way. By the time he was through with them, however, nothing was assured except for their death.

He glanced at his phone, waiting.

He'd missed nothing and could go nowhere until he knew more; he could play in town a little longer.

Who should he play with? The deputy, or the young waitress?

Perhaps he'd save it all for his ultimate prize.

Chapter Seventeen

Rachel tried Dr. Shocking's cell as she sat in the driveway of the older-style ranch that she and Janelle called home.

For now.

Eight months ago, it had started as a place to live while she got her shit together and settled into Misty Pines. She'd sought a job here because of Janelle. This case had her thinking it might be the place she'd stay.

But what happened when it quieted down again? Which it would.

Was she ready for the kind of commitment Janelle asked for? It was a conversation they needed to have, and that Rachel had avoided, never finding the right time.

Including now. Her focus had to be on solving this case. At the least, she had to work it to the best of her ability, whether she'd begun to question if that was enough.

She rubbed her eyes. She'd waited all day to hear more from Dr. Shocking for a clear direction and had heard nothing. The ME must still have nothing to share, but dropping the bomb of a potential serial killer in Misty Pines and not calling back had her on edge.

Especially with the man from the café still unaccounted for.

This was not a case she could fail at.

On her way home, she'd gone to Meddle Beach Park. Brody hadn't been specific where he'd seen the man prior to being in the café, but this was a popular beach amongst the locals, and worth a shot. She parked and stood at the edge where concrete met sand. She'd last been there in January, when a severed foot had been discovered. Now, aside from a few couples strolling along the shore, and one who'd started a small fire, eager to stay out until sunset, there was no signs of the drifter.

The homeless campsite south of town would be another place to check, but easier to navigate during daylight. Considering it a bust, she'd driven past the gas station to see if she could get her final witness statement. Only to find Winona's "places to be" that she'd told her aunt didn't include work.

Now, as the medical examiner's voicemail answered, she left a message, feeling like she'd hit a wall.

She unloaded Koa from the backseat and let her do her business before heading to the kitchen, where she unstrapped her gun and gear, setting it on the kitchen table. Janelle's car had not been in the driveway, and there was no indication she'd been home recently. Or that dinner had been started. She could be at the grocery store. Or still annoyed with their argument from last night about Rachel working too much, and had opted to do something else tonight.

There'd been no time to catch up with her today to find out.

Rachel swooped Koa's bowl from the floor, focused on what she did know. "You've been a trooper today, girl," she said, as she rinsed the porcelain. "But you had me scared to death." Rachel's chest pulled at the thought of losing her best friend. "I'm not sure what I'd do without you, so please don't run off like that again."

Koa cocked her head, then hung it low like she understood.

Koa never asked for anything but love and offered only the same in return. No judgment, future plans not required. She lived in the moment and reminded Rachel to do the same. Everyone needed a Koa in their life.

Rachel filled a bowl with kibble, water in the other, and issued the hand command that it was hers for the taking. As Koa ate, Rachel's thoughts drifted to the case and to what had led the ME to believe they could have a serial killer in town.

The victim, Bruce Hatfield, had a mark on his chest. A jagged X. She hadn't lifted the man's shirt to get a clear look, but the doctor had seemed to home in on the mark and then looked perplexed. Or shaken. That had to be the identifier that led her to believe the crime was like another case.

Unless there were other unseen markings on the body.

Dr. Shocking would know about the duct tape and the victim's mouth being filled with a rag by now. Was that consistent with the old case, too? *Damn.* She'd have liked to talk to the ME sooner than later and before her next call.

Because she, like it or not, owed Jax an update. She'd thought of another resource to call, but she'd pushed not calling her boss, pseudo-uncle or not, too long. Brody might not tell Jax that he'd suggested she do so earlier, but Garrett would if he found out. Better to get it out of the way and avoid the reaction. Even if Abby would be unhappy. Seemed romance always took a backseat to work.

Rachel nabbed a beer from the fridge and punched in the satellite's number. It took several seconds to connect, and then just rang. With no voicemail set up, she disconnected after a minute. If he'd left it on, it might have registered her call.

She took a swig of beer. He probably left it off to avoid Abby's disapproval. At least Rachel had tried; there was no choice but to keep going.

But eat first. Okay, whether Janelle was still annoyed or not, where was she?

About to send her a text, Rachel spotted the note on the corkboard near the coffeemaker. If she hadn't been distracted, she'd have seen it when she walked in from the garage. *Subbing for a friend at the art studio tonight. Class out at 10. See you then.*

Ugh. Ten. A nice dinner to chat and unwind would've been nice. Not that she'd share much about her day, but mundane conversation often helped. She could make them dinner even if Janelle wasn't a fan of her cooking, but by ten, Janelle would've eaten already.

"Looks like we're on our own," she said to Koa while opening and closing a couple of cupboards. The frying pan was somewhere—she'd seen Janelle use it. She'd be damned if she could find it now.

Screw it. She opened the freezer to grab a premade dinner and winced. Abby had told her Jax's freezer was full of ready meals. Maybe they were more alike than she cared to admit.

In front of her computer with her cardboard tasting pizza, and Koa curled under her feet, Rachel logged in. The more she'd thought about it, the more the X sounded familiar. It could be she'd read it in the newspaper or heard something about it on the news.

Dr. Shocking hadn't been specific to how old a case it reminded her of, but she'd worked for the state for twenty years. Rachel would have been a kid then, and too busy playing soccer or softball, or spending time with friends to pay attention to the news if the case went back that far. Her father, of course, brought cases home, but he talked little about them.

As a cop, daily updates of the most disturbing or humorous calls of the day often filled the workplace locker rooms. But it didn't feel like a case that had crossed through her two jobs, either.

Her father might know. No might about it. But whether she'd tinkered with the idea of asking for his help earlier or not, she couldn't call him. Not after their recent fight. He'd only see it as a sign of weakness. A confirmation she was in the wrong place.

Whatever. She tapped in the search and hit enter; a list of Oregon serial killers and their crimes filled the screen. She scanned through each listing and quickly found many of the details left out. Probably a good idea. Talking about specifics like trophies and body marks might worm their way into other cases. Like people could use more ideas on how to hurt each other.

Ready to dismiss this avenue, she glimpsed a series of killings from fifteen years prior. The perpetrator remained at large for quite some time, and authorities only imprisoned him ten years ago. The newspaper article indicated the man's victims were college co-eds. Blonde, pretty girls that he apparently met at a bar near campus. He, an office janitor, regularly made advances toward them that were repeatedly refused.

Rachel enlarged the screen to see the fuzzy picture of a man in glasses, and a fair amount of acne. That said, investigators could only connect him to one killing, although each victim had an X on their chest. Marked for death, or ex'd out, perhaps. No sexual assault occurred on any of the victims.

It might only be a theory that the killer had been involved in the others, but Rachel followed a hyperlink to an innocence project group that had taken on his case. The group's statement didn't include the outcome of their cause. These things could take years, though.

What didn't jibe was that Bruce Hatfield was a man in his late thirties. The X could be random. Or a copycat.

The front door opened, startling Rachel. Koa was no longer at her feet.

"Hey," came a voice from the entry. Janelle was home early?

"I'm in here," Rachel called out, glancing at the computer clock—nearly eleven. She'd gone down the rabbit hole of research. She stretched her arms overhead.

Janelle walked into the living room, Koa by her side. "Sorry, I'm late. Took longer to clean up than I'd hoped."

"No worries." Rachel forced herself out of the chair and wrapped her arms around her girlfriend. She inhaled the combination of mango shampoo and paint thinner wafting off her, then tucked a stray hair that had fallen from Janelle's messy bun behind her ear. Koa wedged her nose, then her entire body, between them. "How was your day?" she said, giving Koa the command to lie down.

"Good. I didn't expect to have to work, but it was a great night. So much talent at the studio. I'm thinking of applying for a full-time job there. The gallery's nice, but I really love working with people in the creative stage."

She did look happy, her face glowing. "Tired of the snootiness?"

Janelle chuckled. "Sometimes. You'd think West Shore wouldn't attract that, but art snobs are everywhere."

People were people everywhere, but Rachel rarely shared the dark side of what she'd seen.

"Anyway, let's talk about it in bed." Janelle moved toward the bedroom. "I'm beat."

Rachel dropped back into the desk chair. "I'll join you in a bit. I have more research to do on a case I'm working."

Janelle pulled the chopstick holding her hair up and let it fall around her shoulders. "You sure it can't wait?"

Tempting, but… "It can't." Not if she wanted to show Jax she could do this. "And honestly, if I lay down, I'd be out in a flash."

Rachel waited for her to say she worked too much.

Instead, Janelle frowned and nodded. "I hope it's nothing like the last case around here. What happened to that poor surf shop owner keeps me up at night sometimes."

That case had kept them all up long after. She hesitated to add to her girlfriend's stress, but this was her job. Her life. "It is a homicide."

"Oh." Janelle's smile disappeared. "Now I have to worry about you more than usual."

Rachel sighed. "That's not nec—"

A crash sounded from the rear of the house. Janelle startled, and Rachel flew out of her seat following Koa, who trotted to the backdoor slider.

"What was that?" Janelle whispered from behind them.

Rachel shook her head, turned off the interior lights. She stood with Koa, staring into the backyard. After a minute, she slid open the door and stepped out with her flashlight, leaving Koa inside.

Nothing stood out at first until she saw one of their patio chairs tipped on its side.

She scanned the perimeter. All clear.

"Probably a cat, or raccoon," she called back to Janelle.

Just in case, she strode to the center of the yard and swung the light along the fence line. Finding nothing didn't stop her stomach from knotting or the hair on her arms from standing on end.

Or like before, the distinct feeling that someone was out there, watching her.

Chapter Eighteen

Jax kissed Abby gently on the forehead and slipped out of bed to watch the sun rise, looking forward to the golden hues it would cast over the trees. On his way to the kitchen, his thoughts drifted to last night and how far they'd come in the past year. The blaming each other for their losses had ceased. They still had their frustrations, of course. Abby still believing she should never be taken off guard, for starters.

But no one could have foreseen Lulu's illness.

Neither of their families had experienced childhood cancer. Aside from a grandfather who'd smoked a pack a day and was diagnosed with late-stage lung carcinoma at seventy-nine, there was no history of the dreaded disease.

Sometimes things just happened—like the cabin.

Abby couldn't have known someone would use the space for their comfort before they arrived. Or that there was a trapdoor, for God sakes.

The same could be said about Hannah, who he couldn't get a read on. As they'd agreed, she was likely the person who'd been in the cabin prior to their arriving. Her sudden appearance last night might've been out of necessity—perhaps she'd forgotten something, or worried she had. Not wanting to admit to trespassing could be at the root of her nervousness.

It was also possible he had it all wrong.

The sun cast stunning shadows against the tree line as it crept skyward. Jax kept eyes on its progress as he made himself a cup of coffee and stoked the fire.

When Abby woke, he'd see if she felt like hiking. He'd done a fair amount of that in Portland before he met her, and she'd come on a few of those treks in their early years together. Usually around Multnomah Falls, or Beacon Rock on the Washington side. The Columbia River Gorge area offered several scenic and easy options, and was the perfect place to decompress, which he and Abby enjoyed.

But like most things in their life, work overtook—and he'd had issues on the job too—which contributed to their move to Misty Pines. Then Lulu came right after, and the moments of being out in nature together dissipated.

It was back to the two of them now. And Abby wanted to talk last night; she'd seemed on the verge of sharing something. Fresh air in this natural setting might be just the thing to reignite that conversation.

"Deep in thought?" Abby's voice drifted from the edge of the living room, startling him.

"Morning, sleepyhead." Even in her sweats, and hair flattened on the right—the side she curled onto when sleeping, always facing him—she stole his breath. Golden sunrises had nothing on Abby Kanekoa.

"How about a walk this morning?" he said, striding to the kitchen to brew her a coffee.

"Like we used to?"

He shrugged. "Might be a nice way to spend the day."

She sighed. "I'm not in the shape I used to be, but let's do it."

Her shape was just fine. He was about to hit the start button on the coffee when she waved him off. "No coffee?" he said.

"I've been cutting back."

"Recently?"

"In the last couple of weeks. Caffeine makes me antsy."

"So can weaning yourself off." Could explain her jumpiness yesterday.

"I'm good. I'll just have a banana."

"That's hardly enough for the day ahead." He pulled jars of peanut butter and jelly from the refrigerator to put together a few sandwiches.

"It'll be fine and looks like you won't let us starve."

He chuckled. "That I won't."

Soon, they were at the front door, packed and ready to go for their hike.

Abby was first out but stopped abruptly before hopping from the top step to the bottom of the stairs.

"What the hell?" she said.

Jax followed her gaze, that landed at his feet. An opossum, its mouth twisted in a horrific grin, was laid out. Gutted.

"What the hell kind of animal did that?" she said. A grimace crossed her face like she might throw up.

He dropped his backpack behind him and squatted to inspect the animal closer. "Maybe not what, but who."

"You think a person did this?" Abby said.

"Hannah's the only one we've seen."

"Now, why would you jump to her?"

"I'm not. Just saying."

"Well, I can't imagine the motivation. It's not like we can control cell service."

"That's true."

"Unless you told her we were in law enforcement. Sometimes that brings out the worst in people."

He looked away.

"You told her we were cops?"

"Not specifically. She asked what we did. I said law." He probably shouldn't have added the part of being in different branches. That was a giveaway. "I didn't see the point of lying." He could read her mind without her saying a word: *so much for not being cops on this trip.* "Anyway, I'm not a wilderness expert, so this could be perfectly normal."

She wrapped her arms around herself. "Me either, but it seems odd with the entire body intact, except for the gut. And I don't blame you for thinking the worst after earlier this year...."

This was not the start he'd hoped for and was desperate to get it back on track. "There are too many species around here to be certain of what did this. I'll just get rid of it."

He stepped over the animal and found a shovel that had been near the woodpile. He returned to the carcass, marching it to the lookout where he stopped a decent distance from the edge and flung the opossum over.

By the time he returned the shovel, Abby was halfway to the tree line where Hannah had disappeared last night. He trotted to catch up, and they turned left down the trail.

"You still look a little green," Jax said.

"Guess I'm more sensitive to things lately."

"Yeah, what's that about? Not much has ever made you queasy." This getaway was exactly what they needed if they could avoid any more gutted animals.

"No idea," she said, picking up her pace.

"Well, let's get far away from here and enjoy a picnic together." He lengthened his stride to keep up. "If Sam drops by again, we can ask him about the opossum then. He'd know for sure one way or another. In the meantime, I won't tell anyone else what we do for a living."

She nodded. "Works for me."

For the next twenty minutes, they walked the trail, taking in the area's beauty. Yesterday's yellowish haze had lightened some, and their footsteps mixed with the clatter of a woodpecker and a gentle breeze through the tree limbs.

"Maybe we can find a creek before this day's over," he finally said to break the silence between them.

"I didn't bring a suit."

He raised an eyebrow. "I don't mind."

"Seriously, Jax—" she started.

A scream pierced the air, cutting her off.

He and Abby shot looks at each other, then outward, trying to track where the scream came from. Not ahead of them. More interior.

"That didn't sound like an animal," Jax said.

"No. It sounded female. Hannah?"

"Possible. She came this way last night."

They listened for other sounds or indicators as they moved together, silently, in the general direction of the scream. They were too far away now to go back for the shotgun. But the scream, while startling, didn't sound panicked or terrified. More frustrated.

But when the next one echoed off the forest, it held more angst. And much as closer. They picked up their pace.

They soon found a path that led perpendicular to where they'd been walking, and then Hannah, slamming the hood shut on a two-door sedan. She startled when she saw them, then turned red.

"Oh shit, I'm sorry. I hope you didn't hear me beating the crap out of this piece of junk."

"Well—" Abby said.

"You did." She grimaced. "Shoot. Again, I'm so sorry. I didn't mean to scare you guys. Or to get you running my way."

"We were out this direction, anyway," Jax said, glancing at Abby, whose tight expression mirrored his own. Their desire to relax and reconnect was being seriously interfered with. "What seems to be the problem?" He returned his attention to Hannah, who was worrying her lip with her teeth.

"My car. I was getting ready to go, you know, call my boyfriend, and it won't start."

"As in dead, or does it turn over?" Jax said.

"Turns, I guess. Doesn't catch."

"I can look at it, if you'd like," Jax said. The sooner she could get that car running, she'd get out of there.

"You know about cars?" Hannah asked.

"Not really," Abby said.

Jax's father, a real son-of-a-bitch, would have agreed, adding he knew enough to be dangerous. "She's right, but I know the basics. Worth a try."

"Thanks," Hannah said, letting out a breath. Relief? "Because honestly, I'm out of supplies and I need to get hold of him. Which I can't do unless I get off this mountain." She was rambling, her voice growing quieter as she went.

Abby stepped toward her. "How about we leave Jax here to work on your car, and you can follow me back to the cabin. We have plenty of food there, and everything looks brighter on a full stomach."

Jax cleared his throat. "Or you could give her one of our sandwiches."

Until he was certain how that dead carcass arrived on their doorstep, he'd rather Abby not be alone with her.

Abby's focus remained on Hannah, clearly not catching his vibe. "It'll be more comfortable back at the cabin. And I'm not feeling up to a hike after all." She turned and raised her brows at him. "You've got this, yeah?"

He hesitated. Abby's eyebrows rose higher. "Sure."

"Gosh, if it's no trouble, I'd appreciate that," Hannah said.

He bet she would. It was interesting that she'd had food last night and nothing today.

Smiling, Abby turned back to Hannah. "No trouble."

He'd have preferred Abby interrogate Hannah right there, but having *girl time* might make her share more. "I'll get to work on this and join you shortly."

"C'mon," Abby said to Hannah, and he watched uneasily as the two disappeared on the trail.

Chapter Nineteen

Rachel rose before sunrise. Not only to avoid more questions and concerns from Janelle about the case she was on, but to get Koa out for a run before tucking her back into the house. Since Janelle had the day off, Koa would have to stay home with her. Rachel couldn't risk another terrifying repeat of her getting loose like yesterday.

After ruffling Koa's fur and a few kisses on the snout, Rachel was on her way to the gas station with a travel mug of steaming coffee and a bagel. From what she remembered, Winona worked weeknights, but with having to relocate due to the fire, it might have required a switch in shifts.

When Rachel pulled into the station, her suspicions were confirmed. Winona was working at the full-service island and inserting a nozzle into a late-model Mercedes. She punched in the gas selection on the pump's control panel as Rachel stretched out of the car, not making eye contact.

"Happy to wash that windshield for you, Ms. Carlson," Winona said, still not glancing Rachel's way.

"That would be lovely, thank you."

Winona hustled to the water-filled bucket, grabbed the squeegee, and began scrubbing the glass.

Huh. Rachel had never witnessed so much enthusiasm in the young woman, and she'd come here countless times in the past months.

"Morning, Winona," Rachel said, approaching.

"Deputy Killian. Going to need a fill today? Better hurry—I hear prices are going up again."

"No need. I came to see you."

Her hand tightened on the squeegee. "What for?" She scrubbed the window with more vigor. "I don't know anything about what happened at the apartments. That's why I left."

"What is it you think I need to know?"

"Well, I'm assuming you think something was left on." She dropped the squeegee into the bucket and strode away from the customer, closer to the station's glass-walled office.

Rachel followed. "The cause is still under investigation, but it appears to have stemmed from a gas leak in another part of the building."

"Oh." Winona's shoulders dropped, almost in relief.

"Why? Did you leave something on you shouldn't have?"

She shook her head a bit too hard.

"You see anyone around the gas meters or connections in the past few days?"

"No, ma'am."

"Winona, it's just Rachel. You know me. There's no reason to be nervous."

"I'm not. It's—okay. Maybe I went into Melissa's apartment and was afraid I'd caused the fire." Her voice had dropped to a whisper.

"What would you have done?"

"I turned on a lamp, but, well, nothing else. I was only looking around."

"What were you looking for?"

"I—"

"Did you have permission to be in her apartment?"

Winona looked away without responding.

"Did you break in?"

"No," she said, quickly. "The door was unlocked. I swear."

"But you knew Melissa wasn't home?"

Winona gave a slight nod as her face reddened.

Rachel rubbed her hands together to warm them. "You're going to have to help me out on why you went in there then."

The girl's jaw clenched. "To find something she took."

"From you?"

"Yes. Melissa acts like she's so put together. Runs ten miles a day.

Volunteers at the library. But the woman steals other people's mail."

Rachel didn't recall a complaint like that coming through the station. "What makes you say that?"

"I've been waiting for a bonus check from corporate for the past month, and they insist they sent it. Last time I called, they said it had been cashed. All I know is it never arrived in my mailbox, and I didn't cash it."

"Isn't most payroll done digitally these days?"

"Not this place. Old school."

Rachel nodded. "What proof do you have Melissa had anything to do with that?"

"She spends a lot of time at the mailbox, and she's always wearing an oversized coat when she goes. I figure she's sorting through people's stuff and takes off with what she wants."

"Anyone else have an issue with her?"

"Chuck's had some random things go missing. Not sure if they were checks or not."

"If I recall, the mail area isn't secured..."

"True," she said, slowly.

"So, anyone could have taken your check."

Winona shifted on her feet. "I guess, yeah, but they didn't."

"Okay—how about tomorrow you go to the station and file a report with Trudy. And call your employer and get a copy of the check front and back. That will move things along. Can you do that?"

She nodded.

"In the meantime, don't enter other people's apartments without an invite, unlocked or not. Otherwise, you'll be the one that gets arrested."

Winona looked away. "Sorry."

Maybe more was happening in this town than she gave it credit for. "Now, did you know Bruce Hatfield?"

"Uh, no," Winona said. Her eyes darted to the customer and back.

"But you knew he lived there?"

"Not sure."

Bruce was young—though older than Winona—but from his pictures, handsome. It seemed more likely than not that Winona would notice. "Have you at least seen him around?"

"Yeah, I guess, but you said *did*. Has something happened to him?"

"You haven't heard?" Rachel said.

"I haven't talked with my aunt since I left her yesterday."

Regardless, she'd expect word of a homicide to have made it through a community hub like the gas station by now. "Mr. Hatfield's deceased."

Her face paled. "The fire got him?"

"The fire didn't reach his apartment."

Winona wrapped her arms around herself. "Did he kill himself?"

Rachel shook her head.

She warbled. "Someone killed him?"

A strong response for someone she'd reportedly never met. "You sure you didn't know him? Or speak with him in passing?"

"No, none of that. But murdered? That's tragic." She straightened. "Is my aunt safe staying there?"

"She's staying with Trudy from the station."

Winona nodded. "Good. That's good."

"Back to Mr. Hatfield. Did you ever see whether he had any visitors? Friends? A girlfriend? Especially in the past few days."

She shook her head. "The other tenants might have information on that. Honestly, I only spend the night with my aunt when I have to. Which isn't often. They'd know better than me."

"They mentioned that Mr. Hatfield worked at the docks."

Winona looked toward the gas pump that was still fueling the car. "No idea."

"How were the other tenants in the building regarding Mr. Hatfield? Any issues you're aware of?"

"Like I said, I don't hang out there. When I do, my aunt asks me to take her dog out for a walk or rub her feet." She curled her lip. "Thankfully, I work a lot."

The pump clicked off, and a horn beeped. Ms. Carlson apparently didn't appreciate waiting.

"Sorry, ma'am," Winona said, running toward her. She replaced the nozzle and handed Ms. Carlson a receipt. The woman eased away from the island. "Anyway, I prefer to hang out at my boyfriend's house whenever I can," Winona said as she returned.

"And who's that?"

"No one you'd know."

"Someone you don't want your aunt to know about, either?"

She shrugged. "She has lots of opinions."

"I'm happy to keep the information between us." Which is a promise she'd keep. Having had far too many people up in her romantic business, she got it.

"His name's Robby. And she wouldn't approve of him because he's a little older."

Huh. "This Robby wouldn't happen to work at the docks?"

She nodded. "He runs a boat there."

A little older was an understatement. Probably a good eight years, give or take. "Did he know Bruce Hatfield?" Rachel asked.

Winona shrugged once again.

"How about drugs?"

She bristled. "Robby doesn't do drugs."

"I mean at the docks. Your aunt's neighbors seemed to think there might be issues down at the marina."

"No idea. Not my thing." Another car pulled in, setting off the chime. "I need to go. Boss doesn't like it when I'm not cleaning in between, and he's got cameras."

"Understood. Thanks for your time." She handed Winona a card. "If you think of anything else."

"Yeah, sure."

But as Rachel ducked into her car, she had had an uneasy feeling about Winona. She'd been quick to throw shade on Melissa, and distance herself from the apartment complex and Bruce Hatfield. She was also sketchy about Robby.

It could be her youth on full display. Could also be she knew more than she was telling.

Chapter Twenty

Jax stared at the sedan and shook his head. What had he been thinking? He knew less about cars than he did about women—Abby, at least. He'd thought with their closeness last night, she'd welcome the suggestion to cool off. It's not like they hadn't found a lake on some of their past hikes, leaving their clothes on shore. Especially on a hot summer day. But her tone had left little doubt she wasn't interested, just before Hannah's scream interrupted the moment.

Nope. He didn't know women at all.

Any more than he knew how to fix this damn car. Dumb to offer. Still, he'd told Hannah he'd try, and almost convinced Abby that he could wing it. Almost.

He ducked inside the sedan and popped the hood and the trunk, right before he caught sight of a pillow and a thin blanket in the backseat. That blanket might take off the chill at a football game; it was hardly enough to keep warm through the night if the temps dropped into the low forties. Which they would at this elevation. On the floorboard, he eyed a duffel that overflowed with a few shirts, a water bottle, and some candy bar wrappers.

No serious camper he'd run across would come to the wilderness with that setup. Ignoring "road closed" signs or not.

Outside the car, he took in the scene for the first time. Plenty of trees surrounded him, but no sign of a tent or shelter. No campfire, which Sam would approve of, but nothing showing Hannah had come here to spend a weekend away, or "set up camp" as she'd claimed last night. At least not that would be comfortable.

If she was waiting for her boyfriend to arrive with the gear, she could at least be clearing the area for a tent and an area to prepare the food. That's what he'd be doing. Unless she was only supposed to stake their spot. What kind of boyfriend allowed his partner to come so unprepared?

If he was a betting man, he'd put money that she was homeless and living out of her car, and there was no boyfriend. If that were the case, living on the mountain wouldn't go unnoticed by the rangers for any length of time. Not to mention the weather would turn soon, and there'd be plenty of snow, eliminating her ability to leave.

Another reason to get her car running now.

Jax propped the hood and checked the oil. Plenty. Radiator fluid. Half-full, shouldn't cause a problem. The battery had a bit of corrosion. He rounded the car to the trunk to look for a rag and found a small toolbox. No rag, but it contained a screwdriver, small hammer, a few wrenches, and a wire brush. After cleaning the battery connections, he tried the engine. It turned, barely. Whined, but wouldn't catch. The gas gauge read a quarter-tank.

He inspected the engine again in case he missed a loose wire. He hadn't. The issue could be with a fuel pump or injector—especially if Hannah had a habit of running her gas tank low—and he had no idea how to fix that.

Whether or not he'd intended to, he'd have to retrieve the satellite phone for Hannah and see if a boyfriend existed. If so, he could come get her and handle the car problem. Let him and Abby get back to their getaway.

A getaway that, with every passing minute, felt further away from possible. Being a cop was in his DNA. He'd been kidding himself to think he could shut it down. This young woman had invaded their lives peripherally, if nothing else, and she was becoming more of an issue than he'd expected.

His strides grew longer and faster on his way back to the cabin. He passed his truck parked below the rock wall, and climbed the steps, his focus on the cabin and the door ajar.

Abby's voice drifted out. "So, you two haven't been getting along?"

"Yeah. I mean, I just needed space, but I did promise him I'd call last night and tell him where I was so he could come, too. I'm afraid he's going to be frantic wondering where I've gone."

Maybe he'd been wrong about the boyfriend.

"I'm sure Jax will have some good news once he's back."

She released a long breath that had a slight tremble with it. "You didn't seem convinced he could fix my car."

"He has a way of surprising me sometimes."

Jax smiled at that.

"That would be awesome. It's important my boyfriend knows I'm okay. And that I know he's okay."

"Why wouldn't he be?" Abby asked. "Would he hurt himself?"

Jax stayed on the bottom step, listening for Hannah's reply. Abby's heart and concern for others had led her into law enforcement—what had led him to fall in love with her. That, and she took no guff from him.

"No, of course not," Hannah said.

"Then sometimes it's good for the men in our lives to worry some. Keeps them on their toes."

He imagined Abby had followed that comment with a wink. The words got a small laugh from Hannah and another smile from Jax. Is that the game she was playing with him? Not that he minded.

Sensing a lull in the conversation, he proceeded to the top of the stairs and joined them inside. "Hey, you two."

"Any luck?" Hannah hopped out of her seat.

He headed for the kitchen and washed his hands. "Wish I had better news. I tried the usuals, but I'm afraid whatever the problem, it's outside my expertise."

Her expression fell. Concerned.

"Look, I have a satellite phone for emergencies, and I'll grab it. You can call your boyfriend. No sense making him worry about where you are any longer."

He looked at Abby and tilted his head.

She rolled her eyes and smirked. Oh yeah, she knew he'd overheard her.

"Thank you," Hannah said, her shoulders deflating, as though she'd been carrying a weight.

"You're sure he's planning to join you?" he said.

"Positive," she said.

"It's just, you don't seem well prepared for even one night of waiting."

Her face reddened. "You saw my blanket."

"I did."

"Yeah, he has all the important stuff, that's why I want to make sure he knows." Her voice had faded.

"I get it." That was fair. Not smart, but fair, and none of his business if she didn't want to share more.

Outside, he trotted down the stairs to his truck. Before he reached the driver's side, he noticed the door was open. As he drew closer, it became clear that someone, or something, had been inside.

"Holy mother of—"

"What's happened?" Abby was at the top of the stairs, Hannah behind her, before he could finish the sentence.

He held back the expletives forming in his head. "Looks like that nocturnal creature—with some heavy-duty claws—caused that problem we found earlier and didn't stop there."

Abby was soon next to him, taking in the same scene. The seats were shredded. "The shreds are thin—not a bear's claw."

"Not a cougar either," he said.

"Bobcat, maybe. You closed your door last night?" Abby said.

"Thought I did." He reached under the seat for his duffle. Tried not to think about what the repair would cost. Or who to call first. Did insurance pay for destruction caused by animals?

"You sure?"

"I was in and out of it when I was changing the flat yesterday. Then Sam stopped by." His conversation about wildfires and potential squatters in the cabin had distracted him. "It's possible, I guess." He patted the floorboard; the bag wasn't under the seat.

He checked the back seat and the passenger side, then rubbed the space between his eyes, thinking.

"Don't tell me," Abby said.

"You didn't take it inside?"

"No."

"What's wrong?" Hannah said, joining them.

"Whatever did this to my truck, took our ability to communicate with it, too."

Chapter Twenty-One

Rachel left the gas station for the south of town and the homeless encampment, replaying the conversation in her head. Winona, having a connection to Robby at the docks, and Bruce Hatfield, having crossed paths with them both, felt relevant. And he *did* cross paths with Winona. Being the youngest in the building, it seemed improbable they hadn't communicated, too, at least once.

Robby, being oblivious that his girlfriend was staying at the same complex as a guy who worked at the marina, seemed no more likely. Especially if Winona stayed there when they were arguing. Robby was too cocky to let that slide.

Yeah, he'd have noticed Bruce Hatfield if he was anywhere near his girlfriend.

But did that mean they were involved in Bruce's murder? Was it a love triangle gone wrong? Or were they serial killers, as Dr. Shocking suggested might be a factor in the case?

That seemed a far reach based on their ages and what Rachel knew so far—she stretched her neck as she hit Highway 101—which was very little.

In over her head or not, she'd keep working the angles until she had word from the ME on exactly what she had, or Jax called in. He'd turn his satellite phone on at some point, and when he did, she intended to prove she'd done what she could.

That meant not discounting anything or anyone.

Including the drifter she'd yet to track down.

As she arrived at the encampment, she rolled through the area at a crawl. Her decision to forgo driving by here last night didn't matter—the encampment had moved on. Though remnants remained. Broken tents. Bottles from each living quarter were piled nearby or strewn about. Tarps mottled with holes, cast aside. Old clothes and random debris used for reasons she could not fathom, left in between. A few grocery carts toppled to their sides.

Despite having seen much of the same in Portland, it never got easier. The County's parks and recreation division would need to be notified to clean the mess. They might already be aware, but she'd have Trudy confirm when she got back to the office.

Right before she gathered the team. If the drifter was on the move, they all had to keep their eyes open for him.

When she arrived at the station, however, only Matt was there finalizing his report.

"I told Trudy I'd be on call last night," she said.

"They changed my shift at the store, so I told her not to bother you." He yawned.

"I appreciate that, but you look exhausted."

"Yeah, maybe."

She shook her head. "No Trudy yet?"

"No. And it was a quiet night. Only a few kids racing down Bull Mountain again, but that's it. The type of night Sheriff would like."

"You're right about that," she said, though she'd never had a patrol night like that until moving to Misty Pines. She tucked her bag under her desk, fighting that unsettled feeling again. The information only underscored the usual pace of this town. Although it's not like she needed another case to compete with the one currently drowning her. "Isn't Trudy normally in at this time?"

Matt checked his watch. "Yeah, suppose she is."

When Rachel arrived and didn't see Trudy's car, she figured she'd caught a ride with Frank. Until she remembered Frank was back east. Trudy never ran late, and after what had happened earlier in the year, Rachel found herself at Trudy's desk, flipping through her calendar.

Nothing was on the schedule.

About to call her, the front door opened. Garrett and Brody hustled in, bringing a cool but smoky breeze in with them.

"Where's Trudy?" Garrett said.

"We were just wondering that," she said.

"Not like her to be late," Brody said.

"I can drive by her house on my rounds," Garrett offered.

Rachel nodded. "That might be a good—"

Before she could finish, the door swung wide and Trudy rushed in—her hair mussed, dark circles under her usually bright eyes. She beelined it for her desk, shooing Rachel from her path. Even moving at a brisk pace, her body language read exhausted.

No one spoke; their eyes locked onto the woman that ran the office like a boss.

"What are all you kids looking at?" Trudy set her gaze on Rachel.

"It's just—"

"What? Can't a woman run behind sometimes?"

"Of course, ma'am," she said. "We were just worried."

Trudy hung her jacket on the coat tree in the corner and yanked her black sweater off the back of her chair, yanking it on. "Well, I appreciate that, but I'm fine." She flopped into her chair and jerked on her headset. "My houseguest might not be if that little yapper dog of hers doesn't quit the barking all night."

"It's always the small guys," Brody said.

"Especially when they're nervous," Rachel said. "Which being in a new location might present."

"Maybe all of that's true. But if Dorothy didn't treat that dog like a child, she might have some control." Trudy waved her hand in disgust. "I've never seen such a spectacle. Sharing her food right out of her mouth."

"Yikes," Matt said before another yawn took hold.

Rachel almost chuckled, then thought better of it. Trudy would have a fit if she knew how she loved on Koa.

Trudy shook her head. "Anyway. You can all help me by getting back to whatever you were doing and making sure that woman gets back into her own apartment quickly."

Rachel had yet to touch base with the Commissioner; she was looking to avoid that a little longer. "If you want to give Troy a shout and see what the status is, that would be a help."

"Honey, I'd be thrilled to."

"And the homeless have abandoned the encampment off Ocean Bluff."

"Let me guess, Parks needs a call?"

"Thank you," Rachel said.

"How about us, Deputy?" Garrett said.

"Follow me." On the way to the strategy room, Rachel gave them the update on the clothes stolen from the Schmidt's backyard. As they filtered in and took their seats, she motioned to Matt. "How about you get out of here and get some sleep. I'll update you when you're back on shift."

"No arguments here. I'm working at the grocery store in five hours."

"How do you work all night, take a nap, and work at the store only to do it again?"

"Lots and lots of coffee."

She was sure of that. But Jax had to get more people on the team if they were ever going to function efficiently.

"That man at the café?" Brody said, taking a seat at the table, along with Garrett. "You think he had something to do with the Schmidt robbery?"

"I do. I've done a precursory look for him, but as I mentioned to Trudy, the encampment moved. So, if you see him, detain him and call me."

Garrett shifted, clearly feeling out of the loop. "Brody updated me some, but any more word from the ME on cause of death?"

She shared what she knew, including that a marking on Bruce Hatfield's chest was consistent with an old case.

Garrett leaned in. "We have a serial killer?"

The idea left her equally uneasy. "Again, that's not confirmed. I stopped by the crime scene last night to speak with the team as they were wrapping up. What I do know at this point is our victim was restrained in the bathroom, and death likely occurred there."

Garrett drummed his fingers on the table. "When are we calling Sheriff Turner?"

He apparently had no more confidence in her than Brody. "I've already called. He didn't answer, so I'll try him again this morning. In the meantime, since you're coming in on day two, why don't you and Brody see if you can find my drifter first until we get some clear direction. I'll be heading to the docks in the meantime."

"After what Brody told me about your last visit, don't you think you need an assist?"

"No, I'm good. Though I'll let you know if it changes. I'm just looking to touch base with Robby again. He and Winona are in a relationship, and I suspect he knows more about our victim than he admitted. If all else fails, maybe the elusive dock manager, Aggie, has returned."

"Night fishermen should be returning to port about now," Garrett said. "Sheriff had an arson case once down there. I remember him saying certain times of the day were like rush hour."

"Then I'd better move. Let's keep in touch."

Rachel opened her case file to put in a few quick notes when the main door sounded. Footsteps headed their direction just before Trudy appeared.

"Rachel, you have a visitor."

She closed her eyes, trying to remember what she'd intended to write before the distraction. And hoping Janelle wasn't out front. She was known to appear on occasion *just to check in.* After their argument about her working too much, and now the homicide that had her worried, Rachel wouldn't put it past her.

"It'll be just a minute."

Trudy cleared her throat. "Maybe sooner than later."

How did Jax do this with the constant interruptions?

Rachel rose from her chair and followed Trudy to the reception area. With his back turned, a man flipped through a magazine on the end table. She didn't need to see his face to know who he was.

"Dad? What the hell are you doing here?"

Chapter Twenty-Two

Jax flipped through the various possibilities for how his duffle bag disappeared from the car as Hannah stepped back. Nothing made sense. And he'd been far too preoccupied to hear much of anything after he and Abby retreated to the bedroom last night.

"I don't see an animal getting into the truck, open door or not," Abby said. "Unless you had food in there?"

"I didn't," Jax said. A human having done this made much more sense. If Hannah believed he'd lied about not having a way to call the outside world, she could have circled back and decided to check herself—especially after he'd admitted they were in law enforcement.

Not his best move.

He stared at the young woman who was shifting her feet uneasily. He had the urge to grill her, but held back any accusations. For now.

Instead, he scanned the open area between the cabin and the forest, then focused on the path he'd taken to get the firewood. He stepped onto the trail and walked several yards. In the grass, a shred of T-shirt caught his attention. He swooped it from the ground, immediately recognizing it as the shirt he'd wrapped the sat phone in.

Balling the fabric, he took another step and spotted another shred. Then another. Before he'd gone a hundred yards, he had the entire shirt in his hand.

As he was about to turn back, he found what he'd been missing stuck in the grass near a boulder: the satellite phone. The battery part, anyway.

He gripped the items and made his way back to Abby and Hannah, who were watching him.

"You found it?" Abby said.

"In pieces, but yes."

She inspected the items in his hands. "Maybe it *was* a bobcat?"

"I have to admit, after seeing this, it could be. Or something along those lines. Might be best if we all get off this mountain." Hannah might be off the hook, but that didn't change the fact their luck had turned south since they'd crossed paths.

Abby met his eye. He knew that look—she agreed with him, but wasn't ready to give up their vacation yet.

He sighed, against his better judgment. Perhaps if he could get Hannah out of the way, they could fix this. The sooner, the better. He tossed the items into the back seat of his truck cab and laid a towel onto the driver's side, covering the damage. "How about this. Hannah, I'll get you closer to town so you can make your call."

"I hate to be a bother," she said.

They'd long passed that. "It's fine. The fact remains, your car needs fixing, and the faster your friend gets here to help with that, the better."

"That would be great." Relief flooded her voice.

He turned to Abby. "When I get back, you and I can decide what next."

Abby's face was drawn. "That'll work. I'll get some stew heated for later, too."

Jax offered a faint smile. "You feeling okay?" One thing after another had gone wrong; it had to be weighing on her.

"I'm good." She smiled. "Just tired."

Hannah was already in the passenger seat.

"You sure?" It wasn't like Abby to be so fatigued. She could be on the edge of a cold.

"Positive. Go."

"It'll get better," he mouthed.

She nodded.

When he returned, he'd stoke the fire with wood, and they could resume cuddling on the couch like last night. Though the next time someone knocked on their door, they'd ignore it. In the meantime, he widened his eyes, conveying his frustration at having to leave.

Abby smiled. She got it.

"I'll be back as soon as I can."

"Don't pop a tire on the way down."

That would be his luck, but he was determined to avoid that.

Hannah focused on her hands, or gazed out the side window, as the truck made its slow roll on the rocky path toward the main road. She finally spoke at the halfway point. "Probably wish I hadn't come by last night," she said. "But I'm not sure what I would've done if you hadn't been out here. Thank you for this."

The smallness in her voice, her sincerity, tugged at him. "I'm glad we could help. But if you don't mind, I'd like to hear more about this boyfriend because I certainly wouldn't let anyone I cared about come to a mountain so ill-prepared."

She stared out the window again. Tapped on the glass with her knuckle. "In fairness, we hadn't seen each other in a long while, and he's a former boyfriend. My showing up was unexpected."

"That doesn't explain him sending you alone."

She didn't respond. It wasn't his place to ask, he supposed, but she'd entangled them in her world, not the other way around. "What broke you up in the first place?"

"That was on me. I don't let people in easily."

A trait he knew something about. "It's always a risk. It can be worth the reward, though."

"You and Abby seem tight."

"We're working our way back to that."

"Really?"

He cleared his throat, not having intended to share anything about his relationship. "All I'm saying is, it doesn't hurt to crack open the door of your heart. Could surprise you. Is he a good guy?"

"Good enough that he dropped everything to gather what we'd need for a week out here. And all that after saying I just needed to get out of town."

"It was your idea to come ahead then?" He'd heard some of that when she was speaking with Abby.

She nodded. "He's supposed to be right behind me today. He might actually be down below waiting to hear from me."

If Jax could hand her off right away, that appealed even more. "Let's hope he is."

She grew quiet. "Yeah, let's hope nothing went wrong."

Her voice was so hushed Jax was unsure he'd heard her right. "What could go wrong?"

"Nothing," she said as they made the last turn off the dirt road and onto the highway.

A few minutes later, a gas station and a supply store came up on the right. As he pulled in, she looked around the premises, expectant. Only a couple of cars were at the island filling their gas tanks. Hannah offered no recognition of them, and Jax saw no signs of a single man with camping gear.

He parked. "I'm going to grab a couple of things while you make your call."

"Cool." She got out and headed to a corner of the building.

Inside the store, Jax grabbed a few items for Abby in case she was starting to get sick. A hot tea cold remedy, some ibuprofen. A crossword puzzle book for her, a Craig Johnson novel for himself, and a few chocolate bars. He'd learned long ago that chocolate had its own healing properties.

When he returned outside, Hannah was frowning at her phone, her other arm wrapped around her midsection. It could be the call hadn't gone as hoped. He slid into his truck to wait.

After a minute, she squared her shoulders and entered the store. He should call the station. Check in. He sank back into his seat. If he had his phone, he could do that. *Damn it.* In his eagerness to offload Hannah, he hadn't gone back in the cabin for his cell.

When Hannah reemerged, she had a bag full of food and what appeared to be supplies. She rushed to the truck and hopped in, setting the full bag at her feet. Her face was red.

"Everything okay?"

"Yeah, yeah. It's good."

"Did you speak to him?"

"I had to leave a message."

"Should we wait to see if he calls back?"

"No. We should get back on the mountain." Her voice shook as she said it.

"What aren't you telling me, Hannah? Maybe I can help."

She drew in a breath. "I just hate being around people. They give me anxiety. I'll feel better once I'm in the woods again."

"If there's someone else to call, it might be best if you stay down here and—"

"No. Please. I'll be fine."

Jax had encountered several types of phobias over the years. From their brief interactions, however, he didn't entirely buy Hannah's dislike of people was her reason to get out of town. She'd come to them right from the beginning. Accepted their offerings of help.

But he also couldn't intervene where help was unwanted or leave her stranded at the store. She'd done nothing that required him to get involved on a legal level. A fatherly one, perhaps, but not everyone appreciated that either.

That had him thinking about checking on his team. He'd promised a week of no work, but he hadn't planned on a wild animal destroying their communication or encountering a stranded camper, or whatever Hannah was.

He glanced her way; she was still clutching her cell. "Mind if I borrow that?" He lifted his chin toward her hands. "I'd like to check in with my office."

She held the phone close. "I—"

"It won't take long. I'm happy to add minutes—"

"That's not it," she said, then handed it to him. "Go ahead."

Not convinced, he'd make it fast. He dialed, a familiar voice answering.

"Trudy, it's Jax."

"Sheriff, hon. Need to put you on hold."

"Okay, sure, but—"

She was gone. He smiled at Hannah and waited. A minute ticked by, and he glanced at his phone. The call had disappeared. Shoot. He pressed redial. It went straight to voicemail. Either the cell towers were toying with him, or she was still on the other line.

He tapped the steering wheel and tried again. That time it rang.

"Where'd you go, hon?" she said, as if he'd been the one disconnected.

"Nowhere. Just checking in."

"All's good here," she said, but sounded harried. "Everything good there with you two?"

"We're fine, yes, but—"

"Happy to hear. Now get back to Abby and enjoy yourself."

"Okay, but—"

"Oh dear, another line's lighting up. We'll see you in a few days, hon. Believe me, rest. You'll have plenty to keep you busy when you're home."

Before he could respond, Trudy disconnected. He handed the phone back to Hannah.

"Wow," Hannah said, chuckling. "She sounded like my mom."

"That's because she's everyone's mother at the station," Jax said, not finding any humor in Trudy's reaction. There'd been an edge to her voice. Her comment that he'd have plenty to deal with on his return had the muscles in his shoulders inching skyward. Had something come from the complex fire, or had something else gone down in Misty Pines in the past forty-eight hours?

Commissioner Marks would know.

But then what? If he returned to Abby stressed out, she might never forgive him. It couldn't be that bad—otherwise, surely, Trudy would have told him. He couldn't imagine a scenario where she believed spending time with Abby trumped the welfare of Misty Pines.

But that fact didn't stop him from worrying whether his team could handle whatever had Trudy stressed on their own.

Chapter Twenty-Three

Rachel waited for her father to respond as he took his time to close the magazine and face her.

"Rachel. You look good." He said it as if he'd expected something else.

She had some idea of what that *something* might be. "Yeah, Dad. I'm a big girl. Know how to take care of myself and everything."

"That she does," Trudy piped in, as she returned to her desk. "So, you're the infamous Jameson. Jax's former partner."

"One and the same."

"I've heard a lot about you. You'd be proud of the work your daughter's doing here."

"I have no doubt." He smiled, though it didn't reach his eyes.

"Wait," Rachel said, suddenly alarmed. "Why are you here? Mom okay?"

He stepped toward her. "She's fine."

Rachel didn't move. "You're not just saying that? You'd tell me if…?" *If* had so many possibilities that she found it hard to breathe. If the breast cancer had returned, worse, spread. If she'd fallen. If….

"I promise," he said. "She's good. In fact, she asked me to bring you these." He held a brown paper bag in the air.

Rachel knew instinctively what was inside. "Brownies?"

"With peanut butter drizzle."

Her father's arrival was unexpected and out of character. Not once had he visited while she worked for the county sheriff's department in Washington. Granted, that job didn't take her a hundred miles away.

But damn if her parents didn't know how to get to her.

She reached for the bag and released her breath. Moved to hug him. Even if their last interaction just a couple of days ago had been less than cordial. Even with his judgment on her lifestyle, of who she was to the core. He was her dad, and while she'd never admit it to him, she'd missed his grounding presence.

"Okay, so what's the real reason you made the drive?" She let him go and took a step back from him. "I've never known you to like cool weather or salty air." She stiffened. "Did Jax call you on his way out of town to keep an eye on us?"

Her father shook his head. "Absolutely not. You'd make a damn good detective with that suspicious mind."

She took another distancing step.

"Then why?" She'd given no indication in their last conversation that she wasn't entirely happy here. But if he'd sensed it, he'd seize the opportunity to try to wheedle his way in, using the brownies as an extra bargaining chip to get her back to Portland.

"Can't a father stop in to see his only daughter without having her think there's an ulterior motive?"

"Some fathers, yes. Not ones that are detectives." Or ones she'd been arguing with almost since day one of moving to Misty Pines.

"Maybe this old man needs to make a few changes."

Had he hit his head? "Seriously?"

He splayed his hands in mock surrender. "Nothing's going on, Rachel. I'd simply love to spend the day with you. See what a day in Misty Pines looks like."

"So, you can convince me it's not worth my time?"

Trudy watched intently; her eyes narrowed. "Now Jax wouldn't appreciate you coming around to do that, especially with him not here. A fact you must know, since you didn't ask for him."

Good point. Rachel cocked an eyebrow at her father.

He shook his head. "Okay. That's fair you'd both think that." He turned to Trudy. "Whatever my former partner and my differences are, I'd never do that to him." And to Rachel. "Look, I had a day off. It's as simple as I don't like this tension between us. I'm here to fix it."

"Wow—Mom must have threatened to kick you out."

He drew in a breath. Maybe not so far from the truth. "So, what's on tap for your day?"

"I was about to leave for the marina. I'm conducting a murder investigation and hoping for another conversation with a potential suspect."

He stuffed his hands in his pockets. "Another homicide? Huh. Seems like there's been a lot more of those around here this past year."

She shifted feet, still not trusting why he'd suddenly shown, or ready to divulge every detail of what she had. She looked at Trudy. "I'll report in later. In the meantime, if you hear from Jax, let him know—"

"Oh, hon, I just did about fifteen minutes ago. I didn't know you wanted to speak with him."

"Yeah, shoot," she said. "I tried him on his sat phone yesterday and didn't get a response. Did he ask about us?"

"Didn't give him the chance. I told him you and the boys were handling things fine, though, and he should enjoy his vacation. If I hadn't, he'd have come running back."

Rachel could feel her father's eyes on her. "That's probably best. We do have everything under control. I just don't want him to feel out of the loop."

Trudy laughed. "Sounds like he was already feeling that, or he wouldn't have called."

"I'll try him later," Rachel said.

"Not sure you'll get through. The sat phone must have been having issues because I didn't recognize the number he called in on."

"Not his cell?"

Trudy shook her head.

Odd. "Everything all right on his end?"

"He said everything's fine."

Good—although she suddenly felt an additional pressure to make sure she didn't have to find him. Without his satellite phone and only an idea of his whereabouts, that might be harder to do. And Trudy clearly believed she could handle this investigation, so she would.

Outside, Rachel's father ducked into the passenger side of her rig. "Where's your girl?"

"She's at home today with Janelle." Rachel started the vehicle.

"Alrighty then. Tell me about this murder investigation. Your first, isn't it?"

She glanced to see if he was serious. "You know I've worked homicide scenes before, just not as lead."

"Gotcha. Well, happy to offer any guidance. Thoughts. Whatever."

She raised her eyebrow again. He couldn't possibly have known about the case before he'd arrived, could he?

"I promise I'm not here to babysit you." He let loose a chuckle. "You truly are a suspicious sort."

"Wonder where I got that from?" She flashed him an all-teeth smile, but her walls lowered some. It would be nice to have someone with experience to talk this through with Jax inaccessible.

She began with telling her father about the apartment fire Koa had run into. Talking work kept them off subjects that she had less energy for. He might be here to make amends. Then again, that could be a ruse.

"That must have been terrifying." He shifted in his seat. "Where are you on the investigation?"

"Waiting to hear from the ME. She's researching an aspect found on the body that might've been consistent with another case."

They pulled into the basin, Rachel's attention immediately drawn to the entrance of the bar where boats were navigating in and out. "Garrett was right that this place could look like rush hour."

Distracted, she parked and got out. The shed where Aggie worked was open this time. An older woman with gray curls sprouting out from underneath a black stocking cap was at the entry with a clipboard, a line of people waiting to speak with her. Aggie, no doubt, and she was writing and ripping sheets out of a notebook of some kind. Receipts, maybe. It was close enough to the first of the month that slip rental might be due about now.

Rachel scanned the docks. The yellow boat that had been dockside and crewless a day ago was now second in line of other boats heading over the bar into the Columbia River. Her eyes drifted to where Robby had been working before. Nothing. Until she spotted him heading up the far dock, closer to where the yellow boat had been moored yesterday.

"I'm going to chat with that guy over there." She pointed. "Be right back."

"Sure," he said.

Robby, a backpack over his shoulder, caught sight of her. She raised her hand to get his attention.

Still a good distance away, she increased her speed to reach him.

As did he. The minute he cleared the deck, he ran.

Chapter Twenty-Four

The man watched the young deputy near the top of the decks, reminding himself that patience is what had saved him as he sat in a prison cell all those years.

It's what led him to his first victim. To his second. His third. To what had led him to his ultimate prize, or so he'd thought.

It turned out to be no prize at all.

It's what had allowed him also to wait as the drugs took effect. He'd watch his victims writhe and squirm, helpless to stop him. Watch as each took their last breath, any remaining tears trickling down their cheeks.

He shuddered now at how he'd feel seeing the young deputy gasp for her last breath. Cry her last tear. Relinquish the fight—as they all should for the torturous pain they'd caused him. Even if not individually, collectively—all women, it turned out, were evil.

But for now, time with the deputy would have to wait. He ached, knowing he couldn't stay any longer. The call had arrived, and nothing could stop his next move. Not even the prospect of having fun with the young woman.

A young woman who now had a shadow of her own, he'd observed. A shadow that smelled like cop even at a distance—and not one he'd counted on being in Misty Pines.

So no, he couldn't wait. Another had to pay a price.

As he set the GPS tracker in motion, he knew the direction he must go.

"Until next time, deputy," he whispered, and drove out of the marina.

Chapter Twenty-Five

"Do I sound like a broken record?" Jax said.

"Just a little."

Jax unloaded the bag of goodies he'd brought from the store into the kitchen's cupboards, Abby nearby. "Okay, but I'm telling you, something isn't right about Hannah."

"She's at that age, don't you think?" Abby ambled to the couch, looking even more tired than when Jax had left. "Relationship troubles. Lost soul. That's how she comes across to me."

"I'd be more inclined to believe that if she were in her early twenties. I peg her closer to mid-thirties."

"Some people don't get it together, no matter what age." She dropped onto the cushion, pulling the blanket over her legs. "We've both seen plenty of examples of that. And we don't know enough about her or her background to judge anything."

Abby had a point. "You're still not feeling well?"

"Like I said earlier, just tired." She snuggled deeper under the cover.

"Are you coming down with something?"

She rubbed her eyes. "You could say that."

He straightened. He'd been smart to think ahead. "Then I have just the thing." He pulled the package of tea-like cold remedy from the bag and ran water into a cup, placing it in the microwave.

"What are you making?"

"A lemon-flavored cold medicine that I picked up at the store below. It should do the trick."

"I don't have a cold."

"If you're feeling rundown, it's best to get ahead of it."

"Not sure it works that way with remedies. Vitamins, maybe." She shifted. "And I don't—"

He met her eye. "Please, let me take care of you."

Abby sat up. Jax expected an argument. The woman hated to be coddled as much, no more, than he did. But if they were to have a fresh start, they had to let each other in. Lower some walls. He'd lead with that.

Instead, she sighed. "Can I see the package?"

His shoulders inched lower as he walked it over. "Anyway, you should have seen Hannah's demeanor after she didn't get a hold of her boyfriend."

"She didn't get through to him?"

"No. She left him a message and told him where she's at, so he can find his way. She's *certain* he'll join her shortly."

"You don't believe her?"

He sat down on the edge of the sofa, watching Abby. Shadows encircled her green eyes. A twinging sensation filled his gut. A sensation he'd felt before when similar types of shadows appeared under Lulu's eyes soon after her cancer diagnosis.

Jax reached over, pressed his hand to her forehead. She didn't look drawn, though, more flush.

"What're you doing?" She swatted his hand away. "I told you I'm only tired." She handed the package back to him. "Thank you, but this has some ingredients that I—" She sank back into the couch. "If I can get some rest, I'll be fine and ready to go again."

The twinge in his gut grew. It was clear she didn't want to talk about whatever had her so tired, and if he pushed, she'd withdraw. The more he reasoned with himself, his dread grew. He stood. "Let me get you a bowl of that stew you heated then."

Her face scrunched, as if he'd offered her a bowl of mud.

"If you're nauseous, I grabbed Pepto, too."

"It's definitely related to my stomach." She swallowed, her face scrunched again.

"Was it something you ate earlier?"

He walked the Pepto to her, figuring she'd want to see it as well.

She scanned the back and quickly shook her head. "No. I don't know. Distract me. Tell me again why you think Hannah's a problem."

It no longer seemed important.

"Please," she said.

He went into the kitchen, returning the items to the bag. "She wouldn't elaborate, but I kept feeling that she came here impulsively. Why else would she have so little?"

"Not everyone's as organized as we are."

"True, but she came out of the market with a bag full of supplies after her boyfriend didn't answer. Yet, all the way back, she kept her eyes glued to the sideview mirror like she expected someone to come up behind us."

"Yeah, the boyfriend she called."

He shrugged. "I can't explain it. It's a feeling." He opened the refrigerator to search for something bland that Abby wouldn't wrinkle her nose at. "You know, we haven't even asked what her last name is."

"What good would that do out here?"

"Nothing, but when I spoke with Trudy, I could have had her…"

"You called the station?"

He closed the fridge door slowly. "I checked in."

"How'd you do that when you left your phone on the coffee table?"

He cleared his throat. "I borrowed Hannah's."

She crossed her arms over her chest. "You have no ability to stop being a cop for two seconds, do you?"

"I wasn't being a cop. I was being—"

"Oh, c'mon. Admit it. First, you have the satellite phone hidden, only coming clean when I told you I already knew about it. Then, from the moment Hannah came to our door, you've suspected her of having some dark motivation. And based on what? That her car wouldn't start? That she came into the wilderness on a whim without being loaded down with gear?"

Seemed enough for him. "Okay, but you think she's odd, too, and you're making my case. It was also smart to check in at the station since we don't have any communication now. I was being responsible."

"You're justifying."

"Damn straight I am."

She shook her head again, her jaw set. "I don't understand how this will work if you can't detach for even one day."

That's what this was about? She'd dragged him out here only to pick apart any chance of reconciliation they might have.

"You know, if you don't want to be together, you could say that instead of finding fault for me caring enough to get you a bag of remedies or thinking ahead to make sure the crew knew where we were." Though they still didn't since he hadn't gotten much more than a few words out of his mouth before Trudy hung up. Beside the point.

"I—"

"I love you, Abby Kanekoa, but I'll be damned if I can do this alone. I'm trying, but it takes both of us." Trying was all he'd been doing. And it wasn't good enough. "So just say it."

"Say what?"

"That this entire trip had nothing to do with reconciling, but for you to find a way to let me down. Although easy couldn't have been your goal. Because nothing about this trip has been easy. So, if you just—"

"Shut up, Jax."

He stepped back at the intensity of her words. Raised his hands in surrender. "Fine. Just tell me it's over first, and we can pack our things and go." The thought had a wedge forming in his throat. Nothing had gone as he'd hoped. Where had it gone wrong?

"Jax."

"It's fine." He couldn't keep the pain from his voice. "We should've gone home the moment something felt off." It would have saved him from this moment.

"It's not that." Her words came out so quietly that he felt dizzy.

The shadows around her eyes. Her fatigue. Her nausea.

His chest gripped.

She was dying…. He steadied himself for the news. Whatever it was, he wouldn't let her push him away if it was *that.* "Tell me, Abby. What is it? Whatever it is. I'm here."

"I'm pregnant, Jax." She wilted into the sofa. "I'm pregnant."

Chapter Twenty-Six

Rachel leaned her back into the chair, waiting for Robby to quit talking.

"That was some serious police brutality," he said for the fifth time from the metal chair he straddled, his hands linked to the table with cuffs.

"Said by someone who thinks it's smart to outrun a cop." Or try.

Robby hadn't gotten far. The slight incline of the parking lot slowed him some, but his rubber boots did him in. She'd known they would be a problem as he took off from the ramp. She might have even let him think he could get ahead, so when she tackled him, it was justified. Because she had tackled him—harder than she intended since she'd tripped in the process—but either way, it brought him to an abrupt halt.

Her heartbeat had yet to fully calm from the encounter. Now she glanced at her father, who sat in the corner chair he'd gravitated to when they'd entered the interrogation room. Uninvited, but since she'd brought him into the case, she could hardly ask him to leave. A case he'd said little about. In fact, he'd remained rather quiet since leaving the marina. Not a bad thing, because he also hadn't commented on how she'd dragged Robby to his feet or led him to the car.

Though his silence might have said more than words about that.

"Well, I want to file a formal complaint with your supervisor," Robby said.

"At the moment, that's me. And anyone would tell you the same thing. If you had nothing to hide, there'd be no reason to sprint across a parking lot to get away or come at an officer of the law."

"I was late for an appointment, and I didn't 'come at you.' I slipped and tried to stop myself. Unlike you." He glared at her.

Jax wouldn't have approved; it was far from her finest moment. Perhaps she hadn't completely forgiven Robby for trying to douse her and Brody with the water hose the day before. Or her need to impress her father had taken over.

She cleared her throat. "Where was your appointment?"

"None of your business. And I have a boat to clean and prep for tomorrow morning with no one to delegate that to but me. So if we could move this along."

"What fish you hauling?" Rachel's father said before she could respond.

"Sardine—until October."

"You returned to port earlier than normal?" he said.

Since when did her father know about fishing?

"Maxed the limit sooner than expected," Robby said. "The warm summer's been prime for them."

Her father nodded at her, like he was handing back the baton.

Rachel stretched her neck, feeling like a live bug under the microscope. "Saw you coming from where the yellow boat had been tied off the day before."

"So?"

"Were you there to help them leave? Saw their vessel getting ready to cross the bar."

"I don't work for them. I run my own boat."

"Then what took you to that side of the docks?"

He didn't answer.

"This will go much faster if you answer the questions," she said.

"Whatever. A few of the crew on board are my buddies. I was checking to see if they wanted to grab a beer later."

"They heading to Sardine, too?" Her father piped in again.

"No. I told the deputy yesterday. They're a guide boat."

"At night, if I recall."

"Yup. But they got a problem with the hull, so were heading to West Shore for repair."

She pulled her notebook out. "Take a full crew to do that?"

"Not my business."

"Fair enough. But you also said you didn't know whether Bruce Hatfield worked for them or the Protocol, or any of the other boats."

He shifted, bringing his feet in front of him and planting them solidly on the floor. "That's what I said."

"See, that's confusing. A long timer like you with buddies all over the marina would possess that information. Or so it would seem."

"Crews vary depending on what the catch is, and that changes on the regular. Not sure you've noticed, but the coast is transient. This stretch more so than others because it's a stop point for men on their way to work in Alaska."

"So, you're standing by your statement that you don't know which boat Bruce Hatfield worked on, but it's definitely not the yellow boat that only runs at night." She glanced at her notes.

"Look, maybe he does, or doesn't. The boat runs mostly at night, but they've been known to fish when there are no ships scheduled. Maybe he worked for them or any number of other boats. I don't—"

"Right, you don't know. Must be a big operation to have so many facets running at one time."

"People do a bit of everything to stay literally afloat down here. If you want details, talk to each one of them."

"Like I needed to talk to Aggie yesterday, but she conveniently disappeared before I could?"

"Your bad timing isn't my problem. She was there today."

"And busy." Then gone by the time she'd caught up with Robby.

He shrugged.

"Let's get back to why you ran," Rachel said.

"Thought you'd have figured that out already."

"You're referring to the unpaid speeding ticket?"

"Tickets. Yup."

"Right. Three, to be precise, and no warrants have been issued on them."

She tapped her pen on the table. "Try again."

"That's it."

"Let's talk about drugs."

He shifted. "Except for a bit of weed in high school, I haven't touched them."

"How about Bruce Hatfield?"

"How would I know?"

"Here's the thing," Rachel said, resting her forearms on the table. "There's a rumor of a drug operation on the docks, but my bigger concern is how that might have tied to my victim. A victim that was found in his apartment, murdered."

He paled a bit. "I was sorry to hear about him. No one wants to hear about one of their own being taken out like that. But I'd never met the guy, and there's no drug running at the marina that I'm aware of." Robby moved enough that his cuffs rattled against the table. "Whatever got him, it had nothing to do with drugs, I assure you that."

"What makes you so certain?"

"Because I've been working there since I was fifteen. I'm twenty-seven and the youngest captain in the bay. Everyone else is an old codger that will *talk your ear off,* as they like to tell me. Now, if alcohol was illegal, then you'd have something. The men love their booze, and I'm sure there's some recreational use of stuff that gets passed around. But hard drugs? Drug smuggling? No way."

"How about the ships that need the tenders?"

"Usually from other countries, and sure, they could be up to no good. But they're usually passing by on their way to West Shore. If something's going on, it would be there."

She slapped her notebook closed. With nothing to substantiate a drug operation, other than the accusations of one tenant from the complex fire and a drifter they'd yet to locate, there wasn't much further to go on the subject. Whether Robby looked like the type to be involved in shady dealings, she wouldn't be guilty of stereotyping, either.

And her gut didn't truly believe drugs had anything to do with Bruce's murder.

"Let's talk about Winona then."

Robby shifted again, those cuffs clanking harder on the metal table surface. "Winona who?"

Rachel waited.

He sighed. "How'd you find out?"

"She told me."

His face wrinkled. "Okay."

"You seem concerned," her father said. "She underage?"

"No, sir."

"Then what's the problem?" Rachel asked.

"Her aunt doesn't think much of me."

"Because?" She could think of a few reasons.

"She and my mom didn't get along. They grew up together. Some high school rivalry thing. And because of that, Winona and I aren't supposed to see each other."

"Yet you do, right? She stays with you?"

His jaw twitched. "No one's going to tell us whether we can be together. But she doesn't stay often."

"Where is she when she's not with you?"

"Her aunt's, of course."

Except that's not what Winona had said, or her aunt. Unless Winona stayed someplace else without either of them knowing. "Bruce was a good-looking guy. Ever worry about Winona while he was living there?"

"Nope. Remember, I didn't know him."

"But you knew he lived in the complex." He didn't answer. "See, the problem is, Winona said she stayed with you most of the time. Only occasionally with her aunt if you two were fighting."

His jaw twitched. "Did she now."

"So maybe she was staying with Bruce?"

"Please."

"Why's that so hard to believe?"

"Because it didn't happen."

"What makes you so sure of that?"

"Because three's a crowd."

"What's that mean?" Rachel glanced at her father, who was paying rapt attention.

"Bruce had a girlfriend," Robby said.

Rachel eased her notebook open. "You didn't mention that before."

"You didn't ask, and I'm making an assumption that it was his girlfriend."

"Based on?"

"Her coming to look for him last week. She said she knew he lived and worked in the area, and the docks were her last hope in finding him."

"And you miraculously knew where to send her to find Bruce while knowing nothing about him?"

"I'd told you I knew of him. People talk about newbies in town. So yeah, I knew where to direct her."

How did Jax do this regularly and not go crazy? "Tell me more about this woman."

"Not much to tell. She seemed desperate to find Bruce, and I told her where he lived. Since I never saw her again, I assume she found him."

Her thoughts turned to the hair tie she'd found in Bruce's bedroom. "You still haven't said why you believe it was a girlfriend?"

"Cute, for one thing, and the vibe she was giving off. It seemed like they were together at one time and broke up, and she was having a change of heart. Just a feeling; guess I can't say for sure."

If he couldn't, Winona or one of the other tenants might. Dorothy had reported hearing someone else upstairs in Bruce's apartment, and she might have seen the woman without realizing who she was.

"Do you have a name of this individual looking for Bruce?"

"Heather, maybe. No. Hannah. Yeah, Hannah."

Rachel made a few more notes. When she looked up, her father had slipped out the door. Must have been bored with the conversation.

"Can I go now?" Robby said.

"I'll have one of my deputies take you back as soon as you tell me the real reason you ran."

"I didn't want to get involved. That woman that came looking, she seemed concerned. Now Bruce's dead. If she was involved in that, then she knows where I work. If I've learned nothing from the old guys at the basin, it's one thing—mind your own business."

"Big muscular guy like you? Hard to believe you'd be concerned about some woman."

"Yeah, well, sometimes it's the cute ones you need to worry about. And I couldn't decide if she was really desperate or a tad crazy. I didn't want to find out which."

Chapter Twenty-Seven

Jax stood motionless in the kitchen, unsure whether he'd heard Abby right. "Say again?"

"I'm pregnant." She enunciated the words, so there was no mistaking. *Okay. Yep.* That's what he'd heard.

"You're sure. I mean, you're…."

"I'm what, Jax?"

"I just thought…how—"

"Tread carefully."

"How could this have happened? It was just the one time before."

"Do you need a reminder of how the birds and the bees work?"

God, he was making a mess of this conversation. "I'm going to shut up now."

"Good idea."

He hurried to the couch, dropped to his knees, and grabbed her in for a hug, determined to make sure she knew how he felt about the news. She returned his embrace half-heartedly. When he let go, he scanned her face. "You're not happy?"

"You are?"

"Of course, I am."

She screwed her face.

"Okay, it's fair to say I'm shocked. I thought you'd gone through menopause or were in the process of that, but—"

"Wow. What would you base that on?"

"Well, we didn't use birth control, and you've been moody."

"Moody?"

Shut up, Jax. "Not yourself, is all I meant. I could sense something was off. Like that perfume you were wearing when I picked you up. When did that start?"

"The citrusy one?"

"Yeah. That is new, right?" If nothing else, she couldn't accuse him of being completely oblivious.

"It's supposed to help with nausea, though it's been hit or miss."

He should have read the signs better. "What's the doctor say?"

"That nausea's perfectly normal at this stage." She pulled the pillow from under her back and tossed it to the floor so she could sink lower into the sofa. "I don't recall feeling so exhausted with Lulu, though."

"That pregnancy was over a decade ago now. You were…"

"I told you—"

"Well, it's true. For both of us. And something we need to be aware of."

"I was much younger, and yes, we do. The doctor's recommending that some tests be done."

He straightened. "Have they already seen something?"

"No, but I'm high risk either way."

"Risk of what, birth defects?"

She nodded, her chin trembling. "What if there's a problem?"

He pulled her in again. "Hey. We'll handle whatever comes our way."

"Will we? Like you did when Lulu died?"

He held her tighter, trying not to take her fears personally. "I understand why you'd feel concerned. I failed you when we lost her, and I regret that a million times over. But I'm not that person any longer. I'm here for you and our baby."

"Still, the odds of me having a child with Down syndrome or some kind of health issue now that I'm older are off the charts. It's best if we know what's coming; I've agreed to the tests."

He shook his head. "It doesn't matter what they say," Jax said, surprised Abby would want that information. "However he or she is when they enter this world, we'll love them with everything we are, regardless."

She placed her palm against his cheek. "Absolutely, we will, and I don't mean to suggest otherwise. That doesn't mean we shouldn't be preparing ourselves, though."

"Nah. This is one area where you're going to have to let go. There's no perfection in this."

She withdrew her hand. "What's that mean?"

Back it up. "Just that we have no control. We may make different decisions, and I'm sure we'll be overly protective and drive our kid nuts, as it should be, but honestly, I'd rather not know or stress ourselves out beforehand."

"Jax, I just—"

"Look, we're getting too far ahead. We should be celebrating this, whether we planned for it or not. What's important now is making sure you're healthy and—" He stopped, realizing she had to have known for a while. "Wait, you must be two months along by now."

"Ten weeks."

"Why didn't you tell me before?"

"I wasn't sure—"

"About what? Whether the pregnancy was viable?"

She looked away.

Ah. "Me."

"Not you, necessarily. About us, yes. And me, and whether I'd miscarry." She closed her eyes. "My ability to raise another child. Which I can totally do alone, but—"

He grimaced. "Why would you have to?"

"Because we're not together. And you're in your fifties and work consumes you. And again, we're not together."

"That's why you were upset about my calling the office. You don't think I'll be there for you."

"Work has always come first for you."

He shook his head. "That's not fair. Yours has too. But never when it came to family, and I feel the same. You've always been important to me. Since the day we met. Then Lulu." His throat tightened. "Now we have a second chance."

Although she was right about one aspect. He was older, and ever since they'd arrived, he'd been feeling every year of his age. Wondering how much longer he could keep going as sheriff. Toying with the idea of slowing down—handing the baton to Rachel.

A new baby would mean anything but a slower pace. It would send their life in an entirely different direction, a shift in priorities in a way they'd long needed.

"I'm ready for it, Abby. I'm here for you. For us."

She said nothing. And he knew.

"It's the other part that's bothering you the most, isn't it? You're not sure if you want to reconcile."

"I didn't say that."

"But that's what this weekend has been for. For you to decide that."

She sighed. "You have to admit, we have history, Jax. It would be foolish not to consider that."

"Sure, I guess, but don't you think that only means we know the pitfalls to avoid?"

She nodded, maybe seeing his point. He couldn't be sure.

"Look, I get it. But know this. I don't want to parent from the sidelines. I love you and you love me. We can make this work."

She smiled, faintly. "There's so much still to talk about."

He stood, squared his shoulders. At least she hadn't rejected him or the idea outright. "There is. Let's get some food in you first. Get you feeling better before we have any more deep conversations."

"Now you're going all Papa Bear on me?"

He grinned. "You bet I am."

The crunch of tires on the road drew Jax's attention.

Abby huffed. "Seriously? For being a private getaway, we sure have had a lot of company."

He headed to the drawn window shade. "Probably Hannah's boyfriend, looking for her. Not sure how she expected him to find her obscure campsite in the first place."

"You think?" she said.

He lifted a blind and peered through. "It's Sam. I'll be right back." Outside, Jax trotted down the stairs and was struck by a faint acrid scent in the air. "Hey, buddy."

"Sorry to interrupt, didn't find anything to report back on, but realized I hadn't mentioned to you about the outdoor fire restriction. With the mountain not being officially open, the signs haven't been reset yet."

"No worries. I already figured as much, and you have nothing to worry about. There are no romantic outdoor fires on the agenda."

"Good. As I mentioned earlier, the damn forest is pure tinder after the summer we've just had. Boys are battling a fire right now across the river."

"Thought I smelled something."

"That would be it. Wind carries the smoke right over, and it gets trapped here."

"Campers?"

"Lightning this time."

Jax's shoulders inched upward. "Should we be worried?"

"Nah. They have a good chunk of it under control, and it won't go much further. Still, you can't be too safe this time of year."

"That's true. And since you're here, I'm hoping to get your expertise on a couple of things." Jax went on to tell him about the gutted opossum and showed him the seats of his truck.

"If the door was left ajar, most anything with claws could've done that kind of damage. Bobcats are particularly territorial. And the condition of the opossum is common around here. Anything from a fox to a horned owl might've been the culprit."

Some of the tension drained from Jax. "Good to know."

"Anyway, better get back to the rounds. At least it's quiet. During a regular summer, I spend half my time making sure outdoor enthusiasts behave themselves. The partiers and first-timers are always an issue."

"Speaking of which. We have a neighbor, Hannah, located to the east. Apparently, she missed or ignored the signs. Now she's here until her friend arrives to get her car started. Either way, you might want to swing through and mention the fire restriction. Not sure she has plans for a campfire, but—"

"Already done. She's who took me out of the watch station. I'd seen two streams of smoke curling into the sky. I knew only one of you was in a cabin."

She was more resourceful than Jax had given her credit for. "She's probably preparing for another chilly night. Had her boyfriend arrived yet?"

He shook his head. "Not that I could tell. And I looked at her car, but I'm not a mechanic."

"You and me both."

"Well, hopefully soon. She seemed awfully jumpy when I came up the road."

"I have a feeling that's her general MO."

"Maybe so. Did seem to have a few questions about you and Abby, though."

"Like?"

"Mostly, if I knew how good your skills were as cops."

Yep. He should never have mentioned it. "What did you say?"

"That there were none more qualified." He winked. "Anyway. She knows not to light any more fires."

Jax hoped she'd follow the rules.

It wasn't just himself and Abby to think about anymore. They had a child on the way. A new beginning. A second chance at being a family. He might be far too old to start again, but if he had to fake it until he got some confidence, he would.

He only had to keep convincing Abby they could work as a couple. The last thing they needed was a fire to put it all in jeopardy.

Chapter Twenty-Eight

From just outside the interrogation room, Rachel watched Brody lead Robby to his patrol car.

"You cutting him loose already?" Garrett said, approaching.

"No cause to hold him."

"Other than he knew Bruce Hatfield?"

"Only in passing." Her lips pursed.

"You don't believe him?"

"Not really, though I'm not sure he's involved in whatever happened to the guy either."

"What's that based on?"

"My gut."

Garrett shrugged his broad shoulders. "Suppose that's about all any of us have to go on some days."

"Appreciate that," she said, expecting him to have challenged her. They really had come a long way. "Well, there was one other thing. He offered another possibility of a young woman named Hannah, who apparently came by the docks last week to ask about Bruce's whereabouts. I found a hair tie on the premises and thought that it had more potential."

"Family?"

"Supposedly a girlfriend. DNA won't be back for at least seventy-two hours, and I'm not sure it will tell us too much, but Robby says he directed this Hannah to Bruce's place here in Misty Pines."

"Could be relevant."

"She's at least worth finding and talking to," Rachel said. "Any word from the ME yet?"

He shook his head. "Not that Trudy's mentioned. By the way, who's the old guy?"

"The *old* guy?"

"The one in Jax's office with his feet propped on the desk, talking on the phone."

Geez. "He's my dad."

"That's the infamous Jameson?"

Is that how they knew him? "I guess. Why do you say that?"

"He helped the sheriff on the first big case we handled around here." He stood a little taller. "It was before your time."

She smiled. They might still have a bit more distance to go with each other. "So, what's next for you?"

"Heading out on patrol," he said.

"Will you ask Winona to come in for a visit on your way back?" She glanced at her watch. "She should be off work in about two hours, and we need another conversation."

"Where you going?" he asked.

"To track down the tenants again. Someone must've seen the woman looking for Bruce. If she was asking for him at the docks, she likely would have asked around the complex, too."

"Makes sense."

"It's a theory. Weird they didn't offer that when I questioned them before, but they were all over the place, and it could be I didn't ask the right questions. Any sign of our drifter?"

"No. Brody had some ideas of places to check. I'm sure he'll update you when he's back from dropping off your boy. In the meantime, you have another old guy, Commissioner Marks, waiting for you up front."

She cringed. "You didn't think to lead with that?"

"No sense you rushing out there to greet him." He lowered his voice. "Never hurts to let him know he's not in charge around this office."

"You're more passive-aggressive than I pegged you for. I like it."

He smiled. "And now I'm headed to the kitchen. Your dad asked for a cup of coffee, one cream, two sugars."

"Making himself right at home," she said, unable to shake the feeling that her father hadn't made the drive to Misty Pines *only* to reconnect. Maybe he had expected Jax to be here and didn't want to disappoint her. During their last argument, he'd said that he'd intended to *talk some sense into Jax*. Referencing her as if she were a child with no ability to decide for herself. She stretched her neck to ease the kink that had settled in.

"Yeah, I was thinking the same thing. Jax is coming back, right?" Garrett said.

"He sure as hell better be."

Suddenly, she was undecided on which direction to go first: to demand answers from her father, or deal with Commissioner Marks. One would probably avoid answering, and the other was no better. Worse would be if they collided with each other. She could only imagine what Jax had shared with his former partner; with no love lost between Jax and Troy, it couldn't be good.

"Commissioner Marks," she said, entering the reception area with her hand outstretched. In charge. Confident.

"Deputy," he said. "How's the fort without the captain?"

"Fort's running fine," Rachel said.

Trudy hopped out of her chair. "Commissioner, how soon before your apartments are livable again?"

"Insurance has already been out to assess, and the arson investigation will be wrapped up soon. Then they'll be working with the county to make sure the building's safe, though much of the building's fine. It's just some smoke damage, and of course, the bottom unit and the utility room are a total loss."

Trudy dropped back into her chair, frowning. "At least a month, then."

"At least."

Trudy slid the headset back onto her head and headed for the copier.

Rachel held back a laugh. Dorothy really must be testing Trudy's limits for her to be so frazzled and looking to keep herself busy.

"As I said, all's good here," Rachel said. "But you were on my list to see. Wondering what you might have on one of your tenants, Bruce Hatfield."

"Very little," he said. "The leasing agent had an application that Mr. Hatfield filled out. Rather sparse, but I'm happy to share it with you."

She'd expected more resistance. "Thanks."

"Well, it doesn't look great to have a murder happen at one of my properties, and the sooner that's behind us, the better. You have any suspects?"

"Not yet. But I was just about to track down some of the tenants and ask a few more questions. The application doesn't specify anyone else living in the apartment, I take it?"

"No."

"When did he move in?"

"A year ago, or thereabouts. He'd lived in Portland for a while and worked for the Port of Portland before coming here. Rent always showed on time."

"Current employer listed?"

"No, just general labor, I believe."

She nodded.

"You must be Troy Marks."

Rachel winced as her father's voice boomed behind her right before he was standing at her side.

"And you are?" the Commissioner said.

"Detective Jameson, Portland PD. Jax's former partner. He's mentioned you a time or two."

"He's mentioned you as well. You here to assist with the murder investigation?"

"No," Rachel said before her father could answer.

He smiled. "Just here visiting my daughter."

He said it a beat too slowly, and her skin prickled. Both men were staring at her like they were there to assist. Or to make sure she didn't screw up. *Damn it, Uncle Jax.*

"With you two having something in common, how about you stay behind, Dad, and I'll swing back after."

"Thanks, but I'll ride shotgun," her father said.

She bet he would. "Trudy, any idea where Chuck Pullman ended up staying?"

"No, hon, but you'll likely find him at the Tip Top this time of day."

She headed for the door, her father keeping her pace.

"I'm here if you need anything else," Troy said after her.

Her lips pursed; she kept walking.

Jax had eyes everywhere.

Chapter Twenty-Nine

By the time Jax rejoined Abby in the cabin, she'd fallen asleep on the couch. He didn't blame her. She'd been keeping the pregnancy to herself and feeling poorly at the same time. She'd now have him to lean on.

Though she was strong—he'd take nothing away from her ability to handle whatever came her way—escaping into sleep seemed the perfect solution.

He found himself pacing the kitchen. The news had left him wired, and wishing he had internet access so he could spend the next hours educating himself on the risk factors of her pregnancy that she'd spoken about. Despite what he'd told Abby, he'd like to learn all he could. To prepare, sure, but more importantly, to have the information necessary to support her since she felt concerned.

Whether the information would make him more obsessive, a place he could feel himself floating towards, it seemed better than not knowing. Though breathing was a risk, he reminded himself. Going outside the front door was a risk. Being in law enforcement shot those risks skyward.

Would Abby still want to continue as an FBI agent? Probably. She'd worked until she went into labor before with no issues. Granted, that was a different time in her life—in both of their lives.

Now, ten years later, he contemplated what bringing a baby into their world would look like. He'd be in his seventies by the time he or she graduated. He winced. Friends of his kid would think he looked more like the grandfather. His own father had been older. And mean as shit.

That, he'd never be. He'd doted on Lulu; this would be no different.

Unless he didn't have the opportunity. How much would he be part of the child's life if Abby chose not to reconcile? This entire trip had been to see if they stood a chance.

They'd been getting along well. Yet, she'd said it herself: she didn't feel certain. What would happen if she never did?

He rubbed the space between his eyes, aware of the answer, and feeling sick about it. Parenting from a distance would be asking the impossible of him. The uncertainty, the questions, had his brain shooting off in a dozen different directions.

Around seven, he stopped pacing long enough to pull a blanket over Abby, who slept peacefully curled in a ball, and he went outside.

The fresh air felt good at first, but the wind bit through his thin shirt. It would be another cold night. The acrid scent he'd caught in the breeze earlier hit his nose again. Stronger this time.

He ambled to the cliff side to stretch his legs and scanned the canyon and across the river, searching for where the forest fire Sam spoke of was supposedly under control. A low haze hung over the trees, but Sam hadn't seemed concerned, and he'd know better than most if there were a problem.

Jax's attention turned toward Hannah's camp. She'd proven not to be a staunch rule-follower so far, but hopefully she'd follow Sam's directives. He shivered, the wind picking up. With it being colder tonight than last, and with only the few supplies she had in that car, he didn't feel confident.

Returning inside the cabin, he found a couple of extra blankets in the closet. As he came back into the living room, Abby stirred.

"Everything okay?" she murmured.

He sat next to her. "I'm going to check on Hannah while there's still light out. If the temps drop much lower, she'll be at risk. We have a few extra blankets."

"That's sweet." She rose enough to kiss his lips. "Should I go with you?"

He hadn't expected the kiss, but he took it in, fighting the desire to crawl next to her on the couch.

"No. Better you stay inside. There's smoke from a distant fire. Not good for you to be in it."

She settled back into the covers. "Okay."

He brushed back her hair. "You hungry? Want me to get you something first?"

She didn't respond.

"Abby?"

A soft snore came in response.

This trust and togetherness were once their life. Every part of him yearned for it to be again—for them to be united. A new life was coming their way. He had to make sure Abby knew he wanted nothing more than to be with her.

"I'll be back soon," he whispered.

Jax slipped into a sweatshirt and headed to Hannah's camp. When he arrived, there were no signs of a campfire. He took a breath, relieved, and glad he'd thought of bringing the blankets.

"Hannah," he called, expecting her head to appear from the backseat of her car if she were sleeping. When she didn't, he proceeded into the camp. Metal clanked at his feet, and he almost toppled onto his knees, but lunged forward, catching himself. He scanned the ground to find what he'd tripped over.

Hannah had pulled a string between two trees, tying two cans to it?

"Hey," Hannah said, appearing on the opposite side of the camp with a rabbit carcass dangling from her hand. "What're you doing here?"

He cleared his throat and lifted the blankets. "Ranger stopped by and said he'd mentioned not lighting any fires. Thought these might come in handy tonight with the temperature dropping."

She set the carcass on the ground. Grabbed a rag from her back pocket and wiped her hands. "Yeah, he did. But kind of a bummer."

"How'd you catch a rabbit?"

"Oh, I didn't. I found it nearby. Looked like a fresh kill, though, and I was thinking of cooking it up. Not now, obviously."

He nodded. "But you do have food?"

"Sure. Like I said, I found it." She smiled, coming closer. "I appreciate the blankets."

CHAPTER TWENTY-NINE

"Sure thing. I'll put them in your car.

"No, that's fine. I'll take them."

"It's no problem," he said, as she hastened toward him.

"No boyfriend yet?"

She slowed her stride; her body tensed as Jax approached the car. "No. But I'm not worried."

He opened the car door. A knife lay on the passenger side. Pretending he didn't notice he tossed the blankets on top.

Hannah seemed to track his moves.

"Everything else okay?" He slammed the door.

"Perfectly. Thanks again. I'm just getting ready to turn in."

Maybe she was fine. And she was armed, and that was good with her being alone. Still… "Why the alarm system?" He nodded toward the string that had nearly taken him down.

"Excuse me?"

"Last time I saw something like that was when I was ten and wanted to keep the neighbor girl out of my stuff."

She chuckled lightly. "Yeah, well, bears and bobcats, right? You saw that rabbit."

He couldn't discount that. "Probably a good idea. You still thinking your boyfriend got the message and will show tonight?"

Her face grew serious again. "He'll be here."

Her tone and body language didn't match. "If there's anything that you're concerned about, or afraid of, you should tell me. I can help."

"You should go now."

"Hannah, I'm just trying to—"

"Leave?" She sighed. "Look, I've got everything under control. It's nice knowing you're close, but I don't want to involve you. I'm sorry I came to ask for your phone. I'm sorry you had to deal with my car. But I'm a loner. It's how I've lived my life for quite some time, and I prefer it that way."

He put his hands in the air. "You know where we are if you need us."

She nodded, then softened. "I'm really okay. Thanks."

He backtracked the way he came. Whatever the reason Hannah had for wanting to be alone, she had no intention of sharing it, or anything else on her mind. Which was her right. Even Abby had said he should mind his own business.

Lost in thought, it took a moment to register when a crackle came from the tree line. Leaves and branches being stepped on? Must be. Probably a deer. Wolf? Maybe. Or a cougar. That rabbit had been taken out by some kind of predator.

Now, the idea of being stalked as prey had Jax lengthening his stride.

Not running would be smart; he wouldn't allow himself to give in to paranoia. Though the sense of being watched followed him all the way back to the cabin.

He stopped by his truck long enough to grab the shotgun and bring it inside. By the time he locked the door behind him, the hairs on his neck were standing so tall they stung.

Chapter Thirty

"When are you going to tell me the real reason you're here?" Rachel held her father's innocent stare for a beat as they approached the edge of downtown.

"I told you—"

"Right. But you disappeared right after Robby started talking about Bruce's *girlfriend* that showed up. Then you're on the phone." She threw her hands up for emphasis. "It seemed to me even Troy Marks wondered if you were here to babysit me. Although I'm thinking he had the same directive."

"I assure you I haven't spoken to Jax. I cannot speak for Troy."

"Hmmm." They pulled into the Tip Top Tavern, and she moved to get out. "I'll be right back." Her father hopped out of the passenger side. He was like gum on a shoe. "Fine, but this is my interview."

"You bet. I'm only here—"

"Yeah, yeah."

They found Chuck Pullman nursing a beer at the bar. "Mr. Pullman," Rachel said. "You have a few minutes." It wasn't a question.

He blinked and swayed on the stool. "Who're you?"

She glanced at the bartender and lifted a brow, who nodded in response. Chuck Pullman was officially cut off. "I'm Deputy Killian. I took your statement at the café."

He nodded. "Oh yeah. I remember." He burped.

"Was hoping you could answer a few more questions."

"I can try." He smiled, all teeth, as a whiff of liquor hit her nose.

She leaned away. At least he was a jovial drunk. As a beat cop, she'd had plenty of experience with both sides of that coin. "I've received information that a young woman might have come looking for Mr. Hatfield in the past week."

"Hmmm."

"Is that a yes or no?"

He wiped a bead of sweat rolling off his glass. "It's a yeah, come to think of it. Pretty thing. A bit on the serious side, like you." He winked.

She sighed. "Did you catch her name?"

"Nope. Didn't ask. She didn't offer."

"Did she end up connecting with Bruce?"

He shrugged. "Guess so. Didn't stick around to find out. I had somewhere to be." A patron walked by on his way out and slapped Chuck on the back. "Hey buddy, see you tomorrow," Chuck said.

Rachel had a feeling that *somewhere* might have been right here on this barstool. "Did she say why she was looking for Bruce?"

He shook his head, closed his eyes. When he opened them, he gulped his beer and set the glass down with a clunk. "Winona might know."

"Winona? As in Dorothy's niece?"

"Yup. Saw them talking."

"Were you under the impression they knew each other prior to that?"

"No, but they were talking about Bruce because I heard his name."

"This happened when?"

"Few days ago. Or so. Don't remember."

She should have known a young woman who purportedly observed mail being taken would be aware of other people around the premises. "Okay, thanks."

"You betcha. Think that deserves another beer," he said. "You buying?"

"How about a burger instead?"

"Make it a club, and you got a deal."

She nodded to the bartender and laid a ten on the counter.

"Mighty kind."

On her way out, she texted Garrett, her father right behind her.

You got Winona yet?

No. Went by to confirm her clock-out time, and she'd left early. Not feeling well.

Shoot. *Did you check Robby's address?*

No one's home.

She gripped the phone, thinking.

What now? Garrett texted.

We'll reassess tomorrow. Get Matt up to speed when he's in. She glanced at her father. *I'm calling it a night. Need to get Dad moving back in the direction of home.*

LOL. Done being babysat?

And then some. She tucked her phone in her pocket without responding.

"Ready for dinner?" she said to her dad. "There's a nice place—"

"I'd like to see where you live."

She swallowed. "I haven't told Janelle you were in town and—"

"No need to fuss over me. Just want to see where my little girl lives. Meet who she lives with."

"Dad."

"Rachel."

"Fine." She sent Janelle a message, who sent back a heart. At least one of them was happy about this.

Rachel dropped her dad off at the station to grab his car, and he followed her to the house.

Koa greeted them at the front door, and Rachel loved up her friend. "Boy, did I miss you today." She stroked Koa's face and then pulled away. "Remember your grandpa?" she said, pointing to her dad, chuckling at the grimace on his face.

Koa trotted over and sniffed his feet. "Hey, pup. You taking good care of our girl?" Koa leaned into him, allowing his hand to run down her back.

Rachel's girlfriend appeared from the living room. "And I'm Janelle, Mr. Jameson."

"Call me Jim," he said. "It's nice to finally meet you." He extended his hand and flashed a warm smile.

Rachel hadn't seen that warmth in quite some time—or heard it in her father's voice. Not with their last interactions being so tense, with him always questioning every move she made.

"Thank you. I'm looking forward to getting to know you better, Jim. Rachel hasn't said too much." Janelle side-eyed Rachel, who looked at her dad for his reaction.

"Well, there's not much to tell, and honestly, I probably haven't been on my best behavior."

Rachel's chest squeezed at his words. "Okay, you two. Let's have dinner before we get too far. It's been a long day, and Dad isn't staying long," she said. "Actually, you didn't say how long you were here for. I'm assuming you're heading back tonight?"

He shifted feet. "Unless you have other plans, I was thinking to stay longer. But I can get a room at a motel if that's easier."

"Oh no, you don't," Janelle said. "You'll stay right here. We have plenty of space, and I'll get the guest room prepared after dinner."

He glanced at Rachel. "I'm happy to get a motel room."

The folds in his face softened, making him look tired and much older. She'd always seen him as indestructible. A force to be reckoned with. She didn't see that now. Time kept progressing, and neither of them were getting younger. She wanted to believe he was here to make amends. To get to know her life by seeing how she lived it. If that was his motivation, she couldn't toss him out, whether having him here felt weird or not.

"Don't be silly," she said. "Of course you should stay."

He smiled. "Then I'll get my bag."

"I already ordered pizza," Janelle said as Rachel watched her father walk out the door. "Should be here in a few minutes." She wrapped her arms around Rachel's waist. "You were okay with me inviting him for the night?"

A loaded question. "Sure. I'm just a little off since I didn't expect him to just show up. You know how I am about surprises."

Janelle nuzzled her neck. "Oh, I do. I learned that the first time I donated that monstrosity of a chair you hauled with you from Portland."

Rachel hadn't thought of that for a while, and it rankled her even now. She'd brought so little with her, and what she had brought meant something.

"Well, it was mine."

"It was a tattered mess. Anyway, it's good he's here. I get to finally learn more about where you came from. It's also clear he worries about you. Like I do."

Janelle caring for her so deeply should be a good thing. Yet it felt like another burden. One more person to worry about letting down.

All things she couldn't say right now. "Maybe you're right. It's all good," Rachel said. "With it being your house, I didn't want to assume it was okay to ask him, but yeah, I appreciate you offering."

Janelle let her go. "That was convincing." She laughed, the way she often did at Rachel's comments. "And it's our house."

Rachel didn't answer, pushing away the memory of her favorite ragged chair, and gave Janelle a hug. She loved her girlfriend; she meant well, but more so, the hug anchored her—she felt herself disconnecting. When her father reappeared with not only his bag, but a pizza box, Rachel let her go.

"Dinner is served," he said.

After grabbing paper plates from the pantry, they settled at the table. "So, tell me about yourself," he said to Janelle. "What do you do for a living?"

"I'm an artist and a teacher in West—"

Rachel's cell buzzed. "Just a second. It's Trudy." She answered. "Everything okay?"

"It's fine, hon," Trudy said. "I was heading out when the ME called."

"Oh, okay. Thanks. I'll call her." The woman had her number, and Rachel expected a call direct, but either way.

"She wasn't calling for you," Trudy said.

Rachel frowned at the phone. "She knows Jax's out of town and that I'm working the case."

"Honey," Trudy said. "She called to speak to your father. She hadn't been able to get through to him and left a message with us."

Rachel turned her focus on her father, who had half a slice of pizza in his mouth.

"Interesting," she said. "Thanks, Trudy. I'll let him know." She crushed the END key. Scanned her father's oh-so innocent face. "Care to tell me why

Dr. Shocking is calling my station to speak with you?"

"I can explain."

"I'd love to hear it."

He set the pizza down and met her eye. "Dr. Shocking was in touch with me yesterday about your case."

"And?" Her heartbeat pounded in her ears.

"She believed your case might be related to something I handled years ago, and she wanted my opinion." He hesitated. "And my expertise."

Heat crept up her neck. "I might be able to understand her not disclosing that to me, but you?"

"Rachel."

"No, Rachel me. Instead of being honest, you appear here under some guise about reconciling when all you wanted to do was take over my case."

"It's not like that."

"Really?"

He cleared his throat. "Please, Rachel. Don't be so damn reactive. Can't it be both?"

The chair legs screeched against the hardwood floor as she stood, desperate not to lose her temper in front of Janelle or her father.

She looked at Janelle. "I'm sorry, but I have to go." She didn't wait for a response. "Koa, come," she said, and they were out the door.

Chapter Thirty-One

Miles away, the man who'd left the marina now eased his rental into a parking slot of a roadside store. The call he'd intercepted could only take him so far. But it had come from this location. He turned off the engine and watched a couple enter the store. The young woman, south of thirty perhaps, was dressed in shorts far too short and a tank top far too tight. Parts of him came to life. The same ones he'd noticed when the pretty deputy had been in view. Lucky for this girl, he was not here for her. Not even her male companion could stop him if he so chose.

Like the man he'd encountered in Misty Pines who'd been powerless against him. And only slightly worth the time it took to persuade his minimal cooperation.

He gazed at the long stretch of road that led further into the coast range. Behind the store, the forest land went for miles. That was surely where the one he sought believed was the safest place to go. There'd be no service or ability to track her once he left the lower roads—he could tell by the density of the trees. There must be thousands upon thousands of acres, the potential locations for hiding endless.

His focus returned to the store entrance, with its faded signs advertising cheap beer, and an ice machine that buzzed like flies on rotting meat.

Unless she'd gone inside the store as well?

Only one way to know for sure.

He waited until the couple left and slid out of his vehicle. Tucked the blade in his back pocket and pulled his jacket low to cover it.

Inside, the smell of pine and a freshly mopped floor tingled his sinuses.

"We're just closing up, mister," the young woman—short dark hair, big green eyes—hollered. She wore a flannel shirt over a tight tank. Her bracelets jangled above a cross tattoo on her right wrist.

Not at all like the pristine college girls that usually required his attention, but he felt the rush of excitement just the same. It had been far too long, perhaps.

He strolled to the worn and rutted counter. "Give me a pack of Camels. And some information."

She huffed, barely looking at him. "Do I look like Siri?"

"Who?"

She grabbed the pack from the shelf above her head and dropped the cigarettes onto the counter. "That'll be eight bucks."

He slid the money her direction, keeping his palm over the top. "I'm looking for someone. A woman. Mid-thirties." He thought back to the last time he'd seen her. "Blonde, mid-shoulder hair, likely worn in a ponytail."

The girl laughed. "Yeah, only a half-dozen of them today on their way back to the city."

Her sarcasm had him teetering too soon. He drew himself back, gave her the time parameters when he expected the woman he sought would have come through.

The clerk tucked a strand of hair behind her ear, the twinkle of a diamond stud catching the fluorescent light. She shrugged. "I don't pay attention."

The diamond couldn't be real. Not working in a place like this, he decided. Cheap knockoffs—like her. Trying to be something she wasn't. Rejecting him like the others. Like she was something special.

"I need you to remember."

"Mister, my shift's about over. Take your hand off the damn money, and take your cigarettes or leave without them. Whatever."

Her voice grated on his nerves. "Here I was, trying to be pleasant."

She smacked her gum. The image of his last *chosen one* flashed through his mind. His smile faded.

She must have sensed the shift. "You can take the cigarettes and go. My dad will be here any time."

They always had someone they were waiting for. Someone who would rescue them. Or so they believed. He'd seen her motorcycle parked in the back.

No one was coming.

He nodded, swooped the cigarettes from the counter, pulled the red tab, and pursed one in between his chapped lips.

He strolled to the glass door. The smallest sigh of relief escaped her mouth as he reached the glass.

Premature, my dear.

There'd be no leaving without the information he came for.

He smiled at his reflection as he switched the lock and lowered the shade.

Chapter Thirty-Two

"Do I even want to ask?" Abby's voice drifted in from the bedroom doorway.

"Morning, sleepyhead," Jax said, the partially dismantled shotgun on the coffee table in front of him. "You feeling better?"

She sauntered into the room dressed in the sweats she'd worn yesterday. When he'd returned from Hannah's campsite, the cabin had been eerily quiet and his nerves on edge. He'd been relieved to find Abby had made her way to the bedroom, and those earlier soft snores had only grown louder. Despite wanting to talk, he had no intention of waking her.

"Much." Lifting onto her toes, she raised her arms overhead and stretched, the slightest swell of her belly showing.

He smiled at the hope that swell represented. Along with the uncertainty. The terror. He stood to hug her. "I'm glad to hear that." He set the barrel he'd been polishing down first and pulled her in.

"Me too." Her heels dropped to the floor; she returned the hug. "You still haven't answered my question." When he fell back onto the sofa, she nodded to the assorted pieces. "What are you doing?"

"Cleaning the parts. Making sure it's in good condition."

"Because?"

"Because you never know."

"Something happen while I was asleep?"

He snapped the barrel into the stock and wiped the rag down the metal to remove smudges. "Went out to check on Hannah last night and took her some extra blankets."

"I remember. Was her boyfriend there and caused a problem?"

"He hadn't arrived yet. But she had a primitive alarm system set at the entry point of her camp, and I think I interrupted her about to skin a rabbit." Jax inspected his work.

"A what?"

"A rabbit. She said she'd found it freshly killed. Anyway, apparently the alarm system is to alert her to animals."

"If she's finding dead things around her camp, and after our wildlife mishaps, that's smart."

"I guess. Maybe it was in the way she told me to leave when I pressed her on her boyfriend's whereabouts that didn't sit right."

"Not everyone appreciates nosy neighbors."

"Clearly. She also had a weapon on her seat."

"Gun?"

"Knife."

"And based on that, you rushed here to pull apart the shotgun?" Abby shook her head.

"I was followed," he said.

Abby stopped. "By who?"

"Not sure if it was who or what."

She smirked. "Sasquatch?"

"Not likely, but whatever it was, it tracked me at least a mile from inside the forest line." Not knowing rattled him again. "Let's just say it had my radar on full alert."

"Well, there's no denying there're plenty of animals in the vicinity." She offered a smile. "Probably a good idea to make sure that gun works."

He got up again, this time setting the shotgun in the corner.

Abby had wandered into the kitchen and was scanning the refrigerator's contents. "I'm starved."

"Eggs?" he said.

"Perfect. And I'm ready to get this vacation in full swing."

"Sounds good to me. What do you have in mind?"

"Let's get out on that hike today and go another direction." She pulled the carton of eggs from the fridge and set it on the counter. "Forget about Hannah and her boyfriend woes. And whatever animals lurk amongst the trees. We'll make enough noise to have them running away from us long before we arrive in their vicinity."

Jax chuckled at the image of Abby yelling, "Hey, bear," with every other step she took. "I like it."

"How's the weather?" she asked.

"Haven't opened the shades yet. Getting more wood to stoke the fire was next on my list."

"I'll get it. Your turn to cook. Wait. You can do eggs, right?"

"If you don't mind a little char." He winked. "But let me get the wood, so you can rest."

"Jax. Stop." She had her hands on her hips. "I'm fine and fully capable of getting a few logs for a fire." He opened his mouth to protest. Closed it when she said, "You know, the only way this will work is if you don't treat me like I'm an invalid."

"I would never—"

"You might not think that's what you're doing, but coddling me will never fly. I had a bad day, but I feel great now, and I intend to take advantage."

He cleared his throat. Headed for the kitchen. He might not be a skilled cook, but eggs he could do. "Well, then get us some damn wood, woman, before it gets cold in here."

She smiled. "That's more like it."

Grabbing a sweater from the back of the dining chair, she opened the door and immediately stopped. "Whoa."

The acrid scent filled the cabin the moment the door swung back. Jax came from behind and stepped past her. A mustard-colored haze clung to the air.

"Sam might've been wrong about that forest fire being under control."

"It's close?"

"Across the river, but the wind gusts were brutal last night and pushing it right towards us."

"Guess the hike is a no-go."

Jax closed the door. "Agreed. I'm also thinking with this stuff hanging around, we should cut our time here short."

She sighed. "You're probably right. The way it looks, it won't clear by tomorrow."

"It could be longer, depending on the state of the fire and the weather. Neither of us needs to be breathing that in."

Abby went into the kitchen. "Then let's have breakfast and get off this mountain. I'm sure we can find a comfortable place on the beach or even a lake area for the rest of our time."

He smiled at the prospect of continuing their vacation. Together. "I'd like that. Maybe we head toward Portland in search of some fresh air."

Within an hour, they'd polished off the eggs he'd scrambled, and Jax had packed the last of their items in his truck, including Abby, who was in the passenger seat. "Got everything?"

"Got you," she said.

His eyebrow arched. She *was* feeling better. "Then let's find us a body of water to dip our toes into."

She chuckled. "That should be easy enough."

He put the key in the ignition and turned.

Instead of the engine turning over, followed by a nice purr, a sickening thud sounded.

"That's not good," she said.

He tried again. Not even a thunk that time. "What the hell?"

"Was it running okay when you took Hannah down the mountain?"

"It was. But there're so many damn rocks and ruts on this road." He hopped out of the truck and dropped onto all fours to peer under the vehicle. A large black stain surrounded a small puddle directly underneath the engine.

"Damn it." He slid into the vehicle and slammed the door. "Fluids everywhere. It's either oil or transmission, I can't be sure."

"A car can still run for a short distance without either, can't it?"

"It would destroy the engine to drive far, but yeah. Maybe. Depends how empty it is, and there's plenty of liquid underneath."

He popped the steering wheel with his hand, trying to rein in his frustration.

Abby leaned into the seat and closed her eyes. "So, no vehicle and no satellite phone." Jax cringed at the reminder. "What now?"

"You're going back inside to relax, that's what. I'll hike over to the new station and get Sam. He's there until tomorrow, and I'll be able to call a tow if nothing else."

Abby nodded, then grew serious. "Isn't the station a few miles away?"

"Over five, but if I take the trail, it's shorter and will save some time. I don't see an alternative."

She nodded. "I'd offer to go...."

"And I wouldn't let you." He opened the door and stretched out, grabbed Abby's bag and the groceries to return them to the cabin. "I know you don't want to be coddled, but in this case—"

"No, you're right."

He led the way. "Then let's get you settled so I can get there and back." And somehow salvage this vacation.

Within a short time, he had a backpack filled with water and an energy bar. He'd just cleared the stairs when Abby ran out after him with the shotgun.

"In case you're stalked again."

"I'd rather—"

"Don't argue. I'm fine here." She kissed his cheek. "Be careful."

He slung the shotgun on his back. "Hey, bear," he said, winked, and headed for the ranger station and Sam.

Chapter Thirty-Three

The run had taken Rachel and Koa to the sea's edge and back. Too many thoughts to settle on one, she instead focused on Koa and the waves, the brackish scent of seaweed and salt on the air. She'd let her bundle of energy run the shoreline, chasing birds, until spent. Eventually, they dragged themselves the last few blocks home.

Only the outside light and a small lamp inside illuminated the house by the time they'd returned. Her father's car remained in the driveway. Knowing Janelle, she'd insisted he stay. Like she'd insisted that Rachel move in when she mentioned there could be a job for her here in town.

Moving in permanently had never been the plan, but things progressed, and it became comfortable. Until it didn't. Despite how wonderful and attentive Janelle had been from the start, Rachel's need for her own space had only grown in the past weeks. Janelle giving away her chair in the beginning hadn't helped, but it was only the catalyst.

She'd not been able to put a finger on why it had bothered her until this case. And this feeling that no one saw her as someone able to make the right decisions. Of feeling the weight of others worrying about her; of not disappointing people.

Now Rachel sat on the couch—Koa curled on the floor chasing dream rabbits—lost in thought. The case of Bruce Hatfield had distracted that part of her that yearned for more action, but it had also triggered her feelings of inadequacy.

Her father showing up unannounced had contributed, sure, but she should have let her father explain further instead of running off.

Was that how she planned to handle every situation that rattled her? Clearly, her life was not working so well with that tactic; she'd have to take a good look at her part in how her life was unfolding.

"Deep thoughts?" Her father had sneaked into the living room.

Rachel startled, though Koa didn't budge. "You're up late."

"You mean early. It's three a.m." He eased onto the cushion next to her, and she made space by pulling her legs close to her chest. As a child, she often stayed awake until he got home. A part of her needed to know he was safe. Another part hoped he'd share how his day had gone and about his cases. He rarely did. Offering cocoa instead, he'd turn the conversation to her day—her ambitions.

She'd had so many, and he'd always seemed proud of her. Until recently. Had she now become one huge disappointment?

"I'm sorry I stormed out earlier," she said. "I needed time to think."

"Nothing to apologize for, but if you'd let me…."

"Let me tell you what I have to say first."

He nodded.

"I've been working to get out of your shadow since the day I entered the academy."

"I—"

"Dad."

He nodded again.

"You might not like the way I live my life. Or who I choose to live it with. But this *is* who I am, and this is my job. Yes, this case has me out of my depth, but it's still mine to solve and to prove."

"Prove what, Rachel?"

"That I'm capable. Jax is counting on me to take care of things while he's gone, and suddenly you show up. Which makes me wonder if he didn't trust me even before he walked out the door."

"I'm not here to babysit you. That's the truth; he didn't contact me."

"Maybe not, but your presence has every one of my insecurities on overdrive." Car analogies. She shook her head for sounding like Brody now.

"That was never my intention."

She slunk into the cushions. "Regardless, I can't ignore that I'm floundering, with no clear direction yet on this case. Everything feels like strands of something, but I'm not sure what."

He chuckled lightly. "Welcome to detective work 101. I feel the same every time I step into an investigation. I'm not sure that ever goes away."

"Except I'm sure the medical examiners in your cases don't call other detectives and leave you out of your own case." He grimaced. "Exactly. Dr. Shocking calling you instead of me didn't help." She shook her head. "Anyway, I left before you could offer a full explanation, so please do." She wrapped her hands around her knees.

He shifted his body toward her. "As I mentioned, she was calling because of one of my old cases, which also ties to yours."

"How so?"

"Dr. Shocking told you that the mark on Mr. Hatfield's chest seemed familiar."

"She did. She also gave the impression it could be linked to a serial killer, but said more research was needed."

"Right. That research was me," he said. "She called soon after she left the crime scene to relay what she'd found because Jax and I worked a case with similar traits about twelve years ago."

"You think they're related?"

"I didn't at first. Our perp was Rodney Backstrom. He targeted young college women who frequented a bar near the campus."

"I don't remember you talking about him."

"I didn't, but you might have recalled my subtle reminders not to get into a car with anyone who didn't know our code word about that time."

"Or not so subtle since you'd been hammering me about that my entire childhood, but yes, I do." She shifted to be more upright. "Are you thinking we have a copycat killer?"

"I'd almost prefer that, but they released Rodney Backstrom two weeks ago on a technicality."

"He's out for good?"

"Unless additional evidence surfaces to tie him to other crimes."

"Okay, but one killing hardly makes him a serial killer."

"There were two other women murdered in the same manner, with the same markings."

"But you couldn't connect Backstrom to them?"

"Correct. Only DNA evidence existed from that one scene, and we secured a conviction based on it. Nothing was found in connection to the other women, except they all partied in the same place."

"Mutual friends?"

"Not that we uncovered, and the bartender who often worked the weekend shifts suddenly disappeared on me."

"Me? You mean Jax, too?"

"He was on suspension at the time. I put tracking down the bartender on the back burner when the DNA came through and the DA had enough to convict."

"Okay," she said, her shoulders tightening. "So, my concern is accurate. Dr. Shocking called you, told you Jax was gone, showed you the similarities, and you didn't think I could handle it."

"Dr. Shocking was an assistant at the time of these murders, but even then, she was determined to see Backstrom fry for what he'd done to those young women. It bothered her that we were unable to tie the other crimes to him, and of course, she's livid that he's out."

"So, she doesn't trust me."

"Rachel, even seasoned detectives screw up. She knows this is your first murder investigation."

Dr. Shocking was right about that. While she could waste time arguing, she had to look at the bigger picture. "I don't blame her; I'd probably have done the same. But what makes you sure my case is tied to yours? Why would this Backstrom guy suddenly arrive in Misty Pines and commit murder? Bruce Hatfield was as far from a young female college co-ed as you can get."

"Because Bruce Hatfield was the bartender's boyfriend. His connection to one of my cases and his murder, with Backstrom's signature mark left behind…"

"And this Hannah that came looking for Bruce, she's the bartender?"

He smiled. "You are my daughter, and yes. If Backstrom was here, it must have been to find her. And when he couldn't, he must have thought Bruce had information as to her whereabouts."

Her face warmed at the praise, despite her annoyance at not being told any of this from the start. "If that's true, then Backstrom knew about Hannah from the beginning and has been waiting until he got out to find her."

"Seems logical. It would explain why she disappeared at the time without a trace the moment she got wind of my wanting to speak with her."

Rachel reached down to pet Koa's head, thinking. "You said Hannah was Bruce's girlfriend. She didn't say a word to him when she left?"

"He claims she didn't. She disappeared from his life at the same time."

"Did you believe him?"

"Not necessarily, but she never resurfaced, and we didn't need her to convict Backstrom. What I feel certain of now is Backstrom came looking for Hannah, and Bruce paid the price."

Rachel nodded. "The poor guy was tortured for information Backstrom thought he had." She shook her head, remembering the blood in the bathroom. "Hannah must have something big on Backstrom if he's willing to go to such trouble after all this time."

"She might. Or he thinks she does. That's why I'd like to speak with her. Backstrom always claimed he'd been set up by someone close to him, too, and I'd like to know more about what that meant. Perhaps she can offer insight."

"That is interesting."

"Hmmm," her father said. "Whatever the connection, if additional evidence comes to light, Backstrom's back in prison."

"Then we need to find Winona. If Chuck was correct, she might be the last person who spoke to Hannah. Maybe Hannah shared about why she was here, or at least where she's gone."

"Agreed." He stood and patted her leg. "Though it will have to wait until daylight. I'm going back to bed. You should, too."

Rachel settled deeper into the couch. "Good idea."

Her father kissed her on the forehead. "By the way, I like your girlfriend."

Rachel raised up on her arms, having forgotten about their alone time together. She could only imagine how that went. "What did you two talk about?"

"You. Life. Some things she and I have in common."

"You have things in common besides me?"

He chuckled. "Yes."

Her eyes narrowed. "Like what?"

"You ever wonder about that bowl in your mother's curio cabinet?"

"The shiny clay piece?"

"That would be the one."

"Thought she bought it at some flea market."

His face wrinkled. "Not sure if that's an insult, but no. I made it for her on our first date."

She laughed. "I meant nothing by it. It's nice, Dad."

"Your mom likes it, and that's enough. But before I applied to the police academy, I thought I might be an art teacher."

"Big jump."

"It was, but it was the right choice at the time to pay the bills. Someday I'd like to get back to it." He cleared his throat. "All I'm saying is Janelle seems good for you."

"She is."

"Sorry that I didn't get to know her before making assumptions."

"Yeah, me too," she said, the protective walls rising in her as she wanted off the subject. "Night, Dad."

She listened for his footsteps to fade down the hall and the bedroom door to click. But sleep didn't come. She'd always sought her dad's approval. Now it felt like more pressure to make everything work for everyone.

What was working for her? Who did she want to become? Making decisions to impress and being what others wanted her to be no longer felt like the answer.

She forced her eyes closed and shook the tumbling thoughts from her mind. She had to be on top of her game to find justice for Bruce.

Equally important, if Backstrom had landed in town, she had to apprehend him before he killed again.

Chapter Thirty-Four

As Jax made his way to Sam, the air quality continued to plummet, stinging his eyes. Had he thought it through, he would've brought a rag to wrap around his face. But his welfare hadn't been among his worries as he'd left. Getting Abby and their baby off this mountain and away from this toxic smoke was all that mattered.

At least he'd remembered to bring his cell. The ranger station should have service. A Wi-Fi signal would suffice, although both the station and tower were as remote as their cabin. He had no idea what he'd find, but there'd be a radio and a vehicle—everything else could be worked out when he arrived.

The dirt road had enough bumps to jar a molar if he were in his truck—far worse than the road down the mountain. His boots kicked and scuffed through the rocky dirt, dust mixing with the haze in each step. Grit covered his hands and found its way into his mouth and eyes.

Branches crunched under pressure; creaks of the old trees bending in the wind became white noise after a mile or so. When the birds lit from the top of a cluster of firs a few yards from him, he startled. Stopped. Heart pounding, he rotated one way, then another, for signs someone, something, was following him.

A squirrel loped up the side of a pine.

The hazy outline of a bald eagle soared overhead.

He relaxed some. The eagle's presence must have spooked the small birds. Could have been a raccoon climbing their tree, too, he supposed. The invasive haze had everything on edge.

Further on, he neared the tree line where deep marks rutted several of the trees' bark. Bear, maybe, a buck sharpening its antlers, or a cougar using the trees as a scratch post.

The idea of the unknown sent the hairs on the back of his neck at attention again. He shifted the shotgun to the front and rested his hand on the shaft. The sense of being watched had returned. He strained to listen; nothing else seemed out of sorts.

Until the sound of grass thrashing and a distinguishable bugling emanated from the woods.

A sound he'd heard more than once coming through Misty Pines.

Elk.

His attention swung to the side as a herd flowed from the deep brush, with what must have been a thousand-pound bull at the lead. Jax backtracked at a fast clip and ducked off the path to allow the herd to pour over the roadway and cross unobstructed.

He'd never known them to be aggressive near town, but with the encroaching smoke they could be agitated; anything had the potential to become so if threatened. With fall approaching, they could also be in their mating cycle, the bull elks full of testosterone and looking to prove themselves. Shotgun or not, he had no intention of being forced to fell a charging male.

When the last cow crossed, Jax grabbed his water bottle and took a long drink. The cool liquid eased some of the scratchiness the sooty air had caused in his throat, and he splashed water on the back of his neck.

By the time he'd tucked the bottle away and finished his energy bar, the herd had visually disappeared. Only the final swishes of grass and a few bugles remained.

The delay had cost him over thirty minutes. He'd not given Abby a time to expect him, but if he took too long, she'd come looking for him, anyway. He increased his pace over the next few miles, drenching him in sweat.

With a little one on the way, he'd get back to running that his therapist had recommended last year, or he'd never keep up. With his age, he still might struggle. If he was around. He'd stayed away from thoughts of his own mortality, but he had to be realistic. His own father had dropped dead of a heart attack in his fifties. Jax had been a grown man by then and about to enter the Navy, and their relationship had always been strained. But that made it no less hard when he died.

A profound sadness hit Jax. What if what happened to his dad was genetic, and his own days were numbered?

The idea had his muscles tight. He was slowing himself down by worrying about his future, about what he couldn't control. It had to stop. He hurried his pace, desperate to tamp down his fears and shake the crippling thoughts. He was fully aware of the stakes and that he had to be different for this new life coming in, for Abby.

Winded and emotionally on edge, he rounded the last corner into an open area where a one-story ranger station sat closest to him—larger, and a definite upgrade from the small cabin he and Abby were staying in. Beyond that, the fire watchtower, standing nearly a hundred feet tall. The full snapshot of the coast range that height afforded would be incredible. A view he had no intention of checking out. A modern zig-zag staircase replaced the old straight ladders, but a hundred feet remained a considerable height.

Cliff edges and towers were in the same category: places he didn't go voluntarily. With Sam's rig parked in front of the station house, it shouldn't be an issue.

Jax trotted up the few stairs of the porch to the station door, anxious for a rest while he explained the situation to Sam. It was locked. Cupping his eyes over the window, he peeked in and knocked. Sam could be behind the reception desk or in the residence. A door blocked the view to the living area.

But Sam didn't appear to be inside…and the lights were out.

Jax hopped off the porch and strode around the building to get a look at the living quarters. There was no rear access, but through the small window, he could tell no one was there, either.

His eyes darted to the tower.

Damn it.

Jax strode to the part of the trail where someone glancing down from the top might see him.

Directing his voice to the sky, he hollered. "Sam, you there? It's Jax."

From his angle, it was impossible to tell if Sam was up top.

Elevating his voice another couple of times proffered no response. The breeze picked up, sweeping his voice away from its target. His options dwindling, Jax kept scanning the tower, willing his friend to appear in the window.

Instead, the slam of wood caught his attention. The wind must be catching the entry door, banging it closed with every gust. Sam might not have sealed it properly; he might not be up there.

Jax skimmed the premises surrounding the tower, and beyond, once again looking for signs that Sam was nearby. He'd said he was on duty for a few days. He had to be somewhere.

The door slammed again, drawing Jax back.

"Sam," he yelled again. "Sam, buddy, you here?"

But the door on the tower slapped continuously now. An uneasy feeling crept over Jax.

What if Sam *was* in the tower? Jax had always known his friend to be responsible and diligent. But he was older than Jax by a decade, and on duty alone. If he had a medical emergency up top, he'd have no way down on his own.

Sliding the shotgun to rest on his back, he headed for the tower's stairs, pushing past the dread in his limbs. He took the treads two at a time for the first couple of flights, not looking down. His heart pounded, filling his ears with static, forcing him to stop and suck in air. He kept his eyes straight ahead. By the time he reached the halfway point, his muscles burned, and the view of only treetops played with his mind.

Suck it up, Sailor. He'd only heard that a few times in his life. Suck it up or not, his leg muscles shook. Hiking on flat ground was no training for this ascent.

Determined not to give in to fatigue, he gathered his wits. Motivation. That's all this was. His kid would want to climb monkey bars and slides. Run like a toddler should. And he'd be there, damn it, so he'd best be getting himself ready for all of it.

He refused to focus anywhere but toward the tower now, pushing himself forward. When he reached the final tread, he thought his chest might explode. The muscles in his back spasmed. His arms ached.

For a beat, he feared he was experiencing a heart attack, until he realized his hand had gripped the handrail so tight his knuckles were white.

Shaking his head, he bent at the waist, gasped for a few more breaths. "Sam, you in there?" he managed.

The door banged in response.

Upright, he caught the door before it hit again and stepped inside the tower. With filtered sun beaming into the windows, the dust particles bobbed and weaved in the air, and the space felt stifling. Oddly stale. Almost coppery.

His jaw tightened with a visceral response as he brought the shotgun to the front.

A large table, an area map spread on top, filled the middle; reading glasses and a magnifying glass on top of that.

On the floor, a shoe attached to a leg that disappeared into khaki pants.

Not good. "Sam, buddy, are you okay?"

He rounded the table, expecting that his friend had succumbed to a medical condition.

Instead, the pool of blood surrounding Sam's head painted an entirely different picture.

Chapter Thirty-Five

Rachel hugged Janelle goodbye, leaving her in bed, and joined her father in the kitchen.

Koa, determined not to be left behind this time, stayed underfoot.

"Your pup is persistent," her dad said.

"One of the many traits I love about her." Rachel ruffled her friend's fur and looked into her eyes. "You're coming with, so don't worry."

That appeased Koa enough to wolf down her kibble, and before ten, they were in Rachel's patrol car.

"Winona first?" he said.

"Agreed. Let's hope she's not out sick again today." Though she'd spend all day tracking her down if necessary, she gripped the steering wheel tighter. If Winona had been forthcoming from the beginning, hunting her down to ask about Hannah would be unnecessary. More important was why she'd edited that portion of her statement in the first place.

"So about last night," her father said.

"I already apologized."

"Not that. I wanted to expand more on Janelle. She sounds serious about you, and I know I've been a jerk about the whole thing."

"Well, since you brought it up—"

He held up his hand. "Look, I've been hard on you, but not because of your sexuality."

She side-eyed her father. "Pretty sure Jax would call bull on that, too."

"I'm aware that's what I'd implied." She raised a brow. "Okay, it's what I'd said. But honestly, that has little to nothing to do with my behavior."

"This I have to hear."

"Admittedly, it took a minute to adjust. Mostly, however, I didn't want you to leave Portland."

"Because?"

"It's near impossible to protect you from so far away."

"Protect me? I—"

"I know what you're thinking—you don't need that from an old man like me. Besides, you have Jax here."

"And Trudy. She wouldn't appreciate the exclusion."

He chuckled. "And Trudy." He leaned back into the seat. "But it's not the same. When you have children, you'll understand. There's nothing a parent wouldn't do to keep their kid safe. And the farther they are, that helplessness becomes overwhelming, causing extreme reactions."

That sounded well and good… from his perspective. "Except instead of telling me that, you attacked my very being in order to control me."

"Never said it was a smart way to approach the matter."

The muscle in her jaw tightened; she stretched her neck, trying to see his view. "Is this you talking? Or did Mom get to you?"

"Me. Though some credit has to be given to your Aunt Renee. She made some good points."

Rachel softened. Along with her own mother, her aunt was another person she'd not reached out to nearly enough. "Which were?"

"That I wasn't owning the actual reason I was upset. Now I am."

"You've always loved Aunt Renee."

"And I love you." His face turned red. "I'm sorry, Rachel. That's all I can say. That, and if you and Janelle want to marry, you have my blessing. You already have your mother's. We'll throw you the fanciest wedding…."

"Whoa." She shifted to get comfortable as she turned left onto the road leading to the gas station. "Let's not get ahead of ourselves."

"But—"

"Look, since we're being honest, I'm not sure what I'm doing here. I'd never intended to stay with Janelle permanently."

His eyebrow shot up.

"Yes, I'm aware that I need to share that with Janelle."

"Good idea. She's making plans."

Rachel winced. "I know." Her father's approval had moved on from pressure to a weighted blanket.

He turned toward her. "Word of advice?"

She drew in a breath. "Do I have a choice?"

"Not on this. Don't wait too long. When you don't tell people what you're feeling, you end up having to make excuses to come see them—even if they're good ones. And it gets harder to be honest with them, and yourself."

"It's also risky because the other person may be too hurt to listen."

"There is that." His stare burned into her. "One hopes they'll take your apology because they love you."

She nodded, hearing him, though not sure what to do with the information yet.

They rode another mile in silence, when a small figure walking on the wrong side of the road, her back to them, came into view. Rachel recognized Winona immediately and pulled over. Got out.

"I was just on my way to see you," Rachel said. Winona wiped her cheeks, that appeared to have been streaked with tears. "Everything okay?"

Eyes on the pavement, she kept walking. "Just late for work."

"Hop in. We'll give you a ride."

"I'm good."

"Okay, well, I can follow behind. At your pace, I'll be moving at less than two miles an hour, and we'll cause a traffic jam. Your call."

Winona rolled her eyes at the empty stretch of road. "Right." She shook her head. "Fine." She trotted to the car and slid into the back seat, where Koa greeted her with a nuzzle. "Thanks."

"No problem." Rachel nodded to the passenger seat. "This is my dad."

"Hey," she said.

"So, what's going on that you're walking? Car trouble?" Rachel pulled onto the road.

"Something like that."

The tears now wiped away said it was more. "You and Robby have a fight?"

Rachel glanced in the rearview that she'd tilted to see Winona.

"Why would you think that?"

"Because we spoke to him yesterday, and your name came up. Did he tell you we'd come by?"

"Yeah. Said I shouldn't be telling people we're together, and it was my fault for being around the complex in the first place."

"Is he so afraid of your aunt that he cares what she thinks of you two?"

"More like he has a reputation of being a player to uphold." She sneered. "He's an ass."

Rachel wouldn't touch that. "He also insists he didn't know Bruce Hatfield. Though I find it hard to believe."

"He didn't…not really."

"But you did."

She shrugged.

"Robby says a woman named Hannah had come to the marina looking for Bruce, and he'd sent her to the apartment complex."

Winona stared out the window.

"We also spoke to one of the other tenants who mentioned that a young woman had come looking for Bruce Hatfield several days ago."

"Don't know what that has to do with me," Winona said.

"That same tenant saw her speaking with you."

Winona stared at Koa as if she was looking for help and rubbed her muzzle. "Yeah, not sure why he'd say that."

Halfway believable if Winona had made eye contact. "C'mon. You're very observant, and I can't think of a reason Robby would make that up, or the tenant who you knew was a man, just to cause trouble."

She rubbed the back of her neck. "Unless he's the one stealing my aunt's mail."

"Or you whip that out to get off a subject you don't want to be on," Rachel said.

Winona frowned and gazed out the window. "So, what if a woman was looking for Bruce? It's not like I knew her or anything."

"Did she identify herself as Hannah to you?" Rachel's father said.

CHAPTER THIRTY-FIVE

Winona shrugged.

"Did she find Bruce?"

"I guess. Never saw her after that," she said, still not making eye contact.

"Winona, if you know something, you need to tell us," Rachel said.

"Okay, maybe we spoke one more time. Not like it matters. There's no way she killed Bruce, if that's what you're concerned about. Instead of asking questions about her, you should try to find the person who did." She almost whimpered. "Because he was a good guy, and what happened really sucked."

"That's what we're doing," he said. "Hannah might have done nothing to Bruce, but she could confirm who did."

"Confirm, as in you know?" Winona swallowed, her eyes wide. "Is that why you were looking for me? You think it was Robby, don't you?" She shook her head. "You're wrong about that, too. He was jealous of Bruce, but he wouldn't do anything like that. He's not violent."

"No, Winona," Rachel said. "We think it's someone who knows Hannah from years ago."

Her brow wrinkled. "No joke?"

Rachel nodded

Winona wilted into the seat. "Ah, like her ex-boyfriend."

Ex-boyfriend? Rachel pulled the patrol car into a nearby parking lot, letting the engine idle. Turned in the seat.

"Did Hannah tell you that her ex-boyfriend was looking for her? Is that what brought her to Misty Pines—to get away from him?"

Her father turned now, too. "If she and Backstrom were former lovers, that would explain a few things about her taking off like she did and leaving Bruce high and dry."

"I—" Winona stammered.

"Enough," Rachel said. "Start talking."

Chapter Thirty-Six

At the sight of Sam's slack face and vacant eyes, Jax flung the backpack to the ground and set his gun against the middle table. He knelt at the ranger's side, searching for the source of blood. The surrounding puddle was still moist.

A quick scan of the surroundings offered little about what happened. No obvious footprints on the floor, bloody or otherwise. A toppled stool near the window. A broken cup once filled with coffee near that.

Could still be warm because Sam hadn't been dead long. Less than an hour, maybe. Had the elk not impeded him, Jax might've been here in time. In time for what, though?

"What happened here, buddy?" Jax said, the idea of having to inform Evie, Sam's wife of forty years, sinking him further into the floor. More precisely, who?

Sam had told him the campsites were empty. Since he and Abby's arrival, Jax had seen only Hannah.

Hannah, who was barely five feet tall and a hundred pounds. Sam could've defended himself against her. Aside from it being odd she was out here in the first place, and her planning to skin and eat a rabbit she'd found, he hadn't sensed anything nefarious about her. In fact, she came across more as a deer ready to bolt.

And Sam was as solid and kind as they came. Jax couldn't make any scenario work where Hannah would feel motivated to cause his friend harm. Certainly not like this.

Her boyfriend, if he'd finally shown, could be another story.

Finding a pen on the map table, Jax leaned closer to Sam's body, inspecting his arms for defense wounds. No signs of trauma. He inspected Sam's cooling hand, scanning the knuckles. Nothing. He tamped the sadness bubbling in him.

It had to be a surprise attack. Sam might have encountered his killer below, and if the person seemed genuinely interested in seeing the world from a high vantage point, he'd have invited them into the tower. Trusting, he likely turned his back on them; the binoculars had been close to the toppled stool.

Jax ground his teeth as he continued his appraisal of his friend, seeing the deep slash across his throat for the first time. The tilt of Sam's head had hidden the wound at first. The medical examiner would provide more information, but from too many years of experience, and the amount of blood, the blade had hit the jugular.

Death would have come quickly—a blessing that would offer little solace to his widow, or his family. Being a ranger was supposed to be less dangerous, though far from safe, when it came to criminal activity. But Sam's love of nature and people had drawn him to this genre of law enforcement. He was a damn good guy. A damn good ranger.

Why had this happened?

On his way upright, Jax glimpsed a splotch of red on Sam's government-issued shirt he'd initially missed, focused instead on the blood around the head.

Jax grabbed a pen from the map table and lifted Sam's shirt enough to inspect the chest. Blood had seeped from the carving, but there was no mistaking the shape of an X.

He hopped to his feet so fast he had to take a step to steady himself. When Jax found his balance, he backed away from the body—he'd seen that mark before.

That was impossible. They'd convicted the man who'd used that as his calling card years ago. He was supposed to be rotting away in prison along with his life sentence.

Although last year he'd read an op-ed piece about an innocence project group working to have the case reopened on a chain of evidence issue. He'd figured it was a pipe dream. No way in hell there was a chain of evidence issue with any strand they'd found. Jameson had assured him of that, and Jameson was a great cop.

Besides, innocence projects centered on cases where the individual was wrongfully convicted with a high probability of being innocent. Rodney Backstrom was neither. Just because Jax and Jameson couldn't tie him to the other women with similar disfigurements to their corpses didn't make the man any less guilty of the crimes.

Backstrom was brutal in his approach. Arrogant. Jax's suspension during part of the investigation left Jameson to handle the preliminary work, but Jax had been there to bring the case over the finish line with his former partner.

Whether Backstrom's quest for freedom succeeded, he had no way of checking from here. Except he would've expected Jameson to reach out and let him know if his release was coming. They might have talked little after hiring Rachel, but that wouldn't be an excuse to leave Jax open. Not like this.

Unless Jameson didn't know? Or worse, Backstrom was making the rounds to go after anyone that had put him away. Had Backstrom gotten to Jameson first?

Bile shot into Jax's throat. Being out of the communication loop in any capacity had been a horrible idea. Backstrom might have followed him and Abby here, for just that reason.

Abby's vulnerabilities had his mind racing in ten different directions. He forced himself to stop, slow down. He could be jumping to conclusions and creating scenarios that didn't exist.

Backstrom could still be in prison.

Jameson, alive and well.

He glanced at Sam. At the "X." It could be a copycat, or some other depraved individual.

Except it was too similar in size to the previous victims. The same side of the chest.

He'd felt a presence, like he'd been followed, and his gut and senses had been on high alert since they'd arrived. He didn't think he had it wrong at all.

"Son of a bitch," he muttered.

At the very least, he couldn't discount it. Backstrom was here or had been. If not him, there was still a killer on this mountain. Jax had to get to the radio and call this in. Get help here now. But he'd have to hike nearly eight miles to the bottom of the mountain to gain reception...

His body ached with tension and indecision, his mind racing to Abby. If Backstrom had come for him, he could know Abby was here, too. The truck not starting this morning might have had nothing to do with rocks hitting the undercarriage. He should've crawled under to see exactly what kind of damage had been done.

Damn it.

Backstrom being outside waiting for him was nothing compared to the thought of him being anywhere near Abby. Her not knowing who he was, what she could be up against, sent Jax reeling down the tower steps, oblivious to the elevation he was descending from. At the bottom, he covered the fifty yards to the locked ranger station like a seasoned sprinter, where he laid a kick an inch below the lock mechanism.

The wood groaned. The second kick, he backed with his weight. The third, the glass shuddered as the door splintered and flew inward, smacking the wall.

The radio was on the other side of the bar-height desk, but what he couldn't see from the front was the destruction that awaited. The wall had wires hanging from it; the receiver lay crushed.

Communication might be eliminated, but Sam's rig sat out front. Jax rummaged through the desk, finding no keys. They might be with Sam. The unease of climbing the tower again, the wasted time it would take, had him tearing through the desk again.

He squashed the impending dread before it took hold. Before going anywhere, he'd check Sam's living quarters. As he moved to the door, he spotted a key hook attached to the wall with two dangling sets. A filled coat tree had obscured it.

Jax raced to the vehicle, envisioning the route he'd take back to Abby and the cabin. If he remembered correctly, the main road was down and right, and back up. He'd seen a T on their way to the cabin, it must connect. But as he settled behind the steering wheel, ready to insert the key, he saw the screwdriver dug into the ignition, the wires ripped through the bottom. To add insult, they'd been snipped so short they were nothing but nubs.

Blood pumping with frustration, Jax exited the vehicle. He could almost hear Backstrom laughing at him. Just as he had years ago when cuffs had been slapped on his wrists.

"You'll never make it stick," he'd said, spitting in his and Jameson's face. "And if you do, one day you'll pay the price."

If Backstrom was keeping to his word, it would explain the weirdness that had plagued them since their arrival.

Though something didn't fit. If Backstrom was here for retribution, why kill Sam? It was possible when Backstrom got into the area, he didn't know where to find Jax. If Sam had sensed anything off, he wouldn't have been forthcoming. Maybe Backstrom then decided he needed the tower for direction, and lured Sam to a place harder to defend himself.

Except there'd been not one defense wound on his friend.

Jax's head spun, trying to put the pieces together. But he was getting no closer to an answer or to why Backstrom would go to the trouble of disabling every way off the mountain. Why not attack directly by now? He certainly had the opportunity on Jax's walk here, and while he'd run around the tower.

Was he playing a game? Or he still didn't know where Jax was, including where he and Abby were staying?

Jax straightened; he might have an advantage. For now.

The haze he'd endured coming to find Sam had only grown thicker in the past hours it had taken to get here. He had to move before all visibility disappeared.

But as he strode from the car, he couldn't shake the feeling that he was missing a key piece. That something bigger was in play.

Chapter Thirty-Seven

Winona crossed her arms. "I got nothing more to say."

"Seems like you have plenty," Rachel said. "But if you prefer, we can go to the station and talk there."

She sat straighter. "I'm already in trouble for being late. If I'm not there in the next twenty minutes, my boss will fire me."

"Maybe he should," Rachel's father said. "No boss likes an employee that holds back the truth."

Rachel hadn't intended for a good cop, bad cop scenario, but she waited for Winona to respond.

Even Koa tilted her head.

"It's not like Hannah and I became friends," she said. "We had a few things in common, so we'd talked for a second. That's all."

"But she was running from someone?"

When Winona didn't answer, Rachel turned in the seat and started the car. She swung the front end toward the station.

"Please, wait. Yes." She sighed. "If you take me to work, I'll tell you what I know."

Rachel U-turned and eased out onto the road. "We're listening."

"Like you already said, Hannah showed up less than a week ago looking for Bruce, but he wasn't home."

"Where was he?"

"No idea, but Bruce was off the day that Robby sent her to the complex."

"You mentioned Robby was jealous of Bruce?"

"He was, but not after meeting Hannah. She's pretty, and Bruce's age, and

I guess he figured he would choose her over me, so no more threat."

"Did he actually say that?" Rachel said.

"No, I could just tell," she said. "And it wasn't like that." She paused. "Anyway, that's why Robby was no longer jealous, and why I said he had nothing to do with killing Bruce."

"Did Robby tell you anything else about her?"

"No. He didn't know much."

"But you just happened to run into her when she got to the complex?" Rachel arched an eyebrow so Winona could see her in the mirror.

"Okay, I liked Bruce, and I didn't appreciate Robby making me feel like I was nothing compared to Hannah. But Bruce had no interest in me, and that's the truth. He was there to work at the docks and was heading to Alaska soon."

"He ever talk about former girlfriends?"

"Not to me."

"Yet you were curious about who she was?"

"Maybe. Yeah. We don't get a lot of new people around here, and she seemed nice."

"But you ran into her a second time, after she'd found Bruce?" Rachel said.

"Only long enough to say hello again."

Rachel's father turned in the seat. "How about Bruce? Did you speak with him after Hannah showed up?"

She nodded. "The next day." Her focus fell to her lap.

"What did he say about it?"

"The same thing she did. That she was an old friend that he hadn't seen in years. That was all, except—"

"Except?"

"Then I spoke to him the night before he, you know." She cleared her throat that had gotten husky. "He'd just gotten off work when I was getting to my aunt's house."

"Another fight with Robby?" Rachel said.

She buried her head in Koa's fur. "Yeah. He asked me if I had any camping stuff he could borrow."

"Where was Hannah during this?"

"He made it sound like she'd left the day before."

"Why did he want camping gear?" Rachel said. "Was he planning to meet her?"

"I assume so."

"Assume or know?"

"Look, sometimes you just take bits and pieces out of what people tell you. Hannah didn't come right out with it, but it was obvious she had no intention of staying indefinitely with Bruce. It was more like she needed his help in finding some place to hang."

"And camping was the solution?"

Winona shrugged.

"Now, you said you spoke to her one other time in passing," Rachel's father said, air-quoting the *in passing*. "Yet you jumped right to her having an ex-boyfriend she wanted away from."

"I just assumed that, too."

He stared at Winona, who shifted again. "I don't think you assumed that at all, or you'd have never suggested it."

"I—"

"I think Hannah told you exactly who was looking for her. If that's the case, you'd better tell us. Otherwise, in my line of work, it's the people who hold back who begin to look guilty."

"What's that mean?" Winona's voice squeaked.

"You liked Bruce. Bruce suddenly has an ex show up you're all up in arms about."

"I wasn't—"

"And you were home, spoke to him the day before he's brutally killed, and you want us to believe you heard and saw nothing?"

"It's true."

"Can your aunt verify that?"

"No, she was gone with friends. I was listening to music with my headphones. The old guy in our building—"

"Chuck?" Rachel said.

"Yeah, he rarely, if ever, comes back until the bar closes."

"So, you were alone, heard nothing, and suddenly Bruce is murdered, and you're spewing lies about your last conversation with Hannah."

"No," she said, her voice straining. "There was some guy with a uniform messing around the utility closet. He wasn't there long, but he could tell you I was just home doing my own thing."

"How could he know that?"

"Because I went to get the mail and he saw me."

"What time was that?" Rachel said.

"Late."

"You didn't think that was strange?"

"It's an old building, and the furnace always has problems."

"Okay," Rachel said, though the hair on the back of her neck tingled. She'd be curious if there was a workman on duty that night, or if it was the killer. The man's quick disappearance might have been because he went upstairs to murder Bruce. "Where was Bruce going with that gear?"

"He never said."

"How about Hannah? What did she tell you about her ex-boyfriend?"

She stopped petting Koa. "In thinking back, I'm not sure I believe he was an ex-boyfriend now," she said.

"Why?" Rachel's father asked.

"Because she never once said he was someone she liked. You know, things start off a certain way in relationships, and it's that beginning stuff that keeps you there. Believing that the relationship can be that again. That's the stuff you talk about when you're describing an ex. Then as it goes to shit, you know, you add that on."

Rachel sensed she was speaking about herself as well. "Did you get the sense that he was abusive?"

"She didn't say."

"Why would she share that with you at all?" Rachel said.

"She seemed scared. Like her life had been floating along for a while, then suddenly got turned upside down. From our short interaction," Winona said, emphasizing *short*, "she regrets having ever crossed paths with the man.

CHAPTER THIRTY-SEVEN

And she needed a place to hide."

"Why didn't you tell us that from the beginning?"

"She swore me to secrecy, which I understood. I think she told me because she wanted it off her chest, but also to make me understand why I should keep quiet. And maybe because if I needed to get away from Robby, I'd hope someone I confided in would not betray my trust."

"We only want to help, Winona," Rachel's father said.

"And I hope you would trust me," Rachel said, offering a lifeline if Winona needed one. "It would beat having to find an old boyfriend and go on the run."

Winona only nodded.

"So, you do know where Bruce was planning to join her?"

"No. She was going ahead to find someplace and contact Bruce with the directions. He was staying behind to gather what they'd need." A tear trickled down Winona's cheek. "He was a nice guy."

Rachel pulled into the gas station. "Thank you, Winona."

Winona got out and ran inside the lobby of the gas station, where a man, her boss, greeted her with a scowl. Her small shoulders hunched, and Rachel's heart squeezed.

Maybe she needed to stop focusing on the pace of this town and start looking at the people who filled it. Bruce Hatfield deserved justice. Winona compassion…. What did she need?

"That was enlightening." Her father's voice broke through her logjam of thoughts.

"We need access to Bruce's cell. If Backstrom was able to break Bruce enough to learn that Hannah would be reaching out to him, then Backstrom has it. We need to know what he knows."

"Have you requested a warrant on that yet?"

Rachel shifted to get comfortable. "No."

"Then let's do that right away. Then we can request a ping. Perhaps find him that way."

Anything she did that could jeopardize a case wouldn't go over well, and she might have erred in not getting those records sooner. Jax probably would have done it by now. "I'll get them ordered when we get back."

"They can take a while," he said.

She smiled. "You don't know Trudy."

Chapter Thirty-Eight

Jax took long strides to the edge of the path, then turned back to the ranger station. As the air thickened and turned rustier than before, his breathing grew labored. It could be the adrenaline receding from traversing the tower and finding Sam, and everything in between, but more likely it was the wildfire smoke.

He'd be useless if he passed out between here and Abby. Abby, who he should have insisted on leaving the shotgun with. The thought of her defenselessness had him hurrying his pace to the station in search of a rag that he could wrap around his mouth and nose. Sam's lightweight jacket hanging on the coat tree he'd spotted before might be an option. The outside polyester layer alone would suffocate him, but he could repurpose the porous mesh lining to allow filtered airflow.

Within a few minutes, and with the assistance of scissors found in the top desk drawer, he had a makeshift mask that would catch some of the fine particulates floating about. It would do little against carbon monoxide or methane, but those didn't pose the immediate risk. It's what you couldn't see that could do him in. His old commander, Grady, had taught him that—he had at least one thing right.

Which brought his thoughts back to Backstrom. He had no idea where he was in the miles between here and Abby, or if he was out there at all. But if so, he could be messing with him like he'd done with his victims.

Men like Backstrom were patient. Lying in wait was how he'd struck, appearing where they least expected him. If that were the case, he might not be heading toward their cabin, and Abby, at all.

Backstrom's victims were a certain type: college-age females, usually blonde, and always attractive. Hannah fit every one of those except her age, which might not matter if he was looking to kill. Even if he was heading for them, odds were he'd encounter Hannah first.

As much as Jax wanted to get to Abby, he'd been watching out for Hannah since the moment she arrived at the cabin, like it or not. Leaving her unaware and unprepared for a vicious serial killer, despite her not wanting his help before, would haunt him.

He began the hike back, finding his flimsy mask no match for the smoke that now shrouded everything around him. The visibility was only a few feet ahead. He strained to listen, but the sound of his breathing filled his ears. His head pounded, and his throat, scratchy before, now burned. His eyes watered, his sinuses were raw.

He didn't slow down. If he could barely breathe, he hoped Backstrom was having as much trouble. That's if he was still on the mountain. Maybe this unforgiving environment was too much even for seeking revenge. Which this must be. Though it didn't make sense to go to all this trouble.

Wouldn't it have been easier to have gotten to Jax back in Misty Pines while he was sleeping?

Why had he chosen not to?

So focused on the why, he almost missed the cutoff to Hannah's camp. A quarter mile later, he found the spot. Through the murk, he could barely make out Hannah's primitive alarm system. Stepping over the rope and metal, he figured she'd be hunkered down in her car.

"Hannah," he hollered.

No response. He scanned the edge of the camp where she'd appeared just last night when he'd brought her blankets.

There was a quiet eeriness to the area.

Checking her sedan, the blankets were neatly folded in the back seat. He opened the door, searched through the sparse contents of wrappers and water bottles. No sign of the hunting knife he'd seen before.

She must be on the move.

Easing the car door closed, he glanced over Hannah's camp with a niggling feeling, like an insatiable itch. Why was she really here? There were several camping grounds along the coastal corridor. Why this mountain? Why on the same weekend as he and Abby?

She'd claimed to have been staying in Misty Pines. Then she'd shown up at their doorstep the first night they'd arrived. The first night she'd *supposedly* just arrived.

But before she'd come to introduce herself, his tire had been flattened, and a dead opossum was left on their doorstep. Not just dead. Gutted.

After, their satellite phone had been decimated, and his seats slashed.

Her car hadn't started, and he'd voluntarily taken her down the mountain to make a phone call to her boyfriend. A boyfriend she said she couldn't reach.

Jax breathed in too deep, a coughing fit ensuing from the inhalation of smoke and dirt.

Right after that call, Jax's truck didn't start.

Now Sam was dead.

With the shock of finding his friend, the fatigue of having to get there, he'd not asked the obvious question: how did Backstrom know Jax was here?

Jax trotted to the edge of the camp, peering at the forest, trying to see through it. He tried to make sense of this.

Nothing connected. There was no way Backstrom could have known to come to the mountain, unless someone had called him there. Someone who'd been up in their business and could keep an eye on them even from a distance.

Lost in thought, he'd dismissed the snap of branches as white noise. The sounds of snorting brought his attention back, and then the roar.

A massive brown bear and three cubs had entered the camp, rooting through garbage Hannah had left behind. He thought to yell *hey, bear!* But mama bears were not easily swayed to find a new path…or easily intimidated.

And she'd not seen him yet.

He eased onto his heels, taking a large step back, waiting. When the bear turned her head away, he slunk into the woods and continued stepping backwards until he was sure she hadn't followed.

When he turned around, he picked up his pace, intending to make a large arc right and to meet the main trail so he could continue to Abby. Instead, he came across a deep and wide ditch, a dry creek bed perhaps, heading off the mountain. Wrong way.

He turned the opposite direction: the tower was on higher ground, not lower. He continued to walk. It was taking far too long, but he kept moving to the right. Forward. Then right again.

Wracked with coughing much of the way, he pushed himself, the thoughts of where Hannah had gone, and how she connected to Backstrom, propelling him.

He had to get to Abby. He couldn't find the main road soon enough.

Finally, he sensed a lightness through the haze and trees a hundred yards over, and he followed it. The route would have taken him off course, but he should only still be a couple miles from the cabin.

But as he drew closer, it became apparent he was nowhere near Hannah's camp or the cabin.

When he emerged from the trees, he was back at the tower.

Chapter Thirty-Nine

Rachel rushed into the station and requested Trudy expedite getting Bruce's phone records.

"Already ahead of you, hon," she said.

"You are?" Rachel's father disappeared into the kitchen.

"Yup. Your case notes didn't say anything about a phone being found at the scene. Checking to confirm if one existed, which it does, and for any available records would be among the first things Jax asked for."

"You're a miracle worker. Thank you," Rachel said on her way to her desk. She'd told her father that he didn't know Trudy. The same was true for her, apparently. She should be grateful. No, she was grateful. But it seemed that Jax had asked Trudy to monitor her while he was gone. Not only what she did, but how. She sat down. "Do you have anything back on the call log?"

"Not yet. I'll push them here in a few minutes. Did you smell the smoke on your way in?"

"Yeah, guess I did. Hadn't stopped long enough to think about it. Wildfire?"

"From Washington. Winds carrying it in." A line formed between Trudy's eyes.

"Jax and Abby are fine," Rachel said.

"I'm sure they are, but smoke isn't healthy… for anyone."

"True." Rachel swiveled the chair in Trudy's direction. "Out of curiosity, did Jax tell you to—"

Trudy lifted her hand, palm out. "Absolutely not, hon. It is, however, my job to take care of him, and therefore, you."

"It's just that—"

"You're supposed to know everything?"

Rachel shrugged. "Would be nice."

"And unrealistic. Jax has plenty of experience, and he still misses stuff." She smiled. "That's why I'm here. And the fact you're asking for the information now means you're doing just fine."

"I suppose."

"Rachel, dear, you were on the right path. My actions only saved you a couple of days. Don't be so hard on yourself. You have what it takes."

It didn't feel that way, but she'd borrow some of Trudy's confidence. "Thanks. Let me know as soon as you hear."

"Will do."

"Where are the boys?" Rachel asked.

"On patrol, but Brody—" She was about to finish, but a call came through her headset, and she popped her finger up to indicate *hold that thought.*

"I'm here," Brody said, emerging from the hallway. "Just on my way out."

"No sign of our drifter?"

"No. But I have a name."

"Rodney Backstrom?" Rachel said.

"How'd you know?"

"We've been uncovering a few facts along the way." And it was *we.* Her father had been treating her more like his equal now. "We're fairly certain Backstrom's our guy. And I have a theory of how he got into Bruce's apartment without a fight." She brought him up to speed on Winona's reference to a maintenance man at the complex the night before the fire. "I'll be checking on that next."

"You think he messed with the furnace that caused the explosion?"

"Would be a classic way to cover a crime."

"Except the fire didn't reach the upstairs."

"Things don't always go according to plan. It's also speculation until we can confirm he's our guy."

"Seems like a coincidence if not, and Chief doesn't think much of those," Brody said.

"Me either, but stranger things happen. Maybe the repairman was legit and simply screwed up."

Brody shrugged. "Or Occam's Razor."

Rachel chuckled. "Where the hell did you hear that?"

"Something Jax and Abby said in their last case. It means—"

"I know what it means. The obvious explanation is likely the truth," Rachel said. "I'm just not sure which one makes more sense. A seasoned repair guy making a mistake, or a killer causing an explosion to cover up a murder that occurred less than twelve hours before."

"I'm going with the Backstrom dude. The way he sent us off course at the café. And he's no friend of the homeless either."

"How so?" Rachel said.

"Took a few laps around the track, but I found someone whose buddy had a run-in with him. I'm heading out now to find that guy. Maybe he'll have something for us."

Garrett might be the one who wanted to be a full-time cop, but Brody made a hell of a good one himself. "Thanks, Brody. Let me know what you find."

"Sure thing."

"Would you like me to make that call to the repair company?" Trudy said, having overheard them.

"You know who the company is?"

"There're a couple of possibilities, but I'll start with the property manager and see if they did call in a repair order."

"If you have time, I'd appreciate it."

"I do, and it'll help keep my mind busy and off other tragedies."

Tragedies? Trudy seemed a little shaken. "Who was on the call?"

"A friend, who's another dispatcher. We keep each other apprised of chatter from other precincts, and she just heard of a woman found dead at a roadside store on the 101."

"Tourist?"

"Employee."

"Foul play?"

"Robbery gone wrong, it appears. All my friend knew was the woman and her father were supposed to have breakfast this morning. When she didn't show, he went looking for her at the store only to find it destroyed inside and his daughter deceased. She'd never left that night." Trudy shook her head, her face tight. "Sounds like she put up one hell of a fight."

Crime touched everywhere, but it had been seeping into Misty Pines and nearby communities far too often recently. Rachel's nerves buzzed. "Let's hope they catch the monster who did it."

"Let's hope. State police will take lead, and they're thorough." Trudy closed her eyes. "Hurts my heart to think someone's baby didn't make it home. Her poor father."

As if on cue, Rachel's dad walked into the reception area with a coffee-filled Styrofoam cup. "What's next?"

From the kitchen, he hadn't heard Trudy about checking on Bruce's cell, and she was just as glad. One thing had become clear: good-intentioned or not, people around her didn't truly believe she could handle this case. She needed to take charge and show what she was capable of. While they were waiting to hear from the phone and maintenance companies, they could be looking into anything and everything else.

"How about we talk to Dr. Shocking together? I'd like to understand more about your previous case involving Backstrom. See if there's anything that would help us figure out if Backstrom's our guy, and if so, why he'd be hell bent on getting to Hannah."

"If that's what you're looking for—"

"Dad, this is my investigation. Jax wouldn't stand for secondhand information, and nor will I. Trudy's pushing for phone records. Once we have those, we'll at least have confirmation of whether Hannah was keeping in touch with Bruce."

"And where will that lead us?" he said. A teaching moment was coming; she could hear it in his voice.

"If Backstrom stole the phone, he's waiting for Hannah to call. Ten bucks says the *track my phone app* is on."

"Reception can be splotchy at best at remote campsites."

"That only means she'd have to get somewhere to make that call. It would bring him within range of her." Her stomach tingled. "Trudy, where's the store where the young woman was murdered?"

"Somewhere on the 101. She didn't say the exact location."

That was an eighty-mile stretch. "Please check."

"My friend was headed out for lunch. I'll ask as soon as she's back."

"Thanks." Rachel strode to the main door, her eyes darting toward her father. "You coming?"

"Yes, ma'am," he said, "but I can save us a trip. I have those files from the old case in my trunk."

Nice of him to now be telling her that.

"Trudy, we're heading to the diner to go over the files." She looked at her dad. "I need food. You're buying."

Chapter Forty

Jax was back at the new fire tower, where he'd started. Frustration and exhaustion battled inside him to take over. If help was on the way, he might have entertained waiting.

But no one was coming.

The ranger scheduled to relieve Sam was at least twenty-four hours out. If there was a system for checking in between, he had no idea. What he was sure of was the encounter with the bear, and getting turned around had wasted precious time.

And parched and weakened, he'd have to waste more to collect himself. He found the bathroom in the ranger station and doused his face and neck with water. The soot and grime that had gathered on his skin turned the sink black.

He cupped clear, cool water over his eyes, offering them relief from the burning. He wet the dry, dirty rag that had stopped a while ago in blocking the particulates, rinsed it several times, and wrapped that around his mouth and nose once again. He scanned the front office for anything else he could use in case he ran into another bear. The smoke was forcing the creatures to move. He had to be prepared.

Inside the ranger's living quarters, he found a locked closet. Grabbing the fireplace poker, he pried it open. The destruction yielded a shelf of bear spray and a secured gun safe. Best-case scenario, the gun remained inside.

Jax took two canisters of repellent, putting one in his pack.

Better prepared this time, he hurried onto the original trail. The main road might be easier to traverse, but it added a mile, and if Backstrom were searching the mountain for them in his vehicle, it would leave Jax far too visible.

His legs wobbled, but this time, no animals impeded his progress. Twice, he caught himself from eating dirt, tripping over rocks, and twisting his ankle in a rut shrouded in haze, but he remained focused. He kept his breath shallow, desperate not to suck in so much smoke that he folded into a coughing spasm.

But as his body continued through the motions, his mind kept returning to Backstrom and the events that had occurred since he and Abby had arrived. What he couldn't decide was if Hannah was the cause? Or if she'd been the one to alert Backstrom of their presence?

It made no sense that she would; based on her look, she'd more likely be one of his victims. What was he missing?

Hannah. Her name had meant nothing when they'd first met, but in connection with Backstrom, it felt familiar.

The more he walked and replayed the last couple of days, he turned her name over and over in his mind. Certain he knew it in conjunction with Backstrom, the *why* remained out of reach.

After twelve years, it was hard enough to recall the events of cases that haunted him without seeing the file. Here, the DNA had been what tied Backstrom to the scene of the murdered college student. Jameson had testified at Backstrom's trial, and Jax had slept well enough after the sentencing with one more sicko in prison where they belonged.

In the ten years since his incarceration, he'd not once crossed Jax's mind. For many of those ten years, he'd wallowed in his own grief after Lulu died. The other years, simply making a new life in a new town.

But if he were being honest, it was that case, and too many like it, that drove his decision to create a quieter life with Abby in Misty Pines.

Yet quiet had been elusive this past year. Now this.

Hannah. He'd encountered her before… where?

Unsure, he took one determined step after another to get back to Abby. The foliage and the boulders set like a bocce court were suddenly familiar. He was near the cutoff to Hannah's camp again.

Only a couple more miles now. Despite the pull in his chest, he kept pushing.

During the investigation, they'd interviewed numerous witnesses, including students, faculty, and employees of the bar. All in hopes of tying Backstrom not only to the murder they nailed him on, but the two other women who'd fallen victim to Backstrom's vile fantasies. No one offered information.

The smoke made his mind spin, but something he'd just thought about seemed relevant.

The bar. Backstrom's victims had been frequent customers there.

Jax wiped the sweat beading across his forehead as a sense of knowing knocked at his consciousness. There'd been one bar employee they'd been unable to locate. One that had disappeared the day of Backstrom's arrest—a young woman herself.

At first, it was undetermined whether she too had become Backstrom's victim or ran because she had pertinent information. Her then-boyfriend claimed they'd been getting along great and was equally concerned. Then her financial accounts were closed, suggesting she'd chosen to leave. With enough evidence to get Backstrom on the one murder, and other crimes wheedling in to consume their time and energy, their search for her stopped. The other two homicides remained cold cases.

Jax's steps hastened. Was Hannah that bartender?

By the time the cabin came into view, he had no idea what he had except his head ached with too many scenarios and rotten air.

Illuminated by outside lights, the cabin on the rocky bluff resembled a beacon on shore. The oppressive smoke played with the light, making the midafternoon feel like dusk. Inside the cabin must be dark…but Abby had drawn the shades, except for one.

When he left, all the blinds were open. Abby could be resting. Unless something had frightened her.

His thoughts returned to Hannah. While he hadn't seen signs of her along the way, she could have returned to her campsite by now. He'd have been smart to check, but he couldn't risk another animal encounter. Getting turned around. Not getting to Abby.

Now, he stayed out of sight of the open shade and eased toward the cabin.

That's when he saw Abby looking out the window. Too far to read her facial expression, her body language said enough: rigid, her stance wide, arms over her chest.

She was on alert.

He squashed the desire to run to her. She could be on guard because she was worried about him—he was well past the time he said he'd return.

That's when he saw the shadow behind her. A jolt raced through his body.

She wasn't alone.

Chapter Forty-One

Rachel gravitated to a booth facing the door. Her father slid onto the opposite bench, passing the two files he'd brought with him across the table.

"It didn't occur to me you'd have these, or I would've asked sooner," she said, gripping the top one, still miffed at only now seeing them.

"That's on me. I should've offered the moment we started talking about the investigation."

"More like when you first arrived with your hidden agenda, which you shouldn't have hidden."

"That too. I was treating you like a beat cop, and a daughter I want to protect. Regardless of my motives, I was wrong."

She straightened at his admission. "Well, I hope you see now that being a sheriff here isn't anything like working patrol in the city."

"I never said—"

"C'mon. Jax told me everything. That you thought this was a step down. That I needed to be in Portland for experience and career movement."

"I did say that."

She shook her head. "Honestly, I thought that too, not that long ago. But I'm realizing that a small town is a master class in law enforcement," she said, letting her own words sink in. She'd been so frustrated about whether she fit here or if the town's slow crawl could satisfy her need for excitement. But nowhere else would she have this opportunity to work a case from all these angles. Fumbling through or not.

"I stand corrected," he said, perusing the menu.

Enough said. Sadie, the young girl Rachel had spoken with before, was working, as was the owner, Milly. She'd yet to speak to her, but it was Sadie who strode over with an order pad.

"The usual, Deputy Killian?" she asked.

Rachel scanned the menu like she might try something new. "You know it. Dad, you want a turkey on sourdough, too?"

"He smiled. "Yes, please, and coffee."

"Make that two. Black, please. And don't forget the wedge of pickle."

"Never." She smiled.

"How you been?" Rachel said.

"Good." Sadie jotted down the last of the order.

"Any more reasons to need your boyfriend to hang out with you?"

Sadie glanced back to the kitchen, biting into her lower lip. Perhaps she hadn't told Milly about the boyfriend coming to work.

"Nah. It's back to normal."

Normal was probably a reach; at least the man hadn't returned to bother her. "That's good to hear." Rachel closed the menu, handing it to Sadie. "If Milly has a few minutes, will you let her know I'd like to speak with her before she heads out?"

"Will do."

Her father chuckled as he handed his menu over, and Sadie disappeared into the kitchen. "Guess you're more like me than I give you credit for."

He could have meant the sandwich—it was one they often prepared together in the kitchen during some of those late nights—but she sensed he meant speaking with Sadie. Rachel blushed. "Yeah, yeah." She flopped open the file. "Let's see what this Backstrom is all about."

Forensic reports and witness statements filled the file, along with photographs. She started with Backstrom's photo first. He didn't look like the man she'd spoken with at the café's counter, but there was something about his eyes that felt familiar. She went next to the crime scene photos. Those had her flipping the pages faster, thankful her lunch hadn't arrived yet. It wasn't just the gore that got to her—it was the terrified mask of death on the girls' faces. What they must have endured in those last moments.

She scanned the transcript of Backstrom's interrogation. His threats of what he'd do to her father if he went to prison. She bristled.

"He threatened you?" she said.

"They often do," he said, without a trace of concern.

"Like this?"

He shrugged. "They're not big on personal responsibility." He grabbed the saltshaker, setting it on its side, spinning it like a top.

"That might be true, but this guy's a serial killer. Not to mention he's out of prison and able to make good on that threat." She lowered her chin and met her father's eye. "Killing Bruce and leaving his calling card might have been to lure you in." She shuddered. "Are you sure he's not after you?"

He sat the saltshaker upright. "It's a good observation, but doubtful. He'd be smarter to have stayed in Portland and murder someone there if he intended to draw me into the open. Regardless, I'm not that hard to find. If he had it in for me, he could've caught me at my favorite coffee bar."

"You have a favorite coffee bar?" She'd never known her dad to be into anything but day-old black.

"You don't have your spots? They knew your order here without asking."

"Fair enough. That doesn't mean he isn't planning to return for you after he gets Hannah, which we have to assume he's doing."

"I'd agree with that last part."

Rachel swallowed hard at the unsettling thought of someone like Backstrom setting his sights on her father. Or the sheriff. "Would he go after Jax?"

He shrugged. "We all know the risks in the work we do. We can't focus there if we're to do our jobs."

"You didn't answer the question."

He shrugged as the front door opened; an older woman walked in. "I just did."

That's what she was afraid of. "Well, the question remains: what does Hannah have on the guy that would compel him to go to this much trouble?"

"Agreed. Bruce was not his usual pleasure kill. He wouldn't have bothered unless he felt it was necessary to get information. And Winona's statement confirms Hannah and Bruce had plans to meet up," her father said.

Rachel looked around the restaurant as he'd ticked off what they already suspected. She did a double-take at the woman who'd slid into a side booth, waving Sadie over.

"I'll be right back," Rachel said and approached the booth. "Ms. Abernathy, hi. It's Deputy Killian."

"Deputy, nice to see you again. And it's Dorothy," she said. "I can't thank you enough for helping me find a temporary home. Trudy's a true saint. Waits on me hand and foot. Loves my little Tiger like he was her own."

Rachel smiled. Dorothy clearly had no clue on how Trudy truly felt about the situation. "She is. But I'm glad you're here. I wanted to follow up on something I learned from Winona. Apparently, the evening before the fire, some maintenance was being done on the HVAC unit at the premises."

"I have no idea, but then again, I wasn't there. I was playing cards at the fellowship hall."

"Winona mentioned you were away. Is it common for the building's system to have issues?"

"Oh, sure. It's an old structure, and that damn commissioner refuses to update anything."

"I see." Perhaps a dead end after all.

"What would be odd, I suppose, was someone coming out so late, and that it wasn't the usual guy."

Rachel perked up. "How do you know that?"

"I was playing cards with him, and he's a sole proprietor. They probably couldn't get a hold of him that night." She shrugged and then chuckled. "He was outbidding everyone and taking every hand. I wouldn't put it past him to have turned off his phone so as not to disrupt his winning streak."

"You mean Roy didn't hire anyone new?" Milly approached the table, a pot of steaming coffee in hand. She filled Dorothy's cup.

"Good to see you, Milly. Thank you," Dorothy said. "No. In fact, the reason he was having such a good time winning was that business has been slow for him lately."

"Huh?" Milly said.

"Huh?" Rachel said.

"Well, you know the day of the fire, you were in and speaking to the man at the counter?"

"Very well." Rachel turned her full attention to Milly now. "I'd intended to speak to you about that. You seemed a bit spooked by him that day, if I read your expression right."

"Not so much spooked, but I did suspect he was one of those guys who likes to be involved in the drama," Milly said.

"What makes you say that?"

"I'd seen him the night before around the complex when I was leaving, in some kind of gray overalls now that I think about it. Then he was here and wanted to speak with you. You can always tell when someone's hankering to be part of the gossip, and he was clearly that."

"Had you ever seen him before then?" Rachel asked.

"Never. Haven't seen him since, either."

But he had been right there, and she'd missed him. "Can you tell me anything else about him?" she asked Milly.

She closed her eyes and rested the pot on the table. "Only that he gave off a strange vibe, and I didn't like the way he looked at Sadie."

Sadie was walking toward the table where Rachel had left her father, two turkey sandwiches in hand. Rachel joined her, Milly following.

"Sadie, the man that gave you the creeps the other night?" Rachel said.

"Yeah." She lowered her voice. "But I told you he hadn't come back."

"He returned after I left?" Milly said, her brow furrowed.

"I don't know if he returned. I told the deputy that he came in after you'd gone for the day."

"Which means he'd been waiting for me to leave." Milly's lips pursed. "He gave you the creeps?"

"Yeah," Sadie said, but gave Rachel a pleading look.

"Right," Rachel said, with no intention of outing Sadie's boyfriend.

"I'm so sorry, Sadie. I should have warned you," Milly said. "I had no idea that he'd continued to lurk."

"It's okay, except I didn't know he'd seen me before."

"Yes, when you'd come up front to ask about ordering supplies." She directed her attention to Rachel. "Being a tourist community, there's always someone coming through. It's difficult to know."

"I understand, but can you confirm at least this is who you saw?" Rachel pulled the photo from the file, showing it to Milly and to Sadie. Perhaps since they'd seen the man for a longer period than Rachel had, they'd recognize him as the same person.

"I don't know. This guy looks much rougher," Milly said.

"Yeah," Sadie said. "The guy I saw was thinner, and his teeth were straight. No acne either. But the eyes…maybe?" Sadie said.

"This photo is ten years old, and it's possible he had work done while in prison," Rachel's father said.

Milly shrugged. "I'm sorry, I wish I could be more helpful."

Sadie shook her head.

What her father suggested could be the case because the man she'd seen at the counter that day matched Milly's and Sadie's description. "More importantly, did either of you see or hear anything that could be helpful in finding him?"

Her father listened intently, as did Rachel, hoping for something.

"Well, if it's the same guy we're talking about, he arrived in a rental car after you'd all left," Sadie said. "I was clearing the table when he was parked right there." She pointed to the front parking stalls.

"You're sure it was a rental?" her father asked, pulling out a notebook.

"I think so. It had a barcode sticker on the front window like the one my dad rented last year when he wrecked my mom's car."

"You catch the make?" Rachel's father asked.

"A newer RAV-4. Black. My sister has one just like it."

"How about the license plate number?" Rachel said.

Sadie shook her head. "But it was Oregon. It had the tree on it."

It was a long shot…

Her eyes widened. "No, wait. I do remember something else. The beginning. It was BLT. It caught me as funny, because, you know…."

"I get it," Rachel said.

"I don't recall the last part."

A start anyway. "That's perfect, Sadie, thank you."

"And you're sure he was driving that vehicle?" Rachel's father said.

"Absolutely. He was talking with Melissa from the complex right before he'd come in. And of course, it's what he got into later that night after creeping me out."

"You saw him again after I'd gone?" Rachel asked.

"Yeah. A few minutes later, he drove past real slow."

He must have been somewhere close when she'd run outside. *Damn it.* If she'd had that information a day ago…. She looked at her father, who nodded. "Can we get these sandwiches to go?"

"You got it," Milly said.

Chapter Forty-Two

Abby disappeared from the window, and the shade dropped.

Jax crouched low and crept toward the cabin. Shade closed or not, the cabin's placement, perched on the rocks, left him exposed in some areas if someone looked out again.

He hurried through those visible points and was in a near army crawl by the time he reached the rock wall surrounding the structure. Opting for the repellent as his weapon, he kept the gun on his back and sprinted the few stairs to the entry.

He flung open the door, the canister cocked and ready.

Hannah shot up from the couch.

Abby, near the kitchen and pacing, startled. Her brow furrowed. "Jesus, Jax," she snapped, a second before she raced towards him and flung her arms around him. "I thought something happened to you."

He wrapped one arm around her, relief sweeping through him, holding her close. He could feel her heart racing next to his. His eyes never left Hannah. "I'm fine. Are you okay?"

"Yeah, of course. Just worried sick and going out of my mind stuck behind these four walls." She released him and glanced at the spray in his hand. "You run into some wildlife?"

"You could say that. In a couple of different forms." He'd aimed the nozzle in Hannah's direction, but now lowered his arm, letting the spray can hang loosely from his finger.

"What happened?" Abby ran the palm over his forehead, over his cheek, her hand covered in soot. "You look like you've rolled in dirt. You need to get out of those clothes and into a shower and—"

"Why are you here?" He directed the question to Hannah, barely hearing Abby's directives.

Hannah dropped onto the couch. "The smoke got to be too much out there. I needed a break."

"Is that so?"

"What's going on, Jax?" Abby said.

"She knows."

"I wanted to say thank you, too," Hannah said, shifting. "It was freezing last night, and the blankets you brought were a lifesaver."

"Cut the crap. Who are you really, and why is my friend Sam dead?"

Hannah blanched. Said nothing.

"Sam's dead?" Abby said.

Jax nodded. "I found him in the watchtower."

Abby went to a dinette chair and sat. "You call it in?"

"Couldn't. Someone destroyed the radio."

"His car?" Abby said.

Jax shook his head, turning back to Hannah. "Start talking."

"About what? I don't know why the ranger's dead. He came to see me yesterday about my campfire, and I put it out and promised not to start another one. And I didn't. That's the last thing… Wait. How did he die?"

The image of Sam rushed back. Finding someone murdered would never be easy, less so when it happened to a friend. "His throat was slit."

Her chin quivered. "You can't think I did that to him." Jax narrowed his gaze. "Please, guys, I don't know anything. I'm here waiting for my boyfriend, who should be—"

"So, you are waiting for Rodney Backstrom?" Jax said.

"What are you talking about?" she stammered, her face pinched. Fear?

"Didn't you put him away over a decade ago?" Abby said.

"We did."

Abby rubbed her temples. "He's out?"

"That's what she needs to confirm."

Abby turned to Hannah. "Who are you?"

Hannah didn't answer.

"I'll tell you who," Jax said. "She bartended at the bar where the victims came from, which means she knows who I am."

Hannah looked away.

He had it right. "Enough games already. Is Backstrom on this mountain for you, or me?"

She wrapped her arms around herself, rocking. "You won't believe me," she said.

"Try us. If you have information to share, then all of us are going to be safer knowing it." Abby said, sounding very much like the FBI agent Jax knew her to be.

Tears formed in Hannah's eyes. "There's no effing way I know the guy personally. And I can't believe you'd think he was my boyfriend. How do you know he's here?"

"He left his mark on Sam's chest."

Hannah started shaking. Tears streamed down her face.

Abby approached the sofa. Her face softened as she glanced at Jax, who nodded. "We can see you're terrified." Abby's voice was reassuring. "But we can only help you if you help us. Why has he come here?"

"I have no idea. But there's only one way he'd have known to come here at all."

"Go on," Abby said, taking a seat next to Hannah.

"I was in town staying with my ex, Bruce. I'd heard Backstrom was released on some technicality over a week ago, so I got out of the area."

"Why would you need to?" Jax said.

"Bruce and I had a plan to leave town for a while," Hannah said, ignoring his question. "I was supposed to set up camp. As soon as I had my location, I was to call him and he'd follow with the gear we'd need. It's not like he camped a lot, so he had almost nothing to bring. But I was too scared to just hang around town and wait in case Backstrom did show. And I thought Bruce would be safer."

"You think he got to Bruce?" Abby said.

"I've tried him twice, but he didn't answer, and he would have."

"Couple of times? You mean when we were down below?"

She wouldn't meet Jax's eye.

Of course. "An animal didn't get into my truck and destroy the seats, did it?"

Her focus remained on the floor. "I just wanted to tell him as soon as I could where I was. I knew you must have had a phone the minute you said you were in law enforcement."

His gut twisted at sharing any details with her. "That doesn't explain why you'd destroyed our only form of communication?"

"I didn't *destroy* it. I dropped it. Hard. Then I got scared you'd put it together and start asking too many questions."

Abby stretched her neck. Even she looked frustrated at the faulty logic.

Hannah's face reddened. "I can see that was a dumb move."

"You think?" Jax said, trying to control his anger. "It might have been salvageable." Not to mention the added destruction of his truck so unnecessary.

"There was no fixing it. Believe me, I tried."

"And to confirm, you were staying here before we arrived, weren't you?" Abby said.

She nodded. "It was so cold that first night. I didn't think it would be a big deal."

Except it had been because it messed with Abby's confidence. Jax had seen it the moment they arrived.

"Did you put the dead opossum on our doorstep, too?" Jax said.

She leaned back. "I wouldn't do that. Though it sounds like someone was sending a message."

"Like Backstrom?"

She frowned. "That's not possible. I didn't even know to be here until the day before you arrived."

"How did you know? Because you being here at the same time as us is just too much of a coincidence," Jax said. "And in my line of work, I don't see many of those."

She stared at her hands. "A girl I met at Bruce's apartment complex,

Winona, mentioned a few places to go, including here, because it was being turned into an Airbnb. Apparently, while the road's been closed, kids have come here to party, and she knew a way into the cabin."

"Winona from the gas station?" Jax said.

"M-hmm. But honestly, I still wasn't planning to come here. Last thing I wanted was to get busted and thrown in jail for trespassing."

"So what happened to change that?" Abby said.

She shrugged. "I might have overheard someone at the coffee shop say your name and that you two were coming up here."

"The coffee shop on the main strip next door to the bookstore and travel agency?"

Hannah nodded.

Abby shook her head. Disappointed? Or disgusted? Jax couldn't tell which but landed on both.

"There aren't so many Jax Turners," Hannah said, "and I remembered you from the case. I realized there was probably no safer place to be than near you guys if something went wrong. But you have to believe me, I never thought Backstrom would find me."

"Well, I believe one part," Jax said. "There aren't so many Jax Turners. Maybe you'd learned Bruce lived in town where I was sheriff, and that's what brought you to Misty Pines from the start. Maybe you heard we were going out of town and you were determined to find out exactly where." Hannah didn't meet his eye. "Like you said, no safer place to be than with a cop, who is also aware of Backstrom's crimes."

"Look, none of it matters now, does it?" she said.

She was right about that. "You mentioned an apartment complex where Bruce lives?" Jax said.

"Yeah, on the edge of town near a cute diner. We hadn't seen each other in a long time, but he loved me once, before. Anyway, I was counting on him to help me, and he planned to. But now—"

Jax nodded, began to pace.

"What?" Abby said.

"Just as I was leaving to pick you up, the team had been called for traffic control at an apartment complex fire. There's only one in that area." Jax should have stayed. Found out more details. Rachel could be in over her head if that fire had turned into something else.

If Hannah's fears proved accurate, Bruce could be that something.

"Backstrom must have found me," Hannah said. "I hope he didn't hurt Bruce, but if he did, and took his cell, and I called him…"

"He had a tracking app installed on your phone?" Jax said.

"Yeah. Since I didn't know the area well, we thought it was smart that he'd be able to map me if nothing else."

Jax had paced from one end of the cabin to the other. None of this made sense.

"We need to get out of here, Jax," Abby said, breaking his thoughts.

"Absolutely. But I'm going to ask you again, Hannah. Why is Backstrom here for you?"

Her mouth opened as if she was about to protest.

"Save it, because he must be. The fact he likely got to Bruce is proof."

"You're right. It's possible."

"Probable is more like it," Abby said. "So, what is it you have on him?"

"I already said—"

"And we don't believe you. The man's going to a lot of trouble to find you, and that can only mean you have something that could put him back in prison."

She started shaking. "Maybe… Or maybe *I'm* just the one that got away."

Chapter Forty-Three

Rachel tossed the keys to her dad on the way to the patrol car. "You drive."

En route to the station, she entered the vehicle information into the relevant databases, including the DMV, typing *exigent circumstances* in the description and black Toyota RAV 4, giving it a small window of newer models, and license plates starting with BLT.

By the time they pulled in, she had a list of nearly one hundred. She'd expected a fair number, just not that many. "This is going to take some time."

Her father leaned over. "That's about the right amount to expect."

"Needle in a haystack," she said.

"Not necessarily. You're looking for something owned by a leasing company. The titles are almost never under the actual name of the rental agency."

"Like I said, needle," she said as they got out, knowing just the guy to help.

Garrett's car was in the parking lot, and he was at his desk when they entered. "I was just about to give you a shout to see if I could assist with the case," he said.

"Glad you asked." She explained the project and the parameters for him to search. "Once we have that, we can work to confirm the identity of the renter and the vehicle they're in."

"Then we can tap into the GPS system of the car," Garrett said.

"You got it," Rachel said.

He nodded and went to work on the list.

"Any word from your friend?" Rachel said, turning to Trudy.

"No, but she's prone to long lunches." She rolled her eyes, having no concept of such things. "I spoke with the property manager, though, about the HVAC system. The fire marshal had already called them for maintenance records on the system. They had the information on hand."

"And?"

"There were no service calls placed that night."

"That tracks." It had to be Backstrom. "By the way, Dorothy thinks you're a saint."

"Only because I didn't kill her over the dog peeing on my tomatoes this morning. I'm moving her into a hotel myself if remodeling takes much longer. Or Frank will when he gets home."

Rachel chuckled. "Thanks for the info." Her father had disappeared down the hall. She went looking for him with the update and heard him on the phone in Jax's office. She stopped just shy of the door.

"Honey, she's fine." He must be speaking with her mother. "Yes, I still believe I was right to come here because it still works within cold case if this is my guy. Which I believe he is, only leaving a trail of new crimes."

"Should I be worried?" her mother's raised voice came through the line, though she wasn't on speaker. The question was rhetorical. Rachel had witnessed many nights her mother worried whether her husband would return. Her worry reminded her of Janelle's concerns. How the people they loved always had the burden of wondering if they'd make it back from their shifts. How unfair that was to them to have to live with that worry.

"Nah," her father said. "She definitely knows what she's doing." Another long pause where Rachel couldn't hear her mother's side of the conversation, but it took little to imagine what it had been when her father said, "I did. But sweetheart, I need to go. We're getting closer on this." Another pause. "We'll be careful. I promise." His voice dropped. "But I don't think she needs me the way I thought she might." There was a sadness in his tone that she hadn't expected—like the water forming in the corner of her eyes.

Was that what his bluster had been about? Wanting to be needed?

She backed away to the edge of the hall and emphasized her footfalls as she came down and approached the office again.

"Dad," she said.

He put up his finger and then put the phone on speaker. "Hon, Rachel's here."

"Hi, Mom," Rachel said.

"Hi, Sweetie. Is your father bothering you? I can tell him to come home. I told him—"

"No, no. It's all good."

Her mother said nothing at first. When she did, her voice cracked. "Well, you two take care of each other and try not to work too hard. You coming for dinner soon? I want to meet this Janelle I keep hearing about."

She'd have to get that situation figured out long before she could let that happen. "Sure, Mom."

"We need to go, hon. I'll call you later," Rachel's father said.

"Be good. Be safe. And I love you." It was something her mother had said to her father before ending every call.

"Always," he said.

"And that goes for you, too, Rachel."

"Always, Mom."

Her father disconnected.

"Sounds like you and Mom were having a serious conversation."

He shrugged. "She knows how I can be."

"I'm sure she does. What did you tell her?" she said, curious if he'd admit what she'd already heard.

"I told her you're a capable woman and a damn good cop."

A lump grew in her throat. "Thank you."

He nodded. "Maybe one day you'll be the sheriff around here when Jax hangs it up."

For the first time, he hadn't said "a detective" like him. He saw her for who she was. Maybe for what she wanted. "He'd be pretty big shoes to fill, but I appreciate that." She shook it off before emotion got the better of her. "But like you said, we should—"

Footfalls came down the hall at a fast clip. Garrett popped his head in the room. "Found it."

"What you got?" she asked.

"It's Avis. Portland branch. The guy's on the line right now. You want it?"

If Jax were working this case, he'd make sure they each had a part in the outcome. She only succeeded if this was a win for all of them. "You talk to him. Get it narrowed down and let's go from there."

"Yes, ma'am," Garrett said, turning on his heels.

She dropped into the seat across from her father. "So, there was no maintenance call to the apartment complex."

"Makes sense."

"And cell phone records are still coming."

"So, we're waiting," he said. "A regular day of investigating."

She smiled. "Maybe, but I want more information on the man posing as a maintenance worker. Witness accounts now put him as the man at the diner. Twice. Though none of them recognized the photo as Backstrom. I still believe he's the drifter based on Brody having seen him a few days before. Working theory, he is who we believe he is, and we'll know that for sure when the rental records come through."

"Maybe Chuck got a look at him. We could go find him, show him the picture."

"We could, but there's still one other witness we haven't spoken with, and Sadie at the diner said she thought she saw her talking to our guy. Plus, the fire marshal stated that her apartment was where the fire started," Rachel said. "Seems like we should at least find out what she and Backstrom discussed. Might be nothing or everything."

"Agreed," he said as they headed to the reception area.

She loved up Koa. "You'll be hanging out with Trudy this round, girl."

"Always enjoy the company," Trudy said, patting her leg as Koa trotted her direction.

"I'll ride shotgun," Rachel's father said.

"Why don't you drive?" Rachel said.

"I'm just a spectator at this point."

"Oh, Dad, you're more than that." She tossed him the keys for the second time in a day. "Besides, as soon as Garrett gets us the information, I'll have work to do."

"What are you thinking?"

"That a guy just out of the joint won't have his driver's license. Even if he did, he's not likely to have a credit card. He might have lifted one, I suppose, or he'd have used a buddy's, and that guy could know Backstrom pretty well if he's willing to do that."

"Did I ever tell you that you'd make one hell of an investigator?"

"Let's see if I'm right first," she said, her face warming. "And whether we can find the other guy."

Chapter Forty-Four

Jax stopped pacing. "What do you mean you got away?"

Hannah hopped off the couch and strode to the window, peeking through the shade. "It's gotten so dark out there."

"It's the smoke."

"Growing thicker by the minute."

"Enough," Abby said. "Answer Jax's question." Gone was the soft approach.

"Just what I said. The night before you arrested Backstrom, he showed up outside my house. He tried to break in, but I escaped out the back door and circled around for my car." She continued to peer out the window. "I've been running ever since."

Something didn't add up. "I may not have been a part of the initial investigation, but why wouldn't you come to the police? It might have helped our case."

"How? He didn't get to me, and c'mon, the police don't always get their guy."

"We're not perfect, but that occurs more often when witnesses don't offer their help."

She shrugged. "I didn't want to be involved in case that turned out to be one of those times." She stared at Jax. "He knew my identity and where I lived. I got away once and decided it was safest to keep going."

Jax could feel the tension emanating from her. "That doesn't explain how he found you, or why he'd want to."

"I've stayed in touch with Bruce off and on over the years. Granted, it had been several since I saw him, but I told him why I disappeared, and he understood. Whether it was for his protection or not, I always felt bad about it."

"Backstrom was in prison for ten years. You could have resurfaced at any time. Changed your name. Started a new life."

"I did, sort of. South of Portland in a small town. I kept Hannah but changed my last name. Then last month, some guy showed up in the diner where I worked. One look at his tats, and I knew he'd been in prison. Said he had a message for me from an 'old acquaintance.'" She swallowed.

"Which was?" Abby said.

"That he hadn't forgotten."

"That you got away?"

"I guess," she said, moving toward the fireplace and rubbing her hands together over the top.

"That makes no sense," Jax said. "Ten years he's away and he's lamenting that you ran out the back door?"

"He's crazy—"

"Or you're not telling us everything," Abby said.

"My thought exactly," Jax said.

"I don't know what to tell you."

Jax stretched his neck. "The truth would be nice."

She shrugged again.

Jax worked his forehead. They were going in circles. "We'll have to hash this out later then. Abby's right. We need to get out of here."

"How?" Hannah said. "Your truck's dead."

"It is. You know anything about that?" He gave Hannah a hard stare.

"I don't. I promise."

Jax huffed. "Regardless, that doesn't solve our problem."

"Maybe not," Abby said, "but is there a possibility that Backstrom hasn't figured out where we are at this point? This is a big mountain, and even with Bruce's phone, that would've only taken him to the store Hannah called from."

"It's possible," Jax said.

Hannah sighed. "I hadn't thought of that."

Jax stiffened. "You didn't mention anything to the clerk about yourself, did you?"

"Only that I was roughing it, and if a good-looking guy showed, to let him know I was about three miles south of the ranger station."

Backstrom wouldn't fall into a good-looking category with his eyes set too small in his head and yellowed teeth from smoking. At least that's what he'd looked like ten years ago. But Jax shifted on his feet with the idea that Backstrom could find a way to get information if he wanted it. "He did start at the ranger station itself. Though I didn't see any physical signs of him on the route here. He could be sticking to the main roads and unaware of this former station."

"Why don't you confirm the leak under that truck was done by a rock just to be sure?" Abby said.

He nodded, grabbed the shotgun, and went outside. The wind had picked up, but the haze had darkened the sky. As he looked over the river, he could sense the slightest amount of clearing. If the wind continued, it might move out most of the smoke by morning, making it safer for Abby and the baby. But could they wait that long?

Trotting down the stairs, he lowered himself to the ground and slid under the carriage, his chest tightening at the half-dozen puncture holes.

He hurried to his feet and scanned the tree line and then returned inside, bolting the door.

"Not caused by a rock, I take it?" Abby said.

"Not likely."

"What's that mean?" Hannah said.

"It means you better come clean because that son-of-a-bitch is on this mountain, and has been here, making sure we don't have a way off."

Abby rubbed her face. He wondered if she regretted insisting they leave their guns behind, and that they come to a remote location. She so desperately wanted to live a normal existence—he wanted that, too. But they were cops. Was there such a thing as ever leaving that reality behind?

"Fuck," Hannah said. "We need to go now. It's not safe to wait any longer if he wants to get to me." Her voice edged toward panic.

Jax turned his attention to her. "Not until you tell me why you're so important to him?"

She shook her head.

"Look," Abby said. "We can defend you, but only if we know why."

Jax nodded. "You want our help, you get real with us, or you're on your own."

Hannah's focus drifted from one to the other before she up and marched to her duffel bag near the door. When she returned, her hand was wrapped around something. She went to Jax and reached for his hand, placing the item in his palm.

An SD card. "What's this from?"

"His camera."

"Excuse me?" he said.

"Backstrom was in the bar a few nights before his arrest, and he was skulking around, as he always did. As a bartender, I could tell when people were there to drink, meet someone, or just creep about."

"And you'd seen him often?"

"Often enough. One night, he had this pocket-sized camera with him that he'd tucked in his jacket. When he got up to use the restroom, he left the jacket on a chair, which some drunk fell into, and the camera went flying. When I went to pick it up, a picture was on the screen." She grimaced like she might be sick. "Then I scrolled through them."

"What did you see?" Jax said.

"His victims."

Jax's jaw twitched. She'd had evidence that could have tied Backstrom to other cases if retrieved at the time. Now, it might be useless having been in the possession of someone else for a decade. Unless... "Please tell me he liked to pose with the bodies."

"Oh yeah. Right next to the big X, he sliced into them."

Chapter Forty-Five

Rachel and her father sat across from Melissa, and next to each other, literally on the same side, hands cupped around their black coffees, at a West Shore coffee shop. Rachel had never thought the day would arrive they'd align on anything. His opposition to who she was had been all she'd felt the past few years. Now if this new version of him could stick.

"Thanks for taking the time," Rachel said.

"No problem. Anything to get me out of my daughter's house," Melissa said, reaching for her fancy coffee, a heart sketched into the foam. "I love being a nana, but her twin two-year-olds are a handful. I can only go out on so many shopping trips. Or runs." She sipped her coffee. "I've been waiting for word on when I can move back into my apartment. I imagine that's why you're here?"

"That would be a question for your property manager. However, we're still in the process of investigating Mr. Hatfield's murder," Rachel said.

"Yes, *we*. I see that." Her eyes fluttered at Rachel's father. "And you're not Sheriff Turner."

"This is Detective Jameson from Portland." Rachel ignored the obvious flirting while her father smiled. "We have a mutual interest in the outcome of the case."

"Portland?" she said.

"Yes, ma'am," he said. "Cold case division."

"I see. That's a distance." She sounded disappointed. "Well, I'm not sure how I can help. Already told you all I knew."

"Perhaps, but in our experience, things often arise later, and in this case, witnesses mentioned they saw you having a conversation with a gentleman outside the diner after you gave your statement," Rachel said.

Melissa's brow wrinkled.

Had the information been wrong? "Do you recall the conversation?"

"They must be referring to when I stopped to chat with Rudy."

Rachel straightened and glanced at her father. Rudy, not so far off from Rodney, but different than the name John that he'd told her when she and Brody asked. "Did you know the gentleman, or had you seen him around before?"

"I didn't really know him, but he'd been near the place prior to the fire. I never can resist a man in uniform."

"Uniform?" Rachel said.

"Well, maintenance, but yes. I believe. He had it on a hanger flung over his shoulder when he stopped to ask me about the empty unit in the back of our complex."

"You say he was carrying his uniform…so he wasn't there to work on the system?"

"No. As I said, he was near the complex, not at the complex. I'd been out running, and just before I rounded the last corner, he stopped me. Said he was new to the area, and he'd heard about the vacancy. We chatted some." She stopped, thinking, then smiled. "He asked me out for that night."

Rachel stiffened. "Did you go?"

"No." She lowered her voice. "I had another date on the books with Joe from the hardware store. A casual sort of thing, you understand. He lost his wife last year. So, when I saw Rudy arriving at the restaurant on my way out, I made sure to let him know I was available for dinner that night if he'd like to take me out."

"Did you know that he was actually at the restaurant at the eating bar when I was speaking to you and the other tenants?"

"No," she said, surprised. "But I wasn't really paying much attention then. We were all just so upset." *And talking about a million other things.* "I only saw him as I was leaving, and he was coming in."

"What did *Rudy* say when you told him you were available to go out?" Rachel's father said.

"He said he wouldn't be in town much longer." She waved her hand, annoyed. "Change of plans. Whatever."

"I'd like to show you a picture," Rachel's father said. "Is this Rudy?"

Melissa scanned the photo as Rachel watched for signs of recognition. The others certainly hadn't given any. Working with a ten-year-old photo had its limitations. She'd looked at Backstrom in that diner herself and didn't recognize him. Prison might change a person in general, but he'd also turned every ounce of fat on his body into lean muscle. Lost the acne. Let the taxpayers who could barely afford their own dental work straighten his teeth. Nothing about Backstrom resembled the unkempt janitor he'd once been.

"Gosh, no," Melissa said. "Rudy is far more handsome."

Her father was not as dissuaded. "Are you sure?"

She didn't look at the photo, as if the idea of the men being the same was distasteful. "Absolutely."

"Let's go back to when you two spoke," Rachel said, certain he could be the same person. "You didn't think it was odd that he'd stop you in the street to ask about the apartment?"

She shrugged. "He seemed sweet."

"Sweet, and yet he'd clearly been watching you enough to know you lived there," Rachel said.

Melissa shifted on the bench and blew on her coffee, which had already cooled enough to drink.

"What did he want to know about the complex?" Rachel's father asked.

"The age of the building itself, the amenities offered—which there are none—and who lived there."

"You didn't think that was strange?" Rachel said.

Melissa shook her head. "Like me, he didn't want to move into a place that hosts parties late into the night. And I was happy he was inquiring. We could use more eligible men in the building."

"Exactly what did you tell him?"

"That the complex was pleasant. Sure, there were some that meddle. Chuck's cranky, and Dorothy's dog can be downright obnoxious, but new blood always helps the dynamics."

"New blood?"

"Like Winona, who occasionally stays with her aunt. And even if Chuck thought Bruce was sketchy, I put that down to jealousy of youth. Bruce was a handsome young man." She lowered her head and turned the coffee cup in a full circle. "It's such a shame what happened to him. I think he was starting to see someone."

"Like a girlfriend?" Probably Hannah….

"Perhaps."

"You didn't mention that before when Dorothy spoke about hearing someone upstairs," Rachel said.

"I didn't? Hmmm. Since I didn't truly know, I must have thought it wasn't relevant."

Rachel held back a frustrated sigh. "He was murdered, Melissa. Everything's relevant."

She sipped her coffee, the foam transferring to her upper lip, which she quickly swiped away. "You're right, but it really was just an assumption. A sweet young woman had come out of his apartment, and I'd never seen her around before or since."

"Did you see Bruce after she left?" Rachel said.

"Oh yes. Soon after, and he was perfectly fine."

"Did you mention anything about that to Rudy?" Rachel's father said.

"He asked about the men in the building, so I told him that Bruce kept to himself but appeared to be a decent sort, and aside from the occasional sleepovers—"

"No, I mean about that woman that visited Bruce?"

She tilted her head to the side. "Yes, because he mentioned something about having a strained relationship with his daughter, and then we got to talking about girls that needed to make better decisions." She shrugged. "Anyway, I ended our conversation with everyone was pretty much to themselves in general. A nice, quiet complex."

"Until there was a murder." Rachel's father scowled.

Rachel held back one of her own. Did Jax have to deal with half-given information on the regular?

"Right. So why the interest in Rudy?" She seemed to think about it, then put her cup down. "You think he's the killer?" She swallowed. "I asked a killer to take me out?"

"Suspected killer," Rachel said. "We believe he disguised himself as a maintenance man the night before the fire to gain access to the building, and then to Mr. Hatfield himself."

"Oh dear."

"Are there any other times you interacted with Rudy?" Rachel's father said.

Melissa pulled the photo of Backstrom closer and scanned it. "No. Just the two times. I did see him briefly at the complex, this time in uniform, but I don't think he saw me."

Or he had, and that's why he'd chosen her apartment to be the torch. The man didn't like loose ends, and had Melissa not run that morning, she wouldn't have survived the blast.

Her face suddenly crumpled, maybe realizing that as well. "Oh God, I did interact with a killer."

"You recognize him?" Rachel's father leaned into the table.

"See the mole on his eyelid?" She pointed to the small mass above Backstrom's right eye. Barely noticeable that Rachel hadn't taken note of it.

But Rachel's father nodded.

"I recall thinking at the time that if we hooked up, that I'd encourage him to have that removed." She shook her head. "He doesn't look anything like this picture, but now that I've looked into those eyes longer…" She shuddered. "I thought at the time they were beautiful. Almost mesmerizing… Now I'm seeing them as cold. Calculating." She turned the photo over. "That's definitely Rudy."

They had the confirmation they'd been seeking. Now to find Backstrom.

As if Garrett had read her mind, a text came through.

CHAPTER FORTY-FIVE

"Got the information you need, and it's not good."

Rachel scanned the rest of the message and slid out of the booth, tugging her dad's arm in the process. "Thank you, Melissa, you've been helpful."

"I'm glad, but if you need me further, I'll be visiting my sister in Seattle for the next month or so."

"Probably a good idea. I have your number," Rachel said.

"What do we have?" her father said as they dropped into the patrol car.

"Another dead body."

Chapter Forty-Six

Jax's hand was wrapped around the SD card as he processed Hannah's revelation of what the card contained.

"No wonder he wants to find you," Abby said to Hannah, interrupting his thoughts.

Jax tightened his grip. "If you'd brought this to us at the time, he wouldn't be free right now."

"I was scared; I'm sorry. But the DA would've forced me to testify at his trial, and I couldn't risk that."

"How's that decision of avoiding risk working out?" Abby said.

Her mouth quivered. "Not so great. Obviously, he wants revenge. I was never safe."

Jax shook his head, wishing she'd have considered the victims and their families for half a second. He took a breath. "When men like Backstrom get an idea, they don't stop."

Hannah cupped the back of her neck and stretched back as if to relieve the tension. "I'm sorry about your friend."

"Yeah. Me too."

"Like most serial killers, Backstrom believes he's too smart to get caught," Abby said. "He doesn't care who's in his way."

Jax nodded. "Or who's a casualty."

Hannah swooped her bag off the floor. "Now that you know what he's after, let's get out of here."

Jax glanced at Abby's stoic face. "Not yet."

"Why not?" Hannah snapped. "If we stay, we're easy targets."

"Winds kicked up enough that breathability might be better in a few hours," Jax said. "It'll be dark soon, which will pose its own problems traversing this mountain, but we'll be better off if one thing is in our favor when we leave."

Abby crossed to Jax and looked him in the eye. Held his hand. "I understand what you're doing, but Hannah makes a good point. We should get a plan together and go. I'll be fine."

Hannah dropped onto the sofa, her jaw set.

"Of course. You're right," Jax said.

Abby straightened her shoulders. "Good. My vote is to keep to the edge of the cliff line and head straight into the forest. We'll have the best cover in there."

"That makes the most sense." He'd have to swallow his fear of heights again, but Backstrom might expect them to come straight down the road, so it could work. "Let's move within the hour then."

Abby nodded.

"Thank you, guys," Hannah said. "I didn't mean to put you in the middle of this."

Abby's look reflected his own. Neither of them bought that for a second. "Let's just focus on the solution and get ready to walk," he said.

After a few minutes, Hannah excused herself and disappeared into the bathroom.

Jax enveloped Abby in his arms. She was so early into the pregnancy, but this stress couldn't be good for either her or the baby, any more than the smoke or being hunted by a lunatic. He had to fix this. To protect them.

"So much for leaving our jobs behind," he said.

Her arms around his body released some of the rising tension in him, if for only a moment. "Let's get out of this alive, and we can talk more about that," she said.

He could feel her heartbeat again; anxiety prickled his skin. "Yes. Alive. But Abby, if something happens to me out there—"

"Nothing will happen."

He peered over her shoulder at the shotgun. The bear spray. "I'd feel better about that if we were better armed."

"We'll make sure we don't put ourselves in a position to need more."

They might not have a choice. "I'm just saying, you don't stop regardless."

"I—"

"You're FBI. I get it. You're well-trained. But you're about to be the mother of our child. Your only focus is getting off this mountain safely. I'll do everything in my power to make sure you and our baby are okay. I need to know you agree with me on this."

Abby's chin crumpled in that way that emotion was about to get the best of her. "Don't be a fool, and I won't have to save you."

"Abby?"

"Whatever. I agree."

He held her for another beat, reluctant to let go. When he did, he looked through the blinds, watching. A year ago, he'd stood at the window of his home, scanning the tree line for a killer that waited beyond it. Nightfall would be upon them in the next few hours, but with the haze, he saw no more now than he had then.

The stark difference—he'd only worried about himself that night. The stakes had grown much higher. Somehow, he'd get them out of there in one piece, even if it took his last breath to do it.

Chapter Forty-Seven

Rachel had Garrett on speaker phone as they crossed the stretch of bridge leading toward Misty Pines. "First off, I want to hear how you figured out who Backstrom's friend was and then how you learned he was dead?"

"The Avis manager helped with that. He remembered the guy who rented the car because he made an impression."

"How so?"

"He provided an Oregon driver's license, but the photo didn't quite match the man in front of him. When the rental manager questioned it, he said the look the man gave him sent chills up his spine."

"Sounds like the Backstrom I remember," her father whispered.

Rachel nodded. "So, what name did Backstrom use to sign the contract?"

"Conrad Porter."

"And he's the man that's dead?" Rachel said.

"Yes. I even sent over the picture of Backstrom to confirm if that's the guy he remembered talking to."

Rachel slumped in the seat, half-expecting the answer to be no. "And?"

"He said he'd never forget the eyes. Apparently, the face had changed some, but he'd stake his life on it being Backstrom."

She straightened. "Good to know. We might not have Porter to get information from, but at least we know it's Backstrom in that car. Do you know what their connection was?"

"I do. As soon as I hung up, I started a criminal check on Porter. Turns out he's an ex-con who's been out for a year. His driver's license was legit, as was his credit card. He was also Backstrom's cellmate for five years."

A thrill skittered through Rachel. From the corner of her eye, she could see the proud look on her father's face, and that sent her heartbeat ticking up. "So Backstrom goes there and convinces him to give up his license and credit card so he can rent a car, thinking he'll be untraceable."

"Sounds about right. Considering he opted to kill his buddy on his way out, he might have been hard to convince at first."

The trail of bodies continued. "Great police work," Rachel said, wondering if Jax felt the same level of pride when the team got it right.

"I appreciate that, Deputy Killian."

She thought to say 'it's Rachel,' but took the sign of respect instead.

"How'd you get confirmation that he was dead?" Rachel's father asked.

"Called in a favor with one of my buddies on the Portland force. He had a friend who knew Porter's parole officer. Guy missed his check-in a few days ago. They found his body yesterday." He cleared his throat. "Hope you didn't mind me following that lead all the way through."

"Absolutely not. We're a team," Rachel said. A damn good one at that. Maybe she should have continued to try to reach Jax early on, but he'd be happy with their progress. "Now that we have confirmation he's in that car, what can they do about getting us his coordinates?"

"Working on it. Manager said he had to get through some red tape, but they'd get it done and back to me as soon as he could." Garrett chuckled. "He was excited to help. Probably watches a few CSI episodes, the way he rambled off terminology to me."

"It's nice when people are willing to help," she said.

"Sure is."

She ended the call. "What do you think?"

"All of what you just said," her father said.

"No. What do you think about Backstrom eliminating witnesses?"

"It's interesting in that it doesn't match his previous crimes."

"Agreed. And we've been approaching this thinking Hannah might have something on him. But wouldn't it make more sense for him to lie in wait until he could isolate her?"

"Killing her ex, someone she ran to for help, in a way, is isolating her."

"True, but he's left evidence, his mark. Now he's killed his former cellmate. It's like he doesn't care if he gets caught."

Her father nodded. "You might be right. He could be looking to burn it all down."

Her throat dried. "That sounds like revenge to me. You and Jax might not be as safe as you think."

"I told you it's part of the job, which you're aware of, Rachel. So, let's not give that any more airtime."

She nodded. Focusing on getting to Backstrom was the only way to make sure there was no more killing.

"There's something that just doesn't sit right with the whole thing, though."

"What's that?" he said.

"Hannah disappeared for ten years. If Backstrom was in town two days before the fire, why not take Hannah then?"

"No opportunity. It also sounds like Hannah didn't stay long."

"Maybe…." The base of her neck tingled. "You know anyone at the prison?"

"Warden Grimes. I've met him a few times at conferences."

"I think you need to call him."

Her dad's eyes widened. "Ah, I see where you're going with that. Say no more."

Her father pulled into a gas station to make the call while Rachel got out and called Trudy.

"I need a ping on Bruce's cell phone like yesterday." A long shot if Backstrom had the battery out—or had already found his target. The thought sent a shudder through her.

No, she had to go with the premise that he hadn't.

There might be nothing to base that on, but until she knew for certain, she wouldn't let up.

Chapter Forty-Eight

Rachel and her father pulled into the sheriff's station a short time later. As Rachel got out, the wildfire smoke that had been wafting in from the Washington side had grown thicker. Every year, it was the same thing throughout the region, but it seemed to only be getting worse.

Koa met them at the door. "She need a break?" she asked Trudy. Her father disappeared into the kitchen, probably for a fresh infusion of caffeine. His earlier call to the prison warden had gone to voicemail.

"Just came back from one. Could barely breathe out there." Her brow furrowed. "And before you ask, I'm working on the ping and cell phone records. In the meantime, I got that information from my friend about the young woman murdered on the 101."

"And?"

"It's near the Camel Mountain cut off."

Rachel stopped. "Isn't that the area where Jax and Abby were headed?"

Trudy met her eye. "The decommissioned cabin is several miles off the 101, but the store is the only one around for miles. Anyone camping nearby would go there for supplies."

What were the odds of a dead woman being in such close proximity to Jax and Abby? Equally disturbing, would Hannah choose that mountain for camping? It had been closed to the public for some time, but that might be exactly why she'd choose it. "What do they know about the killer?"

"Nothing."

"Any marks on her body?"

"None that have been reported. But the ME hadn't arrived yet."

"Hasn't it been hours now?"

"There was some initial confusion on who to call because of the location."

She wondered if Dr. Shocking would know the status. "Well, keep working on that cellphone ping."

"I'm confident the rental company will come through," Garrett said from his desk.

"Which will help, but he could have abandoned it by now. Never hurts to have a couple of things to triangulate to."

Garrett nodded. "Smart."

Smart was far from how she felt. Behind. Catching up. Should have had this figured out by now. She strode to her desk and punched in the ME's number.

"Shocking."

"Doctor, this is Deputy Killian of Misty Pines."

"Deputy, you've been on my list to call."

"Yet you called my father instead."

"I should apologize for that, but he was on the previous case."

She could make a big deal of it, but now didn't seem the time. "It was a good move to bring him back in."

"Still, I should have kept you in the loop. Technically, he was the detective in charge of the previous case and has kept the file active, which was part of my motivation. But it's also personal."

Rachel thought back to her father's conversation the night the doctor had called for him. "My dad said something about you being invested in the outcome of the Backstrom case. He didn't say why."

"One of the victims who died by that monster's hand was my friend's daughter. Whether it could be proven then or not. But I won't let anything get in the way of finding him again and finally bringing him to justice for what he did to Katie. When I saw that mark on the victim, I nearly lost my mind. I'd heard he was out since I follow the son-of-a-bitch like I do my daily horoscope. But I had no idea he'd come into our area."

Rachel had never lost a loved one to murder. "I can't fully understand how that feels, but I'm sorry that happened to your friend, and to you. But I'm calling about another young woman's death." Rachel outlined what she knew so far about the incident at the roadside store. "I'm hearing a medical examiner hasn't arrived at the scene yet."

"That's old information. I deemed it homicide two hours ago. The body will be here shortly for further examination."

"Were there any—"

"None readily apparent. Believe me, it was the first thing I checked," Dr. Shocking said. "That said, there are defense marks all over her body, and I will check further once she arrives."

Rachel's heart sank. It would never get easier to hear of man's inhumanity to man, no matter how many times she was exposed to it. "If you can confirm once you're certain, I'd appreciate it. We believe Backstrom is after Bruce Hatfield's ex-girlfriend, who could be camping in that vicinity. If there's another dead body nearby, it's possible…"

"What's the connection?"

"The woman running was the bartender where Backstrom chose his victims."

"Hannah Cunningham?"

"You knew of her?"

"When you have an investment, there's not much you don't try to find out. Although I didn't know of her connection to Mr. Hatfield." She cleared her throat. "Anyway, she'd resurfaced a couple of years after Backstrom was sentenced."

"How do you know that?"

"She went to the prison to visit Backstrom."

Rachel's grip on her cell tightened. "She did what?"

"Yeah. Weird, right?"

"You're sure she was visiting Backstrom?"

"Of course. We spoke."

"When?"

"Right after her visit. I recognized her name from the file, and I confronted her with why she'd run in the first place and what she and Backstrom had talked about. I guess I hoped he'd confessed to her about Katie's murder, I suppose."

"What did she tell you?"

"Not much. She offered some lame excuse as to why she'd disappeared. She'd never filed a tax return. Had a slew of parking tickets. None of it rang true. When I asked why she'd go see Backstrom knowing what atrocities he'd committed, she said she thought that too in the beginning, but realized he needed compassion. There are women who are attracted to men behind bars, so it wasn't that far-fetched. But she added that it had run its course, whatever that meant."

"Did you tell my father or Sheriff Turner any of this?"

"No. She went one more time, then disappeared again. I hadn't gotten anything from her, so there was little point in wasting other people's time."

Except it was her father's case, and the doctor had let it get too personal. It wasn't her decision to make.

Rachel ended the call, frustrated with the new information and with Hannah's angle. She had ties to Backstrom one way or another.

But had she killed Bruce, or was he a casualty of her connection to Backstrom?

If she and Backstrom had been a couple, a falling out could have sent Backstrom on a rampage to find her. That had some ring of truth, though she couldn't say why.

Koa trotted to Rachel's feet and pressed her chin onto her leg, maybe sensing Rachel's stress. As she stroked the fur between her friend's eyes, she thought about what she did know. A woman was dead, brutally murdered, near where Jax and Abby were spending the week. An area Hannah might have headed to since the mountain and surrounding forest offered several places to hide.

Jax was likely staying on the mountain in a cabin, but where would Hannah be hiding if she was in his vicinity? It could be another proverbial needle in a haystack without more concrete information. The area was so vast.

Another thought pushed at her. What if Hannah wasn't there to hide?

Rachel lifted Koa's face off her and hopped up. "Where are we on that cellphone ping, Trudy?"

"Working on it."

"Please work faster," she said. "And call the ranger stationed on Camel Mountain. If someone's camping in the area, he'd know."

"On it."

"Garrett?" Rachel said.

"Yes, ma'am."

"Gather the team. We have a problem."

"Matt's off and Brody—"

At that moment, Brody rushed in, out of breath. "Was hoping you were back," he said.

"What've you got?"

"Finally tracked the guy that had the run-in with the drifter."

"And?"

"He recognized Backstrom's picture, although he said he didn't look anything like that now. Except for the eyes. No denying it was him because they looked wild, and he'd seen them when Backstrom came unhinged at him."

"We're ahead of you on identification, but did he have any clue where to find him?"

"He said something about he had some hunting to do, and once he got the call, he'd be 'like a rolling stone.' That's what pissed the other guy off. Backstrom said, unlike them, he wasn't about to waste his life sitting around like sea scum."

Call.... God, how had she not thought about it when she'd heard it the first time? "Trudy," she said. "You said Jax called a couple of days ago on a different number."

"Yes, hon, I did."

"What was the number?"

She shook her head. "I'd have to go back and look...."

"Find it. As soon as those phone records arrive, cross-reference them. See if that number was on Bruce's phone."

"You think?"

"Only one way to find out."

Chapter Forty-Nine

Jax lowered the front shade in the living area. Hannah had gone into the bedroom, saying she had a headache, and closed the door. She'd barely slept—might not have slept for days at her camp. He allowed her to rest as she'd need her strength. The eight downhill miles would feel like twice that with the smoke of the distant fire, navigating the untraversed forest, and avoiding Backstrom.

Abby was in the kitchen, grabbing essentials. A small pack of food and water. A knife that might wield minimal damage, but better than nothing. Dishtowels for their faces to filter the smoke.

If Backstrom was observing them, he'd given no indication. He must be biding his time, but what was he waiting for really?

He'd wondered the same about himself this past hour. The old Jax, prior to marriage, and Lulu, would have barreled out of there just as Hannah had insisted, consequences be damned if it meant getting the perpetrator neutralized. He might've done the same after the divorce and his only daughter's death—hopelessness had consumed him then, with little reason to go on.

But those days sat in the rearview. Abby's pregnancy had changed everything, leaving him terrified. Yes, she was fine. Tired, for sure, but smart and capable. She could take care of herself—would insist on it.

None of that quashed the desire, or the fear of failing, to protect her and their unborn child. Their new start. Their new way of being. A chance at true happiness again? He scraped his hand over his scalp. Lulu had consumed every part of his heart. Losing her had nearly killed him.

Jax felt weighed down, paralyzed to move. Afraid to get it wrong. To lose everything again.

But inaction would be worse, and wallowing wouldn't save them. It was time to get off this mountain.

He straightened, went to the side window this time, and lifted the blind. The sky was brighter than he expected, but the view offered nothing else. Perhaps the smoke had cleared some.

"You almost ready?" Abby said, interrupting his thoughts.

He dropped the blind. "Almost." He swooped his own backpack onto the dining chair and tossed two bottles of water into it. "How about you?"

"Ready to roll."

"Let's move then," he said. "Hannah should change out of that light-colored sweater she's wearing so she blends into the surroundings better. It's crucial Backstrom not see us leave."

"I have a black sweatshirt she can use if nothing else."

"That'll help."

Abby took a step to the bedroom, then stopped. "Any concerns Backstrom's armed?"

Jax zipped his pack, shrugged. "Not really his MO. If he had a gun, I'd have expected him to fire a shot by now."

"Unless he's waiting for us to be in the open."

"There is that." Jax's eye twitched at the idea.

"Whatever his plan, it's not happening." Her words were right, but she frowned as she disappeared around the corner.

Jax secured his pack on his back, ready to follow.

"Damn it," Abby's voice carried from the bedroom, her tone on the edge of annoyance. Anger.

"What?" Jax rushed to the bedroom where the bed had been shoved to the side; the hole in the floor lay uncovered and gaping.

"She's gone," Abby said. "Why would she do that if she was scared? It's safer in numbers."

Jax replayed their last interaction. "Maybe she did feel bad about putting us in the middle," he said. "Who knows. Nothing about her has made sense from the beginning."

Abby grimaced. "She said something earlier that's been bothering me ever since. It's when she used the word revenge," Abby said.

"You caught that, too?"

She nodded. "It wasn't a question. It's like she knew that's what this was. And not just against herself for having evidence. But that this was *all* about revenge."

"Which it could be."

"Maybe. But I have a feeling Hannah isn't telling us everything," Jax said.

Abby nodded to the hole in the floor. "Clearly."

"Well, we'll have to worry about her later." He strode into the living space and grabbed the shotgun. Securing the barrel downward and resting between his shoulder blades, he rejoined Abby in the bedroom.

Abby had one foot poised over the hole when Jax grabbed her arm.

"I know you don't like being coddled. But just this time."

She sighed. "Be my guest."

They switched places, him stepping into the hole, making him a foot shorter than Abby. Jax took a moment to linger near her for an extra beat.

"I love you," he said.

"I love you." She closed her eyes and rested her forehead on his. "Let's go home."

He drew in a breath and helped Abby in. Crouched low, he crawled out of the space first, which opened toward the cliff side of the cabin. He averted his eyes from the edge to avoid getting dizzy. Though he knew what was down there. River. Rocks. A tumbling fall with no ability to stop. Sudden death.

He stood, quickly aware the smoke he'd felt so sure was dissipating had only thickened. The Washington fire must have drawn closer. Picked up speed.

Abby emerged from under the house. He grabbed her hand, pulling her to her feet.

She immediately dug into her backpack and withdrew the two wet dishtowels she'd prepared. Tossing one to Jax, she wrapped the other around her head, positioning it over her mouth and nose. "Not as clear as we'd hoped."

"Not even close," he said, after securing his own towel. They inched around the cabin, looking for signs of Hannah. Backstrom. Listening.

The sounds of snaps filled the air.

Crackles. And a loud hum… like a freight train?

As they approached the front of the cabin, the sight stepped them back.

Bright red embers flew into the sky; black smoke billowed from the tree line.

They were standing at the edge of a wildfire.

Chapter Fifty

The seconds ticked past as Rachel and the team waited in the conference room for Trudy to do her search. To push for those phone records one more time.

"What kind of problem do we have, ma'am?" Brody said.

She nearly corrected him, wanting to be nothing more than one of them. But they required her to lead. "The kind that might have the sheriff in trouble. Can we get Matt in here?"

"The grocery store was short-staffed and called him in. I can check, though—" Brody said.

She shook her head, frustrated at facing her own short staffing. But Matt couldn't have gotten much sleep while being yanked in different directions. He'd be more of a liability. "We'll make it work." Somehow.

She explained what she knew. The area Jax and Abby had gone for their time together. That a woman was dead in a nearby store.

"You think Backstrom had something to do with that?"

"It's possible. If the number Jax called in on belonged to Hannah, she's made contact with him and Abby."

"Jax must've brought her down the mountain for better reception, and she would've called Bruce to let him know where she was," Garrett said.

"If I'm right, then yes." *C'mon, Trudy.*

"And Backstrom having the phone would be heading to them, as least as far as the main road. After that, there'd be no cell service on the mountain."

"That's what I'm thinking." She looked to the doorway. "Which makes it more likely that Hannah was trying to get away from Backstrom, although we don't know why." She stretched her neck. There had to be another piece to this. "Either way, Jax and Abby could be in the crosshairs."

"Damn, there're more parts to this than a transmission rebuild."

"Don't I know it, Brody," Rachel said.

"So, what's the play?" Garrett asked.

"We'll head to Camel Mountain," she said. "I've got Trudy calling the ranger station to see if they can offer information. Regardless, we'll be in proximity. Maybe we can get some help from the local authorities once we're there, too. And we'll have Koa."

"Plus one more." Rachel's father strolled into the room and took a seat. "You're not going anywhere without me. I just got off the phone with the warden."

Rachel straightened in the chair. "What do we know?"

"That Hannah came to see Backstrom twice. The first meeting was apparently friendly, like they might have a relationship, but the second time was more contentious."

"That tracks with what Dr. Shocking told me about ten minutes ago. Her investment in the murders, as you'd mentioned, *was* personal, and she'd kept tabs on Backstrom's visitors. Were you aware of that?"

"I was not."

The thought still rankled her. "Did the warden offer theories to what they spoke about?"

"No, and he had to go back through his logs to get the exact dates. It's been several years, but he recalls it because Backstrom had become agitated after she'd left the last time. He claimed, as they always do, that he'd been set up. Others were living free while he rotted. He was furious 'after all he'd done.' He also noted that Backstrom's mental health had begun to deteriorate after Hannah's last visit."

"You think she was involved in his killings?"

Her father sat in the chair next to Garrett. "There was never evidence to suggest that. Of course, there was female DNA at the scenes, but these were college girls who spent time with and lived among other women. And there were no hits in the system."

"I'm still waiting for DNA results on the hair tie found in Bruce's bedroom," Rachel said.

"That might offer something. In the meantime, I have a call into Hannah's former case manager to find out more of what kind of kid she was. See if there is any connection to Backstrom."

"Maybe they were in the system together," Brody said. "I once saw a Dateline episode where these two people had a childhood pact. They went on a killing spree, before one turned on the other."

"Weirder stuff happens," Garrett said.

"Yes, it does," Rachel's father said. "We'd never checked on Backstrom's backstory as it didn't seem relevant or necessary then. But now...."

Rachel had never seen her father question himself. She didn't like it. "We can only investigate what we know at the time."

Garrett's phone pinged. "It's the manager at AVIS."

"Go," Rachel directed.

Trudy came in, frowning. "The ping was no good, hon. The last time the cell was active was yesterday in town. I asked the woman to stay on the other line until I gave you that information because the call logs just came through."

Rachel's heartbeat ticked up. "Did you get a look at them?"

"I was just about to scroll through Caller ID. We had several calls that day, so it might take a minute."

"It's okay, Trudy," Rachel said. "Keep doing that, keep her on the line, and send over the file. I'll look."

Trudy nodded. "One other thing. The ranger assigned to Camel Mountain hasn't checked in. They're sending someone to check on him."

Rachel closed her eyes for a beat, not liking the sound of that.

Trudy hustled out. Within a minute, Rachel's computer chimed with receipt of the new file; she had it open on the screen. Bruce Hatfield had quite a bit of activity overall, but a few were from the local prefix, probably related to work. She recognized a couple of outgoing in the past few weeks to the Italian restaurant. They made a mean pizza.

But one number had been in his activity log multiple times over a week ago and twice in the past couple of days.

"Got it," she said to no one in particular.

She ran to the reception area, reciting the number to Trudy. Trudy held the phone in her hand. "Yes. It's on here. That's the number Jax called from."

The switchboard lit up. "What line is that woman on?" Rachel asked.

"Three," Trudy said while answering the incoming call.

Rachel grabbed the receiver. "Ma'am, appreciate your cooperation. We need a location on this number ASAP. Paperwork showing exigent circumstances on its way." If Hannah's cell was on, there might be some hope to get a ping. They had to try.

Rachel nodded to Brody, who'd followed and knew what to do.

Rachel listened and jotted the information on a notepad. Brody and her father joined her in the reception area, staring at her, waiting for directions. She disconnected the call. "Last ping on Bruce's phone was near that store where the woman was found dead. It's safe to assume that's where Backstrom is, too."

"I can confirm that," Garrett said, coming in from the kitchen. "Manager says the vehicle is sitting on the road leading to Camel Mountain."

Trudy clicked off her call, her face pale. She flattened her palms onto the top of the desk to steady herself.

"Trudy, what's wrong?" Rachel said.

"That was my friend who told me about the store clerk."

"What's happened?" A lump formed in Rachel's throat, her thoughts jumping to Jax and Abby.

"A wildfire has erupted near the top. Wind direction is sending it straight toward the cabin where Jax and Abby are staying."

"Chief will be okay," Brody said. "He's smarter than those self-driving cars. He'll know how to get out of it."

Unless Backstrom had other plans. He'd eliminated witnesses, like Bruce Hatfield and his cellmate. He'd already tried to blow up an apartment complex. Why not ignite a forest? Burn it all down, like her father had said.

"You have to save them," Trudy said.

"We're on our way now. Except you, Brody. We can't leave the town unmanned, and if Backstrom comes back this way."

He nodded. "Understood."

"Garrett, follow in your own car." She looked at Koa, who'd come to her side. Her four-legged friend was not trained to work in a wildfire setting. But any way she cut it, this was search, and she prayed, rescue. "Koa, come. Dad, you're with me."

Trudy shook her head. "You don't understand," she said. "You must get to them. Get Abby to safety."

"We'll get them both out of there," Rachel said.

"Of course, hon. It's that, well, nothing, go."

Rachel stopped. "What aren't you telling us?"

"Just get our Jax and Abby home."

But she'd said to get Abby first… "She's pregnant, isn't she?" Rachel said. "That's why the weekend."

Trudy didn't respond. She didn't have to.

"I'll be damned," Rachel's father said.

"Jax and Abby are going to have a baby?" Garrett said, smiling.

But Rachel couldn't smile. Or feel joy. They were far from safety at this point. "They will if we do our jobs right. Let's move."

Chapter Fifty-One

"That's not good," Jax managed, as a tremor snaked its way from the top of his head into his toes. He reached for Abby's hand.

She took hold and squeezed.

Flames licked the tree line, bringing flashes of another fire years ago that raced through his Navy vessel in the Indian Ocean, the roar of the explosion tearing through. He could still hear the screams like it was yesterday. Smell the bodies incinerate. Scrambling for answers and a way out in the chaos.

"Are you okay?" Abby said.

He shook his head to clear the thoughts that could bury him. Bury them both if he lost focus. "Yes. But that fire's heading our way. We need a new plan." Based on the rate it had evolved, it had an accelerant behind it. Backstrom was looking to flush them out. Get them on the move.

"You're right," Abby said. "I hate to say Hannah's on her own, but with no idea where to start, we can't afford to search."

"Absolutely not." Abby's safety was his only priority.

If only he'd been more aware earlier. There'd been no signs of anything an hour ago. Except for the lightness when he'd looked out. He should have checked further instead of believing the smoke had cleared.

He'd been so far off his game since they got to the cabin. No. Since he learned of Abby's condition. That would have to change if they were to survive.

Jax secured the knot of the damp cloth around his mouth and nose again and made sure Abby's was snug.

She headed to the rear of the cabin and the cliff before he could pick up his gear.

His heart swooped into his stomach. "Where are you going?"

She craned her neck over the ledge. "The fire on the other side looks like it's subsided enough. We can manage the rocks if we take them slowly."

The idea of going near that cliff made him dizzy. "Bad idea."

"Not great, I agree, but Backstrom won't be able to follow, and if we can get across the river—" Her voice trailed off as her foot slipped and gravel trickled down the cliff's edge. She stepped away, shaking her head. "Or maybe not. It would be harder to defend ourselves from a downslope position."

"Yeah, we can't count on Backstrom being gone. I have a better idea," he said when she returned from the edge. "On my way back from the tower, I got turned around." He quickly explained how he'd gotten to Hannah's camp when a bear and her cubs had appeared. How his attempt to get around them got him lost, and, stumbling upon a dry creek bed that moved down the mountain the opposite direction from which they'd come in on. "We'll have a several-mile hike on rough dirt, but it's doable."

"Except the fire will be on us if we can't stay ahead of it."

"It's not a perfect plan, but we'll keep a good pace, and the smoke will make visibility difficult, if not impossible. It could provide the cover we need." Although it worked both ways.

She thought about it. "If we can reach the creek bed, we'll be kept at a low point." She repositioned her backpack. "Backstrom might not expect that you've discovered another way off this mountain, either."

The flames grew, the red dots of fire spreading like cancer through the trees. Sam had been right about this place being a tinderbox. Sparks continued to fly, drifting into the dusky sky, embers landing and igniting the dry grasses. Poisonous fumes would continue to fill the area, and they'd worsen every second they wasted pondering.

"Let's talk and move at the same time." He tightened the straps on his own backpack.

Hunkered low, Jax in lead, they slipped down the rock stairs, heading for his truck for cover. Once there, they assessed the open expanse.

"New plan," Abby said, pointing to a break in the forest in front of them. "There's an opening straight ahead, do you see it?"

"I do."

"Straight down is the fastest way out. You in shape to keep up, old man?"

"It's not me I worry about. But we'll have to be running fast to have a chance. You up for it with your pregnancy hitting you hard—"

"Nothing re-energizes a person more than when the life of their baby's on the line."

That he knew. There were many factors to worry about, being overwhelmed by the smoke, getting trapped with fire on all sides, but they had to at least try the quickest route.

"It's worth a shot," he said.

They listened and watched. Jax shifted the shotgun to his other hand. Keeping his grip close enough to the trigger to be ready, he went out first. They trotted down the rock path that only days before Sam had driven to warn them about sparks.

Hannah was at the crux of everything that had happened since the moment they'd arrived. He'd already gone through the list a few times in his head, the broken satellite phone among the most egregious. But had it been the accident she claimed?

Exactly why had she disappeared when they were getting ready to leave—not warning them about the flames?

Before he could think more, a family of deer charged out of the forest, startling them. Sweat dripped from Jax's forehead as heat scorched even from a hundred yards away. The roar sounded like a jet plane's engine the closer they got.

Abby began to cough. His own cloth around his face dried.

This would never work.

He met Abby's eye; she nodded. They made double time off to the left and found the path that would lead to the creek. Wherever Backstrom had gone, it would be impossible to be anywhere near this flaming forest. This option was hardly better: he could be out ahead of them, somewhere in the dense forest.

Wherever he was, the fire was coming in all directions. They'd have to stay alert.

But as much as they pushed their pace, they had to keep focus on the ground to avoid ruts and rocks. Jax's mind continued to play in an endless loop of what they would encounter. And why them? Why now?

"Something just doesn't add up," Jax said as they got far enough ahead of the smoke and fire to rest for a minute. Sweat poured off him, and exhaustion threatened to settle into his bones. He grabbed a bottle of water, took a long drink.

"I've been thinking the same thing," Abby said, doing the same. "I get Hannah escaping from Backstrom. Being afraid. But to not warn us when she saw signs of the fire was malicious." She took a long drink of her water. "If we hadn't decided to leave when we did, we'd be trapped."

Or dead—those same thoughts had been part of his mind's loop since they'd come outside. And one step further. "Unless she's with Backstrom."

"She's a good actor, then," Abby said. "The fear seemed genuine, but another question's been bothering me since we spoke to her. How *did* Backstrom find her to send a warning that he was coming for her when you and Jameson, with all your resources, couldn't?"

"Good question. She'd become a ghost. If she was truly hiding, changed her name as she said, how *did* he find her?"

"He had to know where to look?" Abby said.

"Seems like there's a connection we're missing."

Abby nodded. "If we make it out of here, we'll be sure to ask her," Abby said.

"When."

She doused her cloth in water from her bottle and wrung it before placing it back around her mouth and nose. "Right...when."

The deep lines between her eyes betrayed any confidence she infused in her words. Adrenalin could only take a person so far, and they'd been walking for a while.

He screwed the cap back onto the water, channeling his frustration into the last twist. So much so, his hand ached. He should've listened to his gut much earlier. Gotten them out long before now.

They were back on the path minutes later. A few more groups of deer and a stray elk trotted across the route in front of them. A couple of coyotes darted from the brush on their way to safety. Only a few birds; the bulk had been smart enough to find other refuge.

The encroaching fire had every creature in a panic.

Hopefully, smoke was all that drove them. He couldn't keep a rapid pace and listen for signs of Backstrom.

He kept Abby close. His gun ready.

As the cutoff came into view for Hannah's camp, he lifted his chin to Abby to signify the direction. It might be shorter to approach from the ranger station side, but they couldn't afford to get turned around. He had to lead them the same way when he'd gotten lost the first time.

At least every step took them closer to the bottom of this mountain.

They were just outside of Hannah's camp when a scream turned his blood cold.

Chapter Fifty-Two

Rachel's foot sat heavy on the accelerator as she took the corners to Camel Mountain with enough momentum that her father clutched the door handle. The radio crackled as the calls to a newly located wildfire made its way through the various channels.

"It's going to be okay, Rachel."

She barely heard her father's voice as she glanced in the rearview. Koa paced in the back seat.

They'd passed by the store where the clerk had been murdered. State police and the crime lab were still on-site. Crime scene tape encircled the perimeter, and two beat cops stood at the door.

She half expected her father to encourage her to stop for more information, but he was laser-focused on the road ahead.

"I've been thinking," she said, breaking the silence.

"Me too." His fingers dug into the armrest tighter. "You first."

She eased her foot on the pedal. "Hannah has to be involved in this somehow. There's no way she dragged herself all the way to the prison because Backstrom needed 'compassion.'"

He nodded. "That's where my thoughts landed, too. She went out of her way to hide from questioning, then resurfaced a couple of years later to see the man she doesn't want to answer questions about," he said.

"She was waiting for the dust to settle."

"The timing would suggest that," he said.

Rachel tapped the steering wheel. "You think something deeper was going on long before she started those visits?"

"There had to be. And given the interaction, and his reaction and comments after she stopped coming, she has something he wants, or something on him. The question is what."

"Yeah," Rachel said. "I can't see the reasoning behind being too scared to hand evidence over to the police, but not too scared to visit a serial killer. Unless she had a death wish. But why go there to taunt him?" Rachel said.

"Maybe it didn't start out that way. Remember, the first visit had gone fine. It was the second where there was obvious tension."

Rachel thought about it. "So she goes there to tell him about what she has, maybe, and they argue. And Hannah would tell Dr. Shocking some made-up story about compassion just to throw her off."

"Possibly. She wouldn't want to implicate herself, and withholding evidence could be seen as that."

Rachel thought about it. "That'd explain her not wanting to hand it over now, I guess. But not why she'd go there to make Backstrom aware of what she had. I don't know, we're missing something. Backstrom's claims that he was set up won't stop running through my head."

Her father rapped his knuckle on the window, something she did herself when contemplating. "Agreed. Something still doesn't quite fit." His phone dinged with a text before Rachel could respond. "Finally," he said as he set the phone on his lap and dialed the texter, putting the cell on speaker. A man answered.

"Gabe, how are you?" her father said.

"Good, good. Hear you were asking about one of my former cases."

"Hannah Cunningham. Would have been about twenty years ago. Totally understand if you need to pull some files."

He chortled. "Some things you don't need a file to remember."

Rachel kept her eyes on the road, her hands gripping the steering wheel with the prospect of good information. "What do you have?" she said.

Her father quickly introduced her.

Gabe said, "Good to meet you, deputy. But Hannah, she was difficult on her best days. Strong-willed. Running away consistently."

"Drugs?"

"Not her thing. Alcohol, some. Boys, always."

"What do you know about Rodney Backstrom?"

"The one that killed those college girls?"

"That'd be the one," Rachel's father said.

"Never dealt with the guy. But at the time of his arrest, it came out that he'd gone to MacClaren Youth Correction."

"That wasn't reported by us," her father said.

"Didn't have to be. Former counselors and social workers recognized the name, and we're a small community. We talk. We knew we'd hear about him on the news at some point. We try to get them on the right path, but this one had a penchant for killing animals so—"

"We get it," Rachel said. "Were there any known connections to Hannah Cunningham?"

"Nothing in the file specific to that. But I do recall Hannah was often caught in that area about the same time Backstrom was housed there. At one point, she was also in a group home for troubled girls real close, until she hurt one of the other residents and was relocated. Still, she'd find her way back to that vicinity on the regular."

"But she never said it was to see Backstrom?"

"No. Boys, just in general, is all I recall."

"Thanks, Gabe. Appreciate the call back," her father said and disconnected. "Nothing definitive, but—"

"But enough. What are the odds they're near the same age, and when she runs, she's making the trip to MacClaren at the same time frame Backstrom was there. I'm not sure it's worth digging into that further now, but the fact she's gone to visit him at all, along with that piece of information, speaks louder than anything in a file."

Once they found Hannah, they'd have more answers. Answers Jax might already have since he'd used her phone. Unless he had no idea who she was. The idea that Jax was unaware of her connection to Backstrom stirred the acid in Rachel's stomach.

They pulled into the staging area at the foot of Camel Mountain, Garrett behind them. Rachel got out and secured Koa on a leash before strapping a search and rescue vest around her. Together, they headed for the group of small wildfire trucks assembled in a row, along with the various crews.

Some of the men's faces were lined and haggard. They'd likely come from the surrounding fires that had been popping up like whack-a-mole this fire season. The leader was growling orders to a cluster of at least a dozen baby-faced boys.

The four of them joined the commander, a tall man of about fifty with graying sideburns and eyes like they'd seen far too much destruction.

Introductions were made. "We have the sheriff out there, and he's with his ex-wife, Agent Abby Kanekoa," Rachel said.

"FBI, right?" the commander said.

"You know her?"

"Worked an arson case at the federal building in Portland. Good lady. Met her husband once."

"Then you know how much we want to get them back alive and well," Garrett said.

"Hundred percent."

"Last we'd heard, they were heading for the converted ranger station, now an Airbnb," Rachel said.

"More like cabin, and that's not good. South appears to have been where the fire initiated, and it's bearing down on everything in that vicinity and spreading."

She rubbed her neck to dispel the tension building. "Then here's more bad news. There's also a suspected serial killer out there, and an unknown accomplice or victim. We're not sure which."

"Jesus," the commander said. "Last thing they need to be dealing with."

Koa barked and pulled toward the trails. She'd heard enough talk, too.

"You have a layout of the area?" Rachel said.

The commander motioned them to the back of the truck, where a map had been rolled onto a flat board. She and Koa had hiked several of the trails in the vicinity since arriving in Misty Pines. As she scanned the map now, she realized had she kept following one of those trails, they'd have begun a climb into the back side of Camel Mountain. Locked gates at the base had detoured them before, but if Jax and Abby were trying to leave, it could be—

"What are the escape routes off there?" Garrett said, as if he'd read Rachel's mind.

"The new road to the fire tower is an indirect route. It ties into the old ATV trail, which is near where the fire started."

"Do we have a cause?" Rachel said.

"It's dry as hell up there, but at the rate this is spreading—"

"There's been a lot of wind," Garrett said.

"Oxygen is helping fuel it," the commander said.

"Like in Lahaina and LA. Wind and fire make a deadly combination," Garrett said.

Rachel's muscles tightened. "Any chance lightning is behind this?"

"No. As I was about to say, at the rate it erupted, there's an accelerant behind it."

"Arson," her father said.

"That'd be my guess."

Rachel straightened as fear prickled her spine. Backstrom. "My team would like permission to assist," she said, having little authority here.

"Far too dangerous—" the commander began.

"Maybe with regards to the fire, but your men are not equipped to apprehend the kind of maniac we're talking about. One, I'm certain, started this blaze in the first place."

The commander huffed. "Goddamn it."

"I know it's not ideal, but there's no other way." She nodded to her father. "Detective Jameson can go with one of your crews. My deputy, Garrett, can accompany another. They'll stay out of your way."

The commander worked his forehead. "I can't be responsible for anything that goes wrong out there, you got that?"

"We can take care of ourselves," Garrett said. Her father agreed.

"Then suit up. You're not going anywhere like that." The commander yelled at one of his men, who hustled over to a truck and drew out a tote of safety gear.

Rachel knelt and tightened Koa's red vest as she became excited. Koa knew what her job would be. That they'd need to work together.

"Wait, what are you doing?" her father said.

She told him about the trails up the backside.

"That's a hell of a hike from here."

"And why we're going alone. We'll make better time."

The commander nodded. "If your sheriff and Abby are smart, they're going to find that back way out. It would make good sense for you to head that direction so you can intercept them."

Rachel nodded, hoping intercepting was all that would be necessary. Though she'd trained for more. She was ready.

The commander returned to the map, sliding his finger along the paper. "There's a dry creek bed that's near the top of that back route. Provided they follow it for about ten miles, it'll feed into another set of trails that takes them closer to Misty Pines' backwoods."

"Rachel, I can't let you—" her father began.

She understood his fear; she felt it at her core. Not for herself, but for Jax and Abby. For her father and Garrett.

For Koa. She was asking her friend to enter a mountain that could soon be engulfed in fire, a situation neither of them had trained for.

Thoughts of Janelle crossed her mind, and what it would do to her if she didn't come back. What it would do her father, and her mother. But she pushed those thoughts aside. She and Koa were in the best shape, and the most qualified to do this.

The idea that this town was too slow for her liking had already dissolved, but it was now replaced with purpose sitting solid inside her gut. She could not fail Misty Pines and Sheriff Turner.

"We'll be fine." She tossed each of them a radio and secured her own. "We report every fifteen. Got it?"

"Yes, ma'am," Garrett said.

Rachel kissed her father's cheek.

"Yes, ma'am," he said.

She and Koa hurried to the trail to the left before he could see the tear sliding down her cheek.

When she looked back, the young teams with Garrett and her father had already disappeared into the haze on the right.

Chapter Fifty-Three

The high-pitched scream had sliced through the air.

Abby dropped to the ground first, yanking Jax down beside her. "That's Hannah."

"Probably." While he had plenty of questions for her, waiting to ask them until they were far away from this damn mountain would have been preferable.

But the scream read surprise, and the sounds that followed were lower and tense. Hannah was arguing with someone. Or something. Above the clamor of the forest, Jax couldn't tell which. It could be she ran into a fire crew. The flames and billowing smoke plumes must be visible from miles away by now.

More likely, she'd encountered Backstrom.

He shifted the shotgun to a better position, barrel forward.

Strained to hear.

A voice came back at Hannah. Just as tense.

Male. Deep. Equally angry.

The words were unclear, but there was no mistaking the tone. The accusations.

Then another scream.

"Please don't hurt me." Hannah. The anger had dissipated; her voice pitched higher again.

Fear.

Abby started to rise, stepping toward the voices, but Jax reached her hand before she took another step.

"Not yet," he whispered.

She ducked again. "We can't leave her behind."

"What if she's playing us? What if this is a trap?"

"We're law enforcement. We don't get to walk away from this."

She met his eye with the steely determination that both attracted and terrified him.

Of course, she was right. But only in that *he* couldn't walk away. Smoke had been stalking their steps and making it harder to breathe. Every second exposed Abby and the baby to risk.

Another scream.

Abby's eyebrow arched.

Damn it. "Stay here," he said. "Please. If things go south…."

She withdrew the canister of bear spray. "Try not to need me."

He squeezed her hand and met her eye again before standing.

Shotgun at the ready, Jax stayed close to the ground, using the landscape as a shield. He was a good distance away from Abby when Hannah came into view. She stood in the middle of her camp, away from her car. A man had her clutched to his chest, a knife at her throat.

Backstrom, although his appearance had changed. If not for the jagged scar along his exposed right arm, Jax wouldn't have been as certain.

He looked for a shot to take him down and to avoid Hannah.

Almost had it. Then Backstrom gazed past Hannah, at the row of trees and shrubs that Jax believed had camouflaged him.

"I know you're out there," Backstrom said. "Best you come out or she's dead."

Chapter Fifty-Four

Rachel climbed the backtrails, making good time, but not seeing anyone. Three check-ins later, Garrett and her father hadn't come across Jax or Abby, either. Or seen any signs of Backstrom and Hannah.

On the fourth check-in, her father's voice came across the mic. "Body found at the fire watchtower."

A lump grew in her throat. "Identity?"

"Looks to be the ranger based on his uniform."

It's what she'd feared when he'd been unreachable earlier. "Jax and Abby?"

"No sign they were here recently, but there are indications Jax might have been since the station has a few of his standard techniques. He probably found the ranger, too."

"Standard?"

"Door's kicked in. Looking for a communication source, likely, but the radio was busted and the car incapacitated. Gun safe hasn't been compromised, and a knife was used to kill the victim. Backstrom might not be armed with a gun, though it's possible he didn't want to draw attention since the sound of a shot would carry for miles. Hopefully, Jax is armed."

Rachel held the radio tighter as she signed off. Abby had wanted to leave their law enforcement ways in town. She didn't expect he would be.

Regardless, the body confirmed that Backstrom was on the mountain.

Had he encountered Jax and Abby already? Was Hannah with them or with Backstrom?

They all had to be out here. Somewhere.

She and Koa had been moving at such a fast clip, she only now realized her chest ached from her heart ricocheting. Koa had kept the pace, but Rachel was struggling to keep up with the change in elevation. Sweat beaded her brow, trickled down her temples, snaked down her spine.

Resting wasn't an option.

She rounded the last of the creek bed and heard voices in the distance.

Talking?

A woman's voice. For sure. Then a man's. Jax and Abby? Maybe. The sounds gave her renewed energy.

Until the voices turned tense. Angry. No—enraged.

Before she could take another step to investigate, Koa took off in a run.

Chapter Fifty-Five

J ax held his position. "You don't want to do that."

"Hell, I don't. I wasn't expecting to be so lucky as to see you here, but it was a pleasant surprise. Just like her to suck you into her game. She's good at using people, aren't you, Hannah? Or setting them up, like you did me."

"He's lying," Hannah said, her eyes narrowed.

Was he? Jax couldn't decide if Hannah was scared, or angry?

Keeping the gun in front of him, Jax stepped into the clearing. "How about you step away from her anyway?" He aimed the barrel at Backstrom's head. "The fire's coming right for us. There're better places to talk this through."

"And miss the grand finale? That doesn't sound like any fun at all. Besides, the fire's on track to destroy the evidence when I'm through." Backstrom pressed the knife blade into her throat. It was the knife Jax had seen on her passenger seat just days ago. A droplet of blood formed.

Jax kept his gun level and looked for a clean shot. "What do you mean she set you up?"

"Tell him, Hannah. Tell him how you were the reason I killed in the first place. That it was your twisted fantasies I fulfilled."

"I'm not the reason, Sheriff," Hannah said. "He's crazy."

Backstrom dug his fingers into her arm. "Stop with the bullshit already."

"Let me understand," Jax said, his heart thumping hard against his ribs. "You get out on a technicality and proceed to squander the chance to remain free by killing the ranger. Why come for Hannah at all?"

"Oh, I've killed plenty, sheriff, but I didn't kill the ranger," he hissed his words, glared at Hannah. "This woman isn't the innocent you think she is."

Jax didn't want to believe he'd read Hannah so wrong, but it would make sense why Sam had no defensive wounds. Having met her before, he would have turned his back, not worried if she walked up behind him while he surveyed the forest from the sky.

Nausea hit him on how easily she could have done the same to Abby, to him. "Who is she then?"

"The instigator. And if she'd kept her end of our agreement, this would have never happened." He sneered at Hannah. "But you couldn't do that, could you? You had to show your pompous face at the prison after a couple of years and tell me you were done with me. Then you disappeared. But you could never escape me, could you?" He licked the side of her face. She grimaced; her jaw flinched.

Jax gripped the barrel of the shotgun tighter, letting them both die crossing his mind. He drew in a breath to control his rage. "Why don't you put the knife down and tell me about that agreement?"

He laughed. "My knife goes nowhere until you drop that gun."

"I won't do that," Jax said.

"Your choice. But I have no problem ending her right here. You and I both know that won't look good on you, whether she's guilty or not."

"Might take my chances." Jax searched again for an opportunity to neutralize him. But the buckshot in the gun would spread. At this close range, it would kill Hannah, too.

Backstrom shook his head, pressed the blade into her neck, and drew the blade across, slicing flesh.

Hannah yelped as blood puddled around the metal. Tears spilled over her cheeks.

Shit. Jax lowered the gun, still desperate to find an opening that didn't exist. He set the shotgun on the ground.

Backstrom relaxed the blade, and Hannah's face scrunched in pain; a steady trickle of red from the cut bled into her sweatshirt.

"That's better," Backstrom said, mockingly. "Now ease that gun closer to me."

Jax used his foot against the butt end to push it to the halfway point.

Backstrom drew closer and, still clutching Hannah's arm, released her just enough for her to grab the shotgun.

Jax scanned her face. Willing Hannah to look at him, toss it back his way. If she ducked, he might have the chance to fire off a round. He'd aim high to avoid her.

Even if Backstrom was telling the truth and Hannah was part of this, he wanted to believe there was some good in her. Desperate to communicate this was her chance to find it and do the right thing, he cleared his throat and tried again to make eye contact.

Toss it and get out of the way.

She lifted the shotgun from the dirt, avoided looking at Jax. Instead, she swayed, trying to break Backstrom's grip. He must have anticipated she'd try. He pulled her upright, swiping the gun out of her hands, clutching her again in his grasp.

"Fuck off, Rodney," she said.

So she *was* part of it.

A branch snapped nearby, along with the metal clank of Hannah's primitive alarm system.

Damn it, Abby.

Backstrom's smirk morphed into a sick grin. "In our sweet reunion, I almost forgot about your wife. Please tell her to join us."

Jax forced his eyes far away from that end of the campsite. "She's not here."

"Oh, but Hannah said she is."

Jax's jaw twitched. "She was. Earlier. She went ahead to get help. She'll be halfway down the mountain by now."

Backstrom scoffed. "FBI agent like her isn't running anywhere, I'm sure of that." He scanned the perimeter. "Mrs. Turner, unless you'd like your hubby to be splattered all over the leaves, you'd best come out."

A flock of birds leaving the mountain flew overhead. The air had grown thicker. The fire would be upon them soon. "I'm telling you, she's gone," Jax said, with more intensity this time. "Whatever happens here is just between us."

Backstrom shook his head, his finger hovering over the trigger, the barrel aimed at Jax, his eyes skimming the perimeter.

The bushes rattled behind Jax, and Abby appeared. Her hands hung at her side, the bear repellent nowhere in sight, as she stepped next to him.

Hannah smirked.

"So, you two were in it together the entire time?" Jax glanced around for another weapon. A way out.

"We were, until Hannah here wanted to be done with me. She forgot there's always a price to pay for one's decisions, and I've come for what she has on me. And then to make sure she pays."

"How many times do I have to tell you, I'm not done," Hannah snapped. "I just got scared. Some doctor approached me and started asking questions after that first time I saw you. You know the cops had been looking for me. If I hadn't run and got asked for my DNA, what do you think would've happened then?"

"You would've been tied to the crimes. Done time, like me," Backstrom said.

She shook her head. "Or you'd be on death row right now when they linked you to the other murders."

He laughed. "You did me a favor then?"

"Yes. I always think of you."

His eyes rolled. "Please. Saving yourself was your only priority. And you certainly didn't want me out to ruin your plans with that loser in Misty Pines. What were you planning with him, anyway? You think you could suddenly be normal and play house together? Or were you just biding time before you asked *him* to kill for you?"

"Of course not," she said. "He was just—"

"What? Helpful? Another pawn on your board?" A sick grin crossed his face. "Well, he was for me. Helpful, anyway. Unfortunately for him, it took some convincing to tell me the plan and give up his phone." He pulled her close, whispered in her ear. "Imagine his despair when he realized you'd only used him. You always liked watching our victims panic, didn't you?"

Hannah's mouth twitched, her face hardened. A coldness seeped through. "Why, Hannah?" Abby said. "Why involve us at all?"

Hannah lifted her chin. "Because I knew he was coming for me, and I wasn't about to spend my life looking over my shoulder."

"So, you did plan all it from the beginning," Abby said.

Jax's teeth clenched. "That's why you made sure we couldn't get off this mountain," Jax said. "Why you went ahead when you saw the fire. You knew we'd encounter you both at some point." Hadn't Sam said she asked about their skills as officers?

Hannah looked away.

"Ah, now you're seeing the real Hannah," Backstrom said. "She wants me dead and you have, or had, the gun." He chuckled. "She had one thing right. I'd never stop hunting her." He glared at Hannah. "Now I won't have to. You wanted it to end here, and so it will."

Hannah writhed in his grip, desperate to get away from him. "Asshole."

Backstrom's face reddened.

"Keep him talking," Abby whispered.

Right. "You said she committed crimes with you," Jax said, quickly. "What were those?" Abby grabbed his hand, and he knew what she was thinking. If they could keep Backstrom's rage focused on Hannah, there might be a moment they could run.

But it was more important for Abby to go and get as far away as possible. If only she'd do what she'd promised and not look back.

Backstrom chuckled. "You want to tell them, or me?" He didn't wait for her to answer. "She chose the girls. Didn't you, Hannah? They were always those haughty women who came in wearing their fancy clothes and expensive jewelry and left shit for tips. Isn't that what you told me?" Hannah twisted in his grip again. "Still, somehow, you befriended them, earned their trust with free drinks. Wormed your way into their world. You've always been so good at that. They never expect you'd bring a friend one night to destroy them. And, there's the matter of the X. Oh, how you loved that mark to be carved into their perfect skin. Your little contribution to the whole affair."

"You carved the X in the women?" Jax said to Hannah.

"I didn't do that," Hannah said.

He laughed. "At least not always. You never truly liked getting your hands dirty, just like when you encouraged me to strangle that cute little yapper dog that your neighbor owned. Clearly, you made an exception with the ranger just to set me up, though, didn't you?" His face darkened as he stepped back from Hannah, pointing the shotgun at her. "Where's the SD card?"

She looked at the ground, then at Jax. "I don't have it, but I can get it."

Backstrom's eye twitched. "You gave it to him?"

"I had to, but only to sell that I was a victim." She lifted her chin in defiance. "Let's just finish them off and go. Enough of whatever this is. We can figure it out like we always have."

"Figure it out?" he said. "Running from me is not figuring things out. Not after what you had me do. And that SD card...I might be plenty guilty, but it was rageful fantasies that I paid the price for. For ten years, I protected you, and this is the thanks I get."

His rage was as strong as the fires surrounding them. "So why put it on film?" Jax said.

"Hannah wanted me to," Backstrom said, his face red. "Though now I see it was to have insurance. Because my taking the fall for you wasn't enough." He raised the gun and looked at Jax. "I'd tell you to give it to me, but I'll get it from you myself."

Hannah paled. "Please, Rodney. Remember when we were kids?"

He shook his head. "You were trouble then and still are."

She smiled. "You liked trouble."

"It was something I relied on. Just never thought you'd turn on me like the rest of the world."

"You're wrong. I never—"

Backstrom leveled the gun, just as a flash of black came out of nowhere. It was the last thing Jax registered before a shot pierced the air.

Chapter Fifty-Six

Rachel's chest tightened as Koa disappeared from her view. They had no idea what they were coming upon, and Koa had flunked police dog training.

Thankfully, almost as quickly, Koa raced back to her before launching forward again.

She'd found something.

Or someone.

Rachel followed, barely keeping up. Then slowed as the voices grew louder and angrier. It took only a moment to home in on the situation unfolding.

Jax was standing in front and to the side of Abby in a patch of clearing surrounded with shrubs and trees. They were talking to someone else, but Rachel couldn't make out who.

Koa remained silent next to Rachel, her sides expanding and contracting.

They needed a better viewpoint.

Keeping below the hedge line, Rachel found a break.

From there, she spotted a young woman, likely Hannah, who stood a few yards from the car, Backstrom behind, a knife at her throat. A shotgun aimed at Jax and Abby.

A well-placed shot could end the situation sooner than later. Rachel frantically searched for it.

If she missed, Backstrom would get off a shot of his own.

She had to quit contemplating. Action. Now. She reached for Koa so they could move, to get a better aim, and got air instead.

Rachel's stomach catapulted into her throat as she saw Koa enter the clearing. Her long, lean body lunged toward Backstrom, her teeth sinking into the arm that gripped the shotgun.

She couldn't lose Koa.

Before she could act, Backstrom shook Koa off and had the shotgun leveled.

A blast rang out.

Jax lunged sideways, his body almost blocking Abby's. Hannah crumpled first—she took the full brunt of the bullet on its way to Jax, whose shoulder swung back as metal tore into his flesh.

He dropped to his heels.

But it was Abby who toppled backward.

Without another thought, Rachel had her weapon out. Aimed. Fired.

Backstrom fell to his side, still holding the shotgun. He fought to get to his feet. To raise the gun.

"Hell no," Jax said.

Blood spewed from Abby's chest area, but she held a cannister in her hand. It seemed she was unable to lift her arm as she struggled to her knees.

Jax got to his.

Abby grabbed the canister with her good hand, and Jax wrapped his hand around hers.

Together, they aimed the nozzle at Backstrom, nailing him in the face with a stream of toxic spray just as another shot rang out.

Rachel's second bullet made sure Backstrom never got up again. She raced to secure him, finding blood on the blades of grass, pooling the ground. His eyes wide, mouth open.

Her attention turned to Hannah, whose tear-streaked face reflected the same as Backstrom's.

Rachel ran to the edge of the clearing, her body shaking uncontrollably. No amount of training had prepared her for how the moment would feel after taking a life. No matter how well-deserved.

The adrenaline pumping through her sent a wave of nausea hurtling through her until there was nothing left in her stomach. Her head spun with confusion. She'd had no choice, but…

"Rachel, that fire's coming, and we need to move," Jax shouted.

His words barely registered through the rush of blood in her head.

"Deputy Killian, pull it together," he said. "Abby's bleeding. Let's go."

The smoke that had only been floating in now poured through the forest like it was a sieve.

Rachel drew herself up, nodded. Wiped her mouth before radioing their location and where they'd be heading.

"Suspects down. Will need recovery."

Her father's voice came across the mic. "Are you okay, girl? How's Jax? Abby?"

She drew in a deep breath. Refocused. "I'm good. Abby needs evac. We'll get off this inferno, but if someone can meet us…."

"On it," her father said, and she could already hear Garrett in the background calling it in.

She grabbed water from her pack and joined Jax, who was packing Abby's wound with his t-shirt.

"I've got a medical team meeting us," she said.

"You think a bullet can take me down?" Abby's voice sounded confident, but her face was pale. Too pale.

Jax stared at Rachel, his entire body radiating fear as he gathered Abby in his arms.

Rachel had never felt more needed than at that moment.

"Koa, get us the hell out of here."

Epilogue

The ambulance had met them at the bottom of the mountain and whisked them all to safety. Teams would recover the bodies as soon as they were able, and there'd be plenty of reports in the days to come. More than Jax had the bandwidth to think about as he sat on the edge of the hospital gurney, allowing buckshot to be plucked out of his skin, one by one.

Soon, they had a bandage wrapped around his arm to stabilize his shoulder, but he was on his way back to Abby when he spotted Rachel pacing, and Jameson sitting, in the waiting room.

"Maybe you should hold off on any more remote vacations in the future," Jameson said, rising to meet him.

"No argument there. You in town for the crab legs?"

"Sure wouldn't be to see you." He winked. "Backstrom, however, I was looking forward to seeing."

God, it was good to see his former partner again. Jax let out a half-laugh before glancing at his arm. "Seems he found us first. Although revenge on Hannah was what brought him into our path, it appears."

Rachel shook her head. "Looking for you or not, what a deranged couple of people they turned out to be."

"How's Koa?"

"Sleeping in the patrol car. I'll need to get her home soon. She deserves a rest."

"And a medal. Her distraction made the difference."

Rachel nodded, then smiled. "Turns out she's more protective of the people she loves than the academy gave her credit for."

"Their loss," Jax said, hugging Rachel. "You pass that hug onto her for me."

Rachel stepped back, her face red. "Will do."

The sliding doors to the hospital opened, and Trudy and Frank marched in like they were on a mission, Trudy with a plate, Frank with a carafe of coffee.

"There you are." She set her chocolate chip trauma relief caramel-marshmallow cookies on an end table before wrapping her arms around Jax's waist in a bear hug only she could muster. "Assumed we'd be here a while and would need sustenance."

Jax held her tight. "You always take care of us."

She pushed him away. "And none of you make that easy on me."

Rachel and Jax chuckled.

"Who's watching the fort?" Jax said.

"Brody's on patrol. Garrett's manning the phone. We'll be losing Matt soon. They keep him too busy at the grocery store."

It would be a shame, but it was important to have people dedicated to the job to be there. He realized that more than ever on that mountain.

"Have you seen Abby yet?" Trudy said.

They'd shooed him away for treatment and taken her into an emergency room a couple of hours ago. "Only when they first brought us in. I was just on my way to find her."

"Bullets lodged above her collarbone and into her shoulder, like you. Deeper though, and lower. Maybe you'll have complementing scars," Rachel said.

"Isn't that sweet?" Jameson said.

Jax frowned. "Since you heard that much, then you know she's pregnant."

"Yes."

"Have they said anything about the baby?"

Rachel shook her head, making Jax's stomach swoop like a roller coaster.

"But I overheard them say they had tests to run. Hopefully, they'll have good news for you shortly," Jameson added.

Jax nodded.

"So, this probably isn't the right time to ask, but what happens next for me, with the shooting?" Rachel said. "There'll be an investigation?"

"Yes. An outside precinct will be assigned to review the matter and determine whether it was justified."

"Which—" she said.

"You have nothing to worry about, Rachel." He placed his hand on her forearm and squeezed. Had she not been there, they'd not be having this conversation. He cleared his throat. "Abby and I'll testify on your behalf. You're still off work for a few weeks pending the outcome, and you'll need it."

Having just gone through a similar situation himself, no amount of justification made the reality of taking a life easier. Rachel would have a hill to climb on that one.

"In the meantime," he said. "Get that full report on my desk."

She nodded. "Don't like that feeling of having missed so much?"

"You know it," he said.

The electronic doors swung open, and a man in blue scrubs emerged. His mask dangled under his chin. "Jax Turner?" he said.

Jax stepped from the group. "That would be me."

"You can see Abby now. She asked that I let you know as soon as she was in recovery."

"Recovery?" He'd not realized she'd been taken in. But with no marital ties, they didn't need to consult him. Or let him know.

"The bullet was deep enough that we had to take her into emergency surgery. She'll be in and out of sleep, but you can see her."

Heart pounding, Jax followed the doctor to the recovery room and slunk into the dimmed space, the sound of machines beeping. His chest tightened at the sight of Abby's petite frame, fragile. The thought of losing her. He could barely breathe. It was Lulu all over again.

His mind reeled back from the mountain just hours ago.

"You are not carrying me out of here," Abby had said ten times in the miles they'd trekked, each one taking them further from the fire and the death on top. But each protest had become quieter as she continued to lose blood.

Too much blood.

He'd ignored his own injury. If only he'd stepped farther to the left, he would have shielded Abby completely. He'd said that to her.

"And you'd be dead," she'd snapped. "You don't get to leave me, Jax Turner."

The bullets would have landed in his chest, killing him on impact, as they had Hannah. But he'd have given up his life in a second if it meant saving her from any of this.

And he could not lose her. He'd get her down the damn mountain if it was the last thing he did.

In that moment, he hadn't thought about the baby.

He couldn't. He had to hold on to who he had in his arms. Save Abby. Without her, there was nothing.

But now.

Abby stirred; her eyes fluttered open. "There you are."

"You know it," Jax said. "How you feeling?"

"Like a truck ran me over and backed up."

"I know that exact sensation."

She reached for his arm. "You okay?"

"Don't worry about me. I'm fine."

"Hannah?"

"Dead."

Her eyes drifted closed. "What a mess."

"And all to be sorted later. What's important is you."

"No, what's important is us, including the little one." A tear squeezed from the corner of her eye, trickling onto the pillow. "Is she okay?"

"She?" he whispered.

"I think so. She's been giving me heartburn like Lulu." She swallowed.

It seemed early to know the gender, but he had no intention of arguing a mother's intuition. And a girl. Damn. "I haven't heard anything other than they're running tests. We should know soon. In the meantime, will we be okay?"

She nodded and reached for his hand, which he took in both of his. "The moment I stepped beside you in that clearing, I knew I couldn't lose you.

Not again. Never again."

He pressed her hand to his cheek, the emotion nearly swallowing him whole.

"But do we know whether Backstrom was telling the truth about Hannah?" she said.

"Appears so. According to Rachel, they met years ago when he was at a boy's correctional facility." He went on to explain the dead animals that seemed to appear when they were together.

"Clearly, Backstrom started his killing streak early." She drew in a jagged breath. "Boy, we missed her by a mile."

"We were preoccupied with other things."

She nodded. "I guess. Were they a couple?"

"At one time, maybe, but it sounds more like a sick duo of friends that fed each other's dark fantasies. They were able to recover the bodies before the fire took that area. Sounds like Rachel was waiting for a hit on some evidence, but now that we have her for DNA, Jameson will be able to cross-reference it with the cold cases."

Abby nodded as the nurse came into the room, heading for Abby to check her vitals.

"You're coming along just great, Ms. Kanekoa."

Jax drew in a breath, relieved at the news. "Can you tell us anything about her pregnancy yet?"

"The ultrasound tech was here earlier, and the ER doctor wanted to chat with you about that when you were ready."

Jax met Abby's eye as she nodded. Whatever the outcome, they'd get through this together.

"We're ready," he said, attempting to project confidence. Be the rock Abby would need, regardless of the news.

The nurse nodded and gave him a look he couldn't read. Was she being sympathetic or assuring? He had to stop, not get too far ahead. Likely neither. There were procedures on how information had to be given out. He knew this.

Abby bit into her lower lip as they waited.

In what seemed far too long, a woman dressed in blue scrubs, her jet-black hair pulled into a messy bun, came through the door.

"Glad to see the patient's awake," she said, grabbing a rolling stool.

"Her pregnancy?" Jax said. "She's had quite an ordeal, and with the surgery, anesthetic—"

"It's okay, Dad," the doctor said. "You'll be keeping your hands full in about seven months with those babies."

Abby's eyes widened, and Jax dropped into the chair. He looked toward the door, where Rachel and Trudy were crowded in, listening intently, and beaming from ear to ear.

"Babies?" Abby and Jax both said at the same time, right before they looked into each other's eyes, and smiled.

Acknowledgments

As always, there are so many to thank, but I'll start with my critique partners, Dianne Freeman and Cindy Goyette. Their keen eyes always see what I miss and help me to elevate the story to another level. Thank you to Dawn Ius, who has championed Jax from the beginning, and for believing in me and this story when my confidence waned.

To my readers who have read and enjoyed my stories, and to all my friends and family who have supported me along the way, a heartfelt thank you.

Many thanks, of course, to my editor, Shawn Riley Simmons, and the team at Level Best Books, for believing in Sheriff Jax Turner and the Misty Pines stories in the first place. Special thanks to Clark County Sheriff Deputy James Lawrence, who is always ready to answer my crazy questions!

And last, but never least, thank you to my husband, Robb. Every day he supports my authorly dreams in a million different ways. I can't imagine sharing this moment in time or my life with anyone else. All my love.

About the Author

Eighteen years in the legal field, and an overactive imagination, led Mary Keliikoa to plot murder—novels, that is. She is the author of the domestic thriller *Don't Ask, Don't Follow*, the "Misty Pines" mystery series which is an IPPY Silver and Bronze Award winner, Silver Falchion finalist, and a Foreword Indies award finalist, and the "PI Kelly Pruett" mystery series which is a Shamus and CLUE Finalist, and has been nominated for a Lefty, Agatha and Anthony award. Her short stories have appeared in *Woman's World* and the anthology *Peace, Love and Crime*. www.marykeliikoa.com

AUTHOR WEBSITE:
  https://marykeliikoa.com/

SOCIAL MEDIA HANDLES:
  Facebook: https://www.facebook.com/Mary.Keliikoa.Author
  Twitter: https://twitter.com/mary_keliikoa
  Instagram: https://www.instagram.com/mary.keliikoa.author/

Bookbub: https://www.bookbub.com/authors/mary-keliikoa

Goodreads: https://www.goodreads.com/author/show/20038534.Mary_Keliikoa

Also by Mary Keliikoa

Derailed (A Kelly Pruett mystery #1)

Denied (A Kelly Pruett mystery #2)

Deceived (A Kelly Pruett mystery #3)

Hidden Pieces (A Misty Pines mystery #1)

Deadly Tides (A Misty Pines mystery #2)

Don't Ask, Don't Follow